FOREST OF THE NIGHT

S.P. SOMTOW

AVON BOOKS • NEW YORK

FOREST OF THE NIGHT is an original publication of Avon Books. This work has never before appeared in book form. This work is a novel. Any similarity to actual persons or events is purely coincidental.

AVON BOOKS
A division of
The Hearst Corporation
1350 Avenue of the Americas
New York, New York 10019

Copyright © 1992 by Somtow Sucharitkul
Cover illustration by Tim White
Published by arrangement with the author
Library of Congress Catalog Card Number: 92-90567
ISBN: 0-380-76628-0

First Avon Books Printing: November 1992

AVON TRADEMARK REG. U.S. PAT. OFF. AND IN OTHER COUNTRIES, MARCA REGISTRADA, HECHO EN U.S.A.

Printed in the U.S.A.

RA   10 9 8 7 6 5 4 3 2 1

To Welby, Betsy
Adrian, Mary Beth,
and Christopher

Row, row, row your boat
Underneath the stream,
Ha, ha, fooled you all!
I'm a submarine.

Contents

book one

---

the forest where things have no names

"I'll tell you, if you'll come a little further on,"
the Fawn said. "I can't remember *here*."

—*Through the Looking-Glass*

TALES OF THE WANDERING HERO
by PHILIP ETCHISON

1: IN THE FOREST WHERE THINGS HAVE NO NAMES

When I was old enough to leave the womb
And seek adventure in the world beyond,
My mother gave me an old iron sword
A loaf of bread, a condom, and a kiss
And told me, "I've just one piece of advice
For you, young Theseus: don't forget your name."

I journeyed far and wide. I forded rivers
And entered the dark forest. I slew all sorts
Of monsters: trolls and harpies, snarks and serpents,
Boars, bears, and dragons; wizards, manticores,
Though they would plead: "Oh, spare me, Gilgamesh!"
"Ulysses, let me live, and I'll vouchsafe you
Three wishes, maybe four." I killed them all,
And each, in dying, apostrophizing me,
Rebounded to the glory of my name.
I ravished maidens, too, and heard them cry,
"Ah, Krishna, you have barbecued my heart,"
Or, "Romeo, Romeo . . ." and my name waxed mighty.
Till one night, sitting beneath the tree of knowledge,
The Bodhi Tree, or Tum-tum, as some call it,
I felt an apple land upon my head,
And realized I no longer knew my name.

I went home to my mother. She embraced me,
Heard me recount my stirring tales of conquest,

Loves lost and won, beasts slain, and castles stormed.
But though I had no doubt of her affection,
Nor of the hearth's warmth, nor the people's love,
I never could be sure this was my home,
Or this the mother I remembered, or the hearth
Where as a child I warmed myself. Perhaps
I never had a name, and all those names
The beasts cried out were merely myths, dreams, eldritch
Fantasies. Perhaps not. Or perhaps
My name was a yet undiscovered thing,
Hiding behind some shadowy bourne, and I
Had really not yet left my mother's side,
Nor wandered in the forest, vanquished beasts,
Loved princesses and warred with wily wizards.

At last, I begged my mother to reveal
The secret of my birth, my one true name.
She gave me a well-rusted iron sword
A kiss, a condom, and a loaf of bread,
And said, "It's time for you to leave the womb.
But this time, Perseus, don't forget your name."

You see:
It is a question of identity.

chapter one

In a Laetrile Clinic

Phil Etchison

It was the nineties, the time before the mad millennium. I was not old then as I am now, but a few weeks had aged me beyond all understanding. I had driven three thousand miles and in that blink's breadth between two points in spacetime I had seen worlds born and unborn; I had seen empires made and unmade; I had sailed the river that spans the universes, from what-has-been to what-will-be to what-could-be to what-might-have-been to what-ought-never-have-been. God, what a journey it had been.

And this is how I came to feel so old: by the end of that journey I knew it was no longer I who was driving the beat-up station wagon of my life across the Arizona desert—not I who had the power to pilot the ship of the river between worlds—not I who controlled my destiny, but my son Theo. Theo whose life was an eternal present, Theo who saw past the accumulated bullshit of our old minds straight through to the heart, who called all things by their true names because he knew no other names for them, Theo whom myriad creatures of other dimensions worshiped as Theo Truthsayer, but who was to me my son,

4

young, tousle-towheaded, blurter of unfaced truths, stripper of illusions.

I loved my son, but it was he who had made me old.

On the second day of November, at the laetrile clinic by the sea, I remembered nothing of our odyssey. My wife was riddled with cancer and my son sulked and did not speak to me, and I had not written a poem in nine months. Our recession-proof money market funds had been trickling away as we whiled away the evenings watching cable television and waiting for my wife to die. We were in a kind of pre-mourning mode.

On the second day of November, at the laetrile clinic by the sea, in a Mexican town manufactured and peopled by gringos, my son and I sat on the veranda of our bungalow and waited for my wife to come back from treatment. We did not speak, but listened to the rhythm of wind and sea and ate our prefabricated pizzas with indifference. We'd been at the clinic for three months and the laetrile wasn't working. No one had expected it to, but we'd thought that maybe the journey would heal all of us, three people who once loved each other but who now stood always apart and alienated.

On the second day of November, the city of Oaxaca celebrates the Day of the Dead—a Zapotec ceremony with a thin veneer of Catholicism—and the people dress up as skeletons, feast over the graves of their ancestors, go on candlelit processions bearing coffins of the living dead, set up papier-mâché altars with images of departed ones and sculptures of skeletons engaged in myriad acts of daily life. It is a Divine Comedy—festive and tragic—and a very big deal.

Oaxaca was a continent away, and there were more Americans than Zapotecs in this Baja town. Doubtless it was for the tourists that the town was doing its own version of the Day of the Dead. I have been speaking of destiny and the control of destiny; yet often what appears to be a serendipitous predestination is only the accidental confluence of the streams of probability.

Perhaps it was only fitting that this Day of the Dead, which was to the genuine Day of the Dead in distant Oaxaca as a Barbie doll is to a beautiful woman, this plastic reconstruction of an authentic darkness, should be the setting for the beginning of our second journey into the world my son made, the world that made my son.

For most of my life I have eked out a living as a second-rate poet, the chair of poetry at a second-string university, handing out secondhand epiphanies to second-class students. I too have been a plastic shell of an authentic poet. I've touched my own reflection in the mirror and wondered which was more real, my face or its imitation. I am my self's own Memorex. The shadow's shadow.

A year, more or less, had passed since we first came to the laetrile clinic. My wife's condition was a little worse than before. I was a year older, but I felt infinitely old. But my son Theo was just the same. For a year he had teetered on the brink of adolescence; but he was no taller now, and his voice had not deepened. It was as if he had chosen not to grow. A late bloomer he would have been called at school in the States, but here at the clinic there was no school as such, only a recreation room with a library where those of us, patients or spouses, our minds on other things, sometimes saw fit to hold impromptu classes for the dozen or so children imprisoned here with us. (I myself had been known to speak on Keats and Whitman.) And so it was that no one really noticed Theo's refusal to participate in the passing of time.

I, it must be said, had not noticed it until that very moment.

Theo wiped the pizza sauce from his lips. The afternoon sun was behind him, over the sea. God he looks young, I thought, younger than when we first came here. I wondered whether I could broach the subject without embarrassing him. With his mother not due back for a half hour, there was a window of opportunity for us to do some male bonding.

"Theo," I began.

He looked at me. He smiled a little.

"What are you thinking, Dad?"

"I'm thinking that we haven't had a real conversation in about a year."

"If this is some kind of warmup to a birds-and-bees lecture, Dad, I think I should warn you that I already know everything."

"No jokes, Theo. Let's be serious."

"But I *do* know everything, Dad. And you've forgotten everything."

"What do you mean?"

"Does the name Joshua Etchison mean anything to you?"

This is what I saw in my mind's eye: a flaming angel leaping into the sea. It seemed to be a memory, but how could it be? A second-rate poet does not see angels, does not have visions of paradise and inferno. I took a sip of Diet Pepsi—the clinic permitted no alcohol on the premises—and I looked my son in the eye and said, "No."

Theo said, "I want you to listen to this poem, Dad . . ." And he began to recite, in a dreamy treble, words that were not quite my own:

> *They are standing at the river's edge; sometimes*
> *I watch them, sometimes*
> *I cannot bear to watch, sometimes*
> *I wish for the river to run upstream, back to the*
>   *mountains,*
> *Blue as the sky, as grief, as delusion.*

But I said, "No, no, that's not how it goes at all." I remembered writing that poem. It was at my parents' summer place. By chance, at sunset, I caught Theo standing at the edge of the creek that borders their property. And I started thinking about how much I loved him. This poem had no "they" in it. It was all "you"—"you" by the river's edge, "you" whom I named God. The "they" was a travesty of what I felt for him, the love so big and deep, I dared not express it save by hints and misdirection.

"You're thinking that you only have one son."

—a flaming angel leaping into the sea—

"I know I only have one son. If I had more than one," I said, "I'd go insane."

"You *are* insane," Theo said.

And suddenly I knew that he was telling the truth. For months now I had been plagued with the notion that the life I was living was somehow not my life. There were the missing pieces in the puzzle of memory—the entire journey between Virginia and Mexico had been reduced to disconnected fragments: a desert highway and a Chinese restaurant that rose out of the sand like a disjunctive Xanadu; a police car that could fly to the top of a mesa; peyote tea and blood-tinged cocktails; and yes, a flaming angel leaping into the sea. All images as real to me as countless other mundane memories, yet images that logically could not be true, even if I could somehow connect the dots into some chimerical hyperimage. "Am I insane?" I asked my son.

"Well, like, if you aren't, you ought to be," he said. "That's why I decided we should have this talk. I mean, since Mom's going to be in treatment for a few hours yet, and we never seem to get a chance to talk. I mean alone. I mean man to man. Man to boy. Whatever."

"Weird," I said. "I thought I was manipulating you into having this conversation, but it turns out you were manipulating me."

"No jokes, Dad," said Theo. "Let's be serious."

This had to be some kind of Möbius-stripping timeloop. We were back at the beginning of the dialogue, but somehow our lines had gotten switched.

"All right," I said. "Assume that I've forgotten everything. Speak to me. Tell me."

"All right. To start off with, how much do you remember about the trip down here? Do you remember the Chinese restaurant?"

"I think so."

"We took a detour. Across a hundred dimensions. And we had a run-in with the Darklings. They're the family that rules the thousand worlds connected by the River. They're what you might call dysfunctional. Like us. They're fighting over the kingdom, you know, like King Lear's three daughters, and I was captured by Thorn, the vampire, because I'm a Truthsayer and I can navigate between worlds; and then Katastrofa—she's a were-dragon—kidnapped Josh because she thought he'd kind of be able to do what I do. And Mr. Stone, that Navajo policeman, he led you to us through a sand painting; and Mom's really an aspect of the One Mother—are you following me?"

I was confused. More than confused. Sullenly, I bit off another piece of pepperoni pizza and wished in vain for a tall, stiff drink. My son was narrating all this very matter-of-factly, the way one might discuss the weather, and every one of the outlandish things he said rang true. But none of it made sense.

"If I really have another son," I said, "where is he now?"

"He's dead," said Theo. "He jumped into the sea. We don't have much time. We may still be able to save him."

I saw the face of the flaming angel. For a moment I almost grasped the truth. Then it slipped away again. I looked at my watch.

"She's not due back for a while yet," Theo said. They were trying out a new procedure on her. "Let's go for a walk."

"You want to go and see the festival?" I said, though the prospect did not fill me with glee.

"Sure." He got up. We didn't clear away our plates— the domestics at the clinic were relentlessly efficient—but started working our way to the edge of the cliff, where a stairway wound precipitously downward to the beach. It was windy and my son moved swiftly, leaping the steps two, three at a time, his hands barely skimming the rickety banister. Now and then, at a landing, he would wait for me. Below, a boardwalk snaked along the shore, from the edge of town, past the clinic and the clustered bungalows, toward the cliffs just north of us, where there was a sacred cave, dedicated to Our Lady of the Sluggish Tears, a limestone statue of the Virgin that, the tourist brochure told us, weeps "so gently that only a few tears may be collected each year, and these precious drops are of miraculous abilities, being imbued with curative powers." (When we first came to the clinic, we'd done the obligatory visit to this tawdry shrine and bought the obligatory postcards and bottles of holy water spiked with a few molecules of those sacred tears.)

As we descended, the wind brought the fish-salt smell of the sea and the sizzle of the salsa music and the crowds and the surf. A black-clad procession moved along the boardwalk, accompanied by a funereal and out-of-tune brass band, punctured and punctuated by the flatus of a bass drum. It was a sorry excuse for a festival. Though I had not, admittedly, ever seen a better. Except—

Moving toward the citadel of Caliosper, a million times a million, human and monstrous, a throng more multitudinous than the extras in a fifties spectacle—

Another misplaced memory.

We had reached the boardwalk. There were stalls that sold candles shaped like skulls, marzipan rotting corpses, skeleton costumes, clay and papier-mâché tableaux of skeletons engaged in such pursuits as golfing, skin diving, driving limousines, and giving one another enemas; there were mestizos hawking fake Rolexes; and everywhere the American families—the children in strident skater pants and the parents with strident voices—strutting about with stereotypical American arrogance. Yet I knew that these families were largely like mine: each had a loved one dying of cancer; each had come to the laetrile clinic in a final, forlorn hope. Perhaps that was why they acted with such exaggerated good cheer, and clung so fiercely to the archetype of the American.

We stopped at a candy stall and I bought Theo a sugared skull with glittering ruby eyes. An old woman begged and a New Yorker with a blue beehive hairdo complained noisily about the poverty and the filth. In the procession, dwarfs with whited faces swallowed fire, and a coffin was borne on the shoulders of masked youths.

In the midst of all this there came a procession of another kind. A cadaverous bald man in an Armani suit was striding through the throng, advancing on each obvious American, shaking hands vigorously, kissing the odd baby. Behind him were a dozen secret servicemen (one can always tell from the suits) and half a dozen flamboyantly pneumatic young women, passing out stickers, buttons, and autographed pictures.

"It's Congressman Karpovsky," I said, suddenly aware that there was a world outside the laetrile clinic—and that back in the States there was an election going on. "Isn't he running for president or something?"

Theo laughed. "But why would he be doing that here? Unless Mexico's like, become the fifty-first state while we weren't looking."

Karpovsky loomed over us suddenly. "Gotta cater to the special interests, my boy," he roared above the pandemonium. "It's a good question, lad, glad ya asked it. I'm getting in a photo-op here because of my national health plan. We're gonna have a tax credit for alternative medicine—ya know, acupuncture, voodoo, hoodoo, faith healers. Gotta break the backs of the medical establishment before they break ours, eh? Ho, ho, ho."

At that moment, one of the attractive women handing out bumper stickers broke ranks and ran up to us. A child-woman, really; she could have been as young as seventeen, except that her suit, her heels, and her sophisticated makeup had metamorphosed her into an ageless *Vogue* cover.

"Hey, Mr. E.! Theo!" she cried, and she and Theo hugged each other as though they were the closest of siblings. I sort of resented it a little. My son had not hugged me in six months. Nor I him. In fact, as I was to learn later, we had not even been inhabiting the same universe.

The woman turned her attention to me, catching me in an almost torrid embrace, while Congressman Karpovsky looked on with a raised eyebrow. I didn't have the slightest notion who she was.

"Just go along with it for now, Mr. E.," she whispered in my ear. "I'll totally explain everything later."

Theo was smiling broadly for the first time in maybe two weeks. He yanked at my sleeve and then whispered, "It's Serena Somers, Josh's old girlfriend. You don't remember her because you don't remember Josh. It's okay. It's all gonna come back to you šoon."

"Congressman," said Serena, "this man's a famous poet— from inside the beltway, no less. Philip Etchison."

"No, really? Met you at the Washington *Post* cafeteria one time. I was giving an interview and you were having lunch with that Dirda fellow. An editor at *Book World*. You remember?"

I didn't remember him.

"Congressman," Serena said, "look, I'm about up for my break and—"

"Sure, dear," said the congressman, "see you back at HQ." He saw a demographically photogenic family and loped off to shake their hands.

Theo said, "I thought you said you were never going to work for him again—that he like sexually harassed you or something."

"Oh, he's in therapy," Serena said. "Keeps his hands to himself now. Chews nicotine whenever his hormones rage too much."

"How's ASU?"

"Oh, I'm not going to ASU at all now . . . I'm taking a year off . . . transferring to Dartmouth . . . well, you know, Arizona . . . I don't like the memories."

"I know what you mean." Theo's eyes darted, as though some ancient enemy stood in the shadows, though the sun had not yet set.

I stood there in a crowd of dancing skeletons. My son and this woman were clearly on terms of the utmost intimacy. They jabbered on, their hands constantly touching, like people who have harrowed hell together and are continually surprised by the miracle of still being alive. I stood in utmost bewilderment. Serena Somers . . . Somehow the epithet *sluglike* came to mind, but it was not an adjective that could easily be applied to this poised young woman.

When she was sure the congressman was out of earshot, Serena said, "Actually, the real reason I came down here was to see you. I hitched a ride on the Karpovsky bandwagon because I couldn't talk my mother into springing for a ticket to Mexico. And it's true he's in counseling, otherwise none of the girls would be working for him—they all know his reputation. But look, there's not much time. Everything's shifting again. We've had a reprieve, but the war's not over."

"Uh huh," said Theo. "I've been feeling it too, I guess."

"What war?" I said. "What reprieve?"

"I've been getting like weird vibes for about six months now. Like one day last week, I knew for a fact that Ronald Reagan was president of the U.S., not Mondale."

"He *is*, isn't he?" I said.

"And then there's the right-left thing. One day I wake up and we're driving on the left, and we've always driven on the left, and we've always had a bay window that faces the sunset and a dog named Buffy, but then other days it's the cat who's named Buffy and there's no bay window."

"It's the Darklings," Theo said. "They're sifting through reality again. They want me back. Or maybe it's Josh, trying to claw his way back to the land of the living. But he can't because we've all turned away from him, because he doesn't exist here, never has, never will."

"I haven't turned my back on Joshua," I said. "I'm not even sure who he is supposed to be."

"You really have forgotten everything, haven't you, Mr. E.?" asked Serena.

"He sure has," said my son. "I've been trying to break it to him gently all day, but he's not really grasping it."

"Mr. E., you have to think about Joshua."

—a flaming angel—

"All right. I'm thinking. I'm thinking."

—a flaming—

"Come on, Dad, this won't wait, stop playing mindgames."

—flaming—

Dark angels roared past us, their black robes flapping in the wind. The sun was setting at last and they were breaking out the candles for the vigil of the dead. I bought a Corona from a passing vendor and slugged it down. I *was* starting to remember. Didn't want to remember. The pain. Better to block it out. (That's why I will always be a second-rate poet. I don't have the guts to face my pain. I have the words, but I have nothing to say.)

"He was your son, Mr. E. He flew away on the wings of a gold-scaled dragon woman."

—a shadowy figure stood behind Theo, his face mottled by the cottonwood leaves as they speckled the sunset, and—

Flaming.

Serena took my hand. And Theo took my other hand. I shrank back from his touch, which had become unfamiliar over the past months. But he gripped me hard, demanding. Perhaps it was I who had withdrawn from him, I who had failed to give. Serena's hand was warm, Theo's cold and uncompromising.

"We're gonna fucking *make* you remember, Dad. Come on. We're taking you to Mom."

"But the clinic's south of here," I said, for I saw that they were leading me north, along the wooden path that led past the makeshift bazaar toward the grotto of the limestone Madonna.

"We know where we're going," said Serena softly. "It's you who are lost."

chapter two

Stealing the Madonna

Theo Etchison

When I see Serena Somers elbowing her way through the crowd toward us, I know it's finally time to get back to the River. Because if Serena has somehow contrived to come here, then she must know about Joshua. Which means I'm not the only one who's managed to keep sane while the universe tries to boomerang back on itself and to unchange the changes in reality.

"Go easy on my dad," I tell Serena. "He's old. It's hard for him to leap tall universes in a single bound."

"Weren't you fat once?" Dad says. I can tell that another image has surfaced in his mind.

"Yeah, I guess," says Serena. "But I like myself now."

"Dad, they're coming back for us. They can't play their game without me, and . . . if I get sucked in, you will too. And there's Josh, floating around in limbo, not dead, not alive."

My father looks terrible. Before Mom got sick, before I began having the dreams that all turned out to be true, Dad used to charm us with words . . . not charm as in flirt or being cute but charm as in what you do with a snake;

15

he'd make words dance around you till you're dizzy. Since Mom was diagnosed . . . well, kind of since the chemo-therapy started I guess . . . he's been losing the gift. Now's another time when words fail him. He looks around and I bet anything the one thought that's racing through his mind is like, I want a drink. I don't want these memories to breach the placid surface of my mind. Because each one hurts.

Dad says, "I see a flaming angel. He is leaping into the sea."

"Come on, Serena," I say. We still haven't loosed our grip on his hands because we feel he's going to slip into what Ash calls disjunctive fugue, when the universe *twang*s back and forth on itself like a guitar string and your brain can't keep up with the changes.

We lead him gently north toward the cave. And as we move, we're kind of like a magnet moving through a pile of iron filings. I mean, the crowd begins to align itself, begins to get a direction. It's darkening and they are lighting candles and falling in with the procession. Over the ocean's tangy smell there's a hint of incense.

Dad says, "Let's start with an hour ago, when Theo and I were sitting on the veranda waiting for Mary to come back from treatment."

"Dad, you've been waiting for her to come back for three days now. Maybe it was only a few minutes for you, but the world has shifted like half a dozen times and you've just been sitting there, in a little puddle of your own private time. We had a nuclear holocaust yesterday and all life was destroyed. You don't remember that, of course. The world was wrenched back on course and everyone's memories have been erased. Except mine, because I'm a Truthsayer. I had to twist back the course of the River so that the war never happened. It's okay. Some of the more sensitive people in the world will have a vague feeling that it happened . . . like they've woken from a nightmare but they can't remember the details."

Serena says, "Wow. I dreamed I was in a forest fire. The

trees were crashing all around me and I was all, No! No! but no one could hear me screaming."

"That wasn't a dream," I tell her. I know that she believes me. She's been able to swallow a lot of inconceivable truths. It's because she loves Josh so much, this love has clung to her like the strand of wool that showed Theseus the way out of the labyrinth.

God I envy people their dreams. Recently I came to the realization that I've never really had a dream. I can't dream because I'm a Truthsayer. For me the very act of dreaming makes it true.

"Anyway," I tell Dad, "it's all over now, and it's not even that important. The main thing is us. We're at the center of this storm. The Darklings are trying to throw our world out of phase, but it's only because they want *us*. They could give a shit about one tenth-rate planet in a distant corner of a Z-grade galaxy. You'd better start remembering soon, Dad, because they're chasing us down."

As I'm saying this, darkness is falling—wham!—like a fade-out in a movie. And the candles are everywhere—tall candles, short candles, scented candles, and the special Day of the Dead candles shaped like human skulls—most of them in like these glass holders to keep the wind from blowing them out. I suck my sugar skull. The sugar tastes bitter. Maybe it's my mood and maybe it's another reality shift. I throw the skull into a trash can heaped with Corona bottles. And suddenly the night is scary. The crowd's pressing on us. It's carrying us toward the shrine whether we want to go or not. Dwarfs and mutants and skeletons dance past us and the candlelight flickers so their whitefaced features seem to bob up and down in the sea of night. Musics clash: salsa music, funeral brass music, and in the distance a church choir singing words in Latin that sound like *libera me, domine, libera me, domine*. And the wind is roaring now, though we can't feel it much because there's this line of market stalls with canvas awnings shielding us from the sea.

There were like a whole bunch of American tourists

out, but they all seem to have melted into the shadows. I don't know, this afternoon the festival seemed all fake and plasticky and now it's starting to feel real. I can smell death. I'm scared. Even more than when I reversed the holocaust, because that was an impersonal kind of thing, feeling the glitch in the flow of the River and steering hard to starboard to get the world back on course—Truthsayers do things like that all the time, they nudge the universe, and mostly the universe snaps back by itself, like a rubber band.

So here we are being sucked into the flow of a human river. And it reminds me of the trek to Caliosper . . . it's easy to imagine in the pandemonium the beating of aliens' wings. I wonder when the Darklings will start to appear.

"Why don't we walk by the beach?" Dad says. "We'll get there quicker."

"No, Dad. Don't you remember? Water could be a gateway."

"Yeah. Right." I think he sees, or is starting to see at least. We move swiftly, the three of us, threading our way through the throng. Pallbearers dance and the coffin lid goes *bang bang bang* as the cadaver within pops up to crack jokes and strum his guitar. Flamenco dancers leap and twirl. The air is a collage of gasoline and incense and fish and tamales and old puke.

"Hurry, hurry," I tell him. But there can't be any hurry, really. The whole crowd is headed the same way. Up ahead is the Madonna's grotto, its entrance glittering with thousands of twinkling Christmas-type lights. Of course the Madonna has nothing to do with the Day of the Dead, but here in this Disney-style Mexicoland all the traditions are tossed together like a Waldorf salad. There are the black-robed women mourning the tears of the world . . . they don't belong here at all . . . I last saw them on Thorn's world . . . in another cave next to a different sea. But they are here, palms folded, floating alongside the parade. And there . . . whirling through the skeleton celebrants . . . isn't that Cornelius Huang, towering Fu-Manchuishly over the dancers? He lifts his conch to his lips . . . I hear its savage blast rip through the salsa cacophony. "Oh, Jesus, hurry, hurry."

There's the entrance to the cave. All of a sudden, inexplicably, there's silence. The crowd has fallen reverently to its knees. Not a whimper except the battering of the surf against the shore. The three of us are the only ones standing. The lights around the entrance shimmer and then they're all like the lights in Times Square in New York where they have the newspaper headlines scrolling across, and the lights flash:

WELCOME THEO TRUTHSAYER BACK TO THE FRAY

and

ONLY YOU CAN SAVE THE UNIVERSE

and

**THOUGHT YOU COULD ESCAPE, EH?
MUAHAHAHAHA!!!**

which prompts my Dad to say, "Hm. I suppose this might be considered sort of the comic book interpretation of the cosmos."

"Yeah, Dad, but . . . in a way . . . the cosmos is what I dream. And maybe I'm bright, because you always read poetry to me and make me watch foreign movies on PBS and shit, but . . . I'm still a kid underneath and I still have a comic book kind of a mind."

"My son, the solipsist!"

"Better pay attention to what he's saying, Mr. E.," Serena says. "The weirder it gets, the truer it is."

The three of us are the only ones standing. Half the town is prostrate around us. The sea of backs stretches all the way to the sea of water.

"Come on, Dad, hurry the fuck up," I say. I'm really scared now. I've seen a shadow flitting at the periphery of my vision.

And then we're at the entrance to the cave.

And then we're inside. There's so much incense that we seem to be standing in the clouds. Serena coughs. Through the mist we see the pinprick flames of a thousand thousand candles. A choir is singing. It's those same words: *libera me, domine, libera me, domine . . . free me, Lord.* Could they be addressing themselves to me? Oh shit I hope not. In this world I'm just a kid, frail and powerless. Sure, I wrench the course of time back on track once in a while but hey, it's all in the dreaming, it's not supposed to leak out into the real world. I can't free anyone. Not here. Not yet.

I feel in the pocket of my shorts. I'm looking for the plain glass marble that is actually a schematic chart of the entire River. I touch something cold. That's probably it, but in this world it's probably only a marble.

There's an altar rail, but there's too much smoke to see what's behind it. We only see the tall man with the Chinese features and the mandarin hat, with the conch tucked under one arm. Apart from the hat, he is clothed in the vestments of a priest.

"Cornelius," I say softly.

"You," he says to me, "I expect you to know my name. But these others . . . they shouldn't remember anything. They're not part of this scenario. You'd better get rid of them before we're forced to eliminate them completely."

My father lets go of my hand suddenly. "I remember now! There was a Chinese restaurant . . . You said you were a fan of my poetry . . . You kidnapped my son." There's so much anger in him. It's all coming back at once. The hurt. The grief. The fury. "You took him away and you and that . . . that vampire master of yours . . . and you were using him for . . . for something."

Cornelius Huang smiles.

" . . . and my other son . . . you've done something to him."

"Not my department," says Huang.

Behind the wind and the surf we hear another sound . . . yes . . . the beating of mighty wings and the hollow roar of a dragon's breath. So I know Katastrofa is in the vicinity too, circling above the cliffs maybe, waiting to pounce.

Huang holds out his hand and a crystal goblet materializes in it. It fills with a frothy red liquid.

"You're just in time for communion," he says.

Oremus, the choir thunders.

Huang raises up the goblet. "The Holy Grail," he says. "But are you worthy of it?"

The grail sparkles in the candlelight.

Ave verum corpus, shrieks the choir.

My father is staring at the chalice. He's hypnotized by it. I know the power it has over him. "Don't take the wine, Dad!" I scream. "It's gonna make you blind again, you'll forget everything—" But Dad's moving toward the altar rail and he genuflects in front of Cornelius Huang as his lips widen in an orca smile. Serena runs forward and dashes the goblet out of Huang's hand and it crashes somewhere, we hear the tinkle and the long long echo of it through the cavern as above our heads the stalactites seem to whirl and Huang's standing there, looking at his bleeding hand, still clutching a shard of glass that has sliced into his palm, and the blood is spurting up, spritzing my father, moistening his lips, and my father's all, "Howl, howl, howl," like he was wandering through a high school production of *King Lear*. And Cornelius Huang says, "Children, children; you force me to take dire measures."

He blows one shattering blast on that conch of his and that's when the cave kind of splits apart like an egg. The tide must have been rising or something because now seawater's sluicing in through the cracks in the cave wall. People are screaming. I think we're having a flood. I can hear the ocean battering at the cliffs. And all of a sudden we're moving . . . I mean we're still in the cave but the cave has been unmoored from the world and the cave's become part of a big old ship and I *know* that ship . . . it's Thorn's ship, and I know we're

adrift once more on the great River that runs between the
worlds, and that the cave is nothing more than another inlet
of that River . . . and there's Dad, still kneeling at the altar,
baptized in the blood from the herald's hand. Oh fucking
Jesus I am scared because I hadn't wanted it to happen that
way. I didn't want to see Thorn again, to fall into his power.
I don't see him now but I know he's got to be close.

Just then Serena tugs at me and yes, we're still enveloped
in mist, but through a break above our heads we can see
Thorn and Katastrofa, brother and sister, battling in the sky.
Thorn is a monstrous bat and Katastrofa a crystal dragon
coiled and uncoiling around the bat's torso. Blood rains
from Thorn's lips. "You don't have me yet," I cry to
Cornelius Huang. "And you don't have Dad or Serena.
Your master's desperately fighting for control of me."

"But it is I who have custody," Cornelius says, without
ever unclenching his teeth.

"Not yet. I appeal to the Madonna for protection," I say,
and I leapfrog over my Dad and into the outstretched arms
of the Madonna.

The mist around her clears. Mom's face looks down on
me. A single tear has been moving down her cheek for
many months. She is pale and veined in pink; she is stone
and flesh at the same time. She used to have a stone child
in her arms, but now she has only me.

Dad looks up. "Oh, my God," he whispers. "It's Mary."

Serena says, "That's what we've been trying to tell you,
Mr. E. On Earth, which is like only a shadow of the greater
world, Mrs. E.'s a middle-aged woman with cancer, but like
in the *real* universe your wife is like the great mother goddess of everything. She only seems to be a statue because
time moves so slowly for her that sometimes she doesn't
take a breath in a thousand years. And your wife has
cancer because, in the *real* universe, everything's falling
apart because of the war between the Darklings."

I don't think Dad really has time to assimilate this because
the battle in the sky seems to have finished in a draw and
both bat and dragon are plummeting towards us, talons

outstretched, and we're like three blind mice, or maybe sitting ducks, nowhere to run or hide . . . so I put my arms around the statue and I say softly, "Help me . . . Mom . . . wherever you are . . . if you can hear me . . ." as Huang advances toward me with a butterfly net in his hands . . .

Something happens to the statue. The tear, which was glistening on her cheeks, begins to race down it, and more tears come welling up, and the stone heats up so it almost burns me. And what happens next is incredible because her arm comes flying up and it sort of hits Huang in the face and he goes flying into a wall of candles. It's a supreme effort of her will to condense time like that. Somewhere in the universe a sun has died to fuel her gesture. Then, well, the statue like freezes up again, this time in the new posture with its arm upraised, and the brother and sister Darkling are still hurtling down toward us, but the statue's movement's bought me maybe a split second to act.

I pull the marble out of my pocket. I home in on our location inside the twisted strands of the River which are all folded up inside the marble. I forge a new rivulet. Not for me, because I know I must stay and fight and maybe bring my brother home. But Dad and Serena have to go home. They're not involved. They shouldn't get stuck here. They're not Truthsayers. No one has the right to make them pawns in all this. It was selfish of me to try to drag Dad into this, I realize. Better to leave him back on earth, to have him lose all memory of me or Joshua . . . for then, if we don't return, he will never know how he once loved us, or the pain of losing us. Oh, God, why did I have to remind him about Josh? How could I have wished the pain of remembrance on him? No. No. I summon the wall of water and it rises from the sea.

"Don't fight it, Dad . . . Serena . . ." I say. "Go with it. It'll take you back to where you started from."

I force the water in over Dad and Serena and watch the current carrying them away, toward home.

Then I wait for the shadows to swoop down and carry me away.

But that doesn't happen. Instead, I feel the statue heave, uproot itself, and me along with it, raising itself slowly into the air. Bat and dragon plunge into the water. The salt spray soaks me. I look around me. The statue, the altar, the railing, the limestone floor of the cavern, all these things are hovering above the sea. We're cupped in the palm of a hand a hundred feet wide, and the palm is attached to a gigantic elbow which is connected to a monstrous arm which is bending as the hand rises up toward a human face which is gradually blotting out the entire sky . . .

It's a weatherbeaten face, with long white wind-whipped hair and now I see the lips parting and the stench of the giant's breath billows around us. I know the face. It's Strang, the mad king, the one whose kingdom the three children are battling over, the one who once caged the darkness in a crystal scepter and was given dominion over all the worlds fed by the River that leads every place.

"Mom . . ." I say. "It's Strang."

The jaws gape. Snap shut. With us inside, coasting on a stream of saliva. The statue of the One Mother and I are rolling down the king's esophagus. *Dad! Serena! Joshua!* I try to cling to their memories as we slide down the monster's gullet. I'm choking on the fetor. I don't think I'll ever see them again. At least I've saved Dad and Serena, I think. The universe can wait for someone better than me, stronger, more compassionate. Blackness engulfs me, and I'm full of despair.

chapter three

Renewable Virginity

Serena Somers

We broke through the wall of water. Me and Mr. E., that is. I knew that Theo had done it. He probably thought he was saving our lives. If you can call it living.

We were back in the cave, but there was no statue behind the altar rail.

About a dozen choirboys were chanting listlessly, and censers were being swung. An old Indian woman prayed beside the rows of candles. From outside came the sounds of the festival. There had never been a flood. The Darklings had never come.

"Where's—" said Mr. E., rubbing his eyes as though wakening from a nightmare. "Where's—" I suddenly realized that he couldn't remember Theo's name.

Theo had never existed.

Even I, who loved Theo like a brother, couldn't remember the color of his eyes. That's the remarkable thing about all these reality shifts. They edit the whole past as well as the present. A universe vanishes and another replaces it. In the world where I used to go out with Joshua Etchison and he had this weird, introverted brother who had an uncanny

habit of blurting out the truth at the wrong moment, where
he lived with his poet father and his dying mother in a
Virginia suburb of Washington . . . in that world I'd been
a virgin. Not that I'd wanted to be. I was too scared not to
be. I made myself fat so that I could stay a virgin. In the
minutes between wakefulness and sleep I'd fantasize about
Joshua.

Then I learned that this whole universe was a backwater
tributary of the River that flows from universe to universe,
and that Theo was a Truthsayer, one of the few beings with
the talent of being able to navigate from world to world . . .
and that his services were being fought over by the Darkling siblings as they battled each other for control of a
mega-universe, a cosmic egg that was rapidly splintering
into pieces that King Strang's horses and men couldn't put
together again, not without Theo's ability always to see the
truth, and to know the true names of things. He alone could
hear the original music of the universe, of which every
other universe is only an echo. Oh, yeah, Theo was special.
Some might even call him God, since it couldn't really be
determined whether it was him dreaming the universe into
being or just him seeing the truth at the center of the infinite
onion skins of illusion. He was the key to everything. The
still point of the turning world, Mr. E. would probably say,
since he always quotes other people's poetry in moments
of confusion. Theo the God. Theo $= mc^2$. And all this time
we'd just thought he was weird.

They came and took Theo away, and the world, rushing
in to fill the vacuum of his absence, made it so that he never
existed. And Phil, his father, had no memory of him at all.
Mr. E.'s a poet, and poets are supposed to be Truthsayers in
a way, but Philip Etchison would've been the first to admit
that he wasn't that kind of poet. He was always down on his
own poetry, ever since he got passed over for the Pulitzer.
But Joshua remembered. Because he had a piece of Theo's
talent, a watered-down version of it.

So they took Joshua away. But the journey into other
worlds is a kind of death, and Joshua wasn't properly

prepared for it, and by the time Mr. E. and I found him, he was already dead. But he was also undead.

I sacrificed my virginity to save his life.

I guess I have a bit of the talent too, though not as much as Joshua and certainly not like Theo, who's like a totally different kind of being, I mean, he doesn't even *think* in past and present, everything's always present to him, and every possibility is equally real, equally unreal. Yeah.

Well, we all came back from the River. Me and Mr. E. and Theo and Joshua, and Mrs. E., who had gone from a terminal cancer patient to a hallucinating schizophrenic to the goddess of the universe and back again to a dying woman. But see, Joshua had kind of gotten used to being dead.

That's why he leaped into the sea.

Joshua had never existed. Which meant I had never made love to him to save him from the dragon woman Katastrofa, second child of the mad King Strang. Which made me a virgin again. Reconstituted my hymen and everything. I hadn't had a physical examination, but I was sure of it. That was something that made me different from my other friends in school. I never really went out with anyone. I just radiated this hands-off thing, I guess. Which was strange since the boy I loved had never existed.

Okay. I was thinking all this out, trying to get it all straight because I was giving it all to Mr. E., in chronological order, as we walked along the boardwalk in Baja down to the asylum. Theo and I *had* been trying to explain it all to him before, but it always came out jumbled because we never knew how much he could actually remember or how much he could take before his mind would go off into a labyrinth of disjunctive fugue.

Did I say the asylum?

"I thought we were at a laetrile clinic," Mr. E. said.

We'd walked about half a mile and I had already eaten three of those sugar skulls they were selling in every stall. That meant I was scared, so scared I'd forgotten my pledge—I'd stuck to it for a year now—no more eating disorders. I knew I was going to chomp down enough candy skulls so I'd be up half the night puking in the hotel room.

"You don't understand, Mr. E. There *is* no laetrile clinic, because Mrs. E.'s not dying of cancer anymore. Don't you remember? I told you five minutes ago . . . when you lose your sons, your wife's disease usually changes to something else. Last time it was schizophrenia."

"This is madness."

"Yeah. It is."

At least it was still November 2, in the last decade of the twentieth century, on a beach in Baja. I was pretty sure of that. When reality changes it takes the path of least resistance. So I was probably still here working for Congressman Karpovsky and all that. I wasn't certain of that, but I told Mr. E. that even though the clinic was gone, the Hyatt would still be there.

We worked our way through the crowd of celebrants. There were a lot of tourists. Even though they were wearing the skeleton outfits too (they were selling them in the hotel for $5, one size fits all) the tourists had like this corn-fed look about them, you know, you can take the boy out of Idaho but you can't take the Idaho out of the boy, that kind of thing? And that was different. Because when we were walking toward the shrine the tourists had like all faded away and there was this sense of menace . . . maybe because the minions of Thorn and Katastrofa had infiltrated the festival. Okay. It was back to normal now. Muzak and fakery. Popped another candied skull. Sucked another soul. It was hot and sticky on my tongue.

We walked on without talking for a while. A sandy street led away from the boardwalk, into town. Just a few feet from the festival and there wasn't a living soul. I guess the whole town was out there playing "puttin' on the tourists." We walked uphill. The street wound a lot, hugging the contour of the landscape I guess. The music was faint now.

"I don't remember this cemetery," Mr. E. said. "In fact . . ."

I could tell that the disjunction was hitting him hard. I guessed that the laetrile clinic must have been here last time he looked. Now, instead, there was an adobe-walled church, a graveyard . . . with a great view of the sea and the fireworks display, far away, over the water, strangely quiet.

"Remember," I said, holding his hand. "You never came to any clinic."

"Then what am I doing here?"

"Reality takes the path of least resistance. Theo explained it to me once. It's like the way matter curves the fabric of space, making a big gravity well around itself, you know? Well, you and I, Mr. E., with our sentient souls, we curve the fabric of perception around us. So even though there may be no logical reason for you to be in Mexico anymore, it's easier for it to give you some wild serendipitous excuse for occupying this bit of space here than it is to send you careening across to Virginia. Know what I mean?"

We found ourselves opening the wrought-iron gates and entering the churchyard. The place was full of people . . . it would be, being the Day of the Dead . . . and many of the graves were brightly lit with candles. There were like clusters of people around each of the candlelit graves, and they were eating and drinking . . . The air smelled of flowers and corn tortillas. This was a lot closer to the real thing than the revelry by the beach. A solemn-eyed kid sat on a tombstone, chugging a Corona and puffing on a cigarette. There was a subtle war of musics . . . three or four ghettoblasters playing everything from Menudo to Metallica . . . but softly, unobtrusively. Each of the families was doing its own thing, whether it was weeping over the dead relatives' photographs or leaving offerings of tamales and even, on one grave, a neatly stacked pyramid of unopened Big Macs . . . or just sitting around catching some rays . . . moon rays, that is . . . there was a full moon in a cloudless sky.

"But Serena . . ." said Mr. E. "Our bungalow used to be over there. This wasn't a cemetery at all, it was where our family was staying, you know, during the treatment." He pointed to a patch almost flush with the cliff edge. Now there were only grave markers. "My car was right there. If that's disappeared, and never existed, how the hell am I supposed to have gotten here in the first place?"

"How should I know?" I said. "Let's check it out."

We walked through knee-tall grass. The grass tickled the holes in my jeans. It suddenly occurred to me that I hadn't been wearing jeans before—I'd been in my designer uniform, the one all of Congressman Karpovsky's campaign flunkies wore—relentlessly yuppie-looking. Did this mean I wasn't with Karpovsky? Was there a new set of memories that I hadn't cottoned on to yet, a whole 'nother reason why I happened to be in Mexico and not in Tucson studying for a literature test?

At the cliff's edge, a low wooden railing was all that stood between us and a sheer drop into the ocean. We could see the parade going on far below, an undulating snake of candlelight from the town to the Virgin's shrine.

There weren't a whole lot of graves on this end of the cemetery and none of them was decorated with flowers, lights, and foodstuffs. In fact, Mr. E. and I seemed isolated from the others all of a sudden.

"This is where we were sitting, on white chairs with wrought-iron backs," Mr. E. said. "I and . . . someone. You're telling me it was my son."

"Your son Theo."

"I think I see him in my mind's eye. He's slender and small for his age, almost as though he'd willed himself not to cross into puberty country. His hair's a mess and . . . dirty blond and . . . I think . . . a Redskins T-shirt. Too long. Hugging his knees almost. I wish I'd picked up a Corona down there at one of the food stalls."

"No, no, no alcohol. Hang *on* to that memory, Mr. E.! Sometimes, when these disjunctions happen, the only thing left to anchor you to the last reality is . . . you know . . . a face, a landscape, maybe even just a smell."

"God! I just remembered how Theo smelled."

"Yeah. Smells don't lie."

"He wasn't grubby. His T-shirt was always soaked in sweat but it had a kind of sweet smell. A residue of the Teenage Mutant Ninja Turtles bubble bath that kid Jesus gave him for Christmas."

"Jesus?"

"Yeah . . . a scrawny little Mexican kid who used to hang out by the veranda. He and Theo ran around together a lot. I mean, they didn't exactly *communicate*, because he didn't speak a word of English. Maybe Theo taught him a few words. I don't know. Jesus Ortega. Yes."

"You sure remember a lot, Mr. E. Considering the evidence of your eyes, which totally contradicts everything you're saying. I think you must have a little bit of the talent after all. Well, it's not surprising that it'd be in the genes, is it, now?" But I was pretty frustrated because I knew there was so much more that he *couldn't* remember. What is it about people when they hit middle age? Memory becomes slippery. Images slide away like eels.

"I remember that I'm supposed to be waiting for my wife. And we have a car, a battered old gas guzzler, and it's parked about there . . . by that headstone."

A firework went off overhead. It lit up the headstone and we both read the name at the same time:

Mary Etchison

"Oh, God," said Mr. Etchison. "Oh, God, she's dead."

chapter four

Free-Falling

Theo Etchison

So it's like I'm plunging down this well. I think it's a well because of the way it echoes. But it's dark and I've lost my hold on the Madonna. I fall and fall. Eventually . . . though I know I'm still falling . . . I get a grip on myself . . . it's free fall. There's no gravity. I'm weightless. Maybe I can maneuver a little bit if only I can get rid of the notion that my feet are *down* and my head is *up*.

The way I figure it, Thorn and Katastrofa were both trying to kidnap me and the One Mother. Strang intercepted them and swallowed me up. I'm inside him in a way. But that's an illusion, like everything else in all the universes, and I know that I can see through it if I use my gift. I fumble in my pocket for the marble. This is hard because of course I'm still falling . . . probably somewhere near the velocity of light by now . . . and I have to make myself perfectly still inside before I can reach for it.

But it's there. It's cold and my hand is clammy as it wraps around it and pulls it out. There's a faint blue glow about it, and that's how I see the walls of the well for the first time. It's all massive blocks of odd-shaped stone

cunningly fitted together like the Cyclopean walls of Troy
and Mycenae. Here and there is a niche in the wall or a
shelf, and each one is crammed with an entire world. But
I'm falling too fast to recognize them. I hold the marble
up to my face. Inside are the million strands of light that
chart the course of the River. And the filaments are twisting,
writhing, weaving in and out, changing color . . . I can see
that the whole structure of the universe is spinning out of
control. Worlds are leaking into other worlds so fast that
the cracks don't have time to heal.

I can't fix it all by myself. I'm just one of me. But I know
that if the streams all fuse into one, there's not going to *be*
a universe. Every world will be every other world all at the
same time. It's a chain reaction. Disjunctive fugue will hit
everything that has consciousness. Every reality will be true
at the same time. We can't survive that. Don't the Darklings
understand that they're fucking up the whole cosmos?

And I'm still falling. Falling. Falling.

Somehow I'm going to have to reach my Dad . . . to call
to him across the chasm that separates our worlds. I've got
to find him first. It's hard because when I try to focus on
him, to think myself deep into the heart of the marble, the
image shifts and shimmers and won't stay still. It's because
Dad's becoming a different person with every split second
that passes, because he's at the intersection of a dozen
lifelines and he has a dozen pasts and he doesn't have
the gift of picking among them. I see him now. He's
standing at the edge of the cliff. That's just where he was
earlier today when I started trying to explain everything to
him . . . and when the worlds started leaking out all over
each other.

They're in a cemetery with low adobe walls. It's party
time there. There's people feasting, praying, decorating the
headstones, and some of them have fallen asleep in the
tall soft grass. It's a little windy up there. There's kids
running around like crazy in their little skeleton costumes.
I don't see any of this that clearly . . . it's more like a kind
of radar . . . the people are like little blips against a 3-D

screen, and my Dad and Serena are big blips, because to
them I still exist, and they're thinking of me.

That's when I notice that Jesus Ortega's one of the kids
who are playing tag, weaving in and out of the headstones,
sucking on corpsicles, laughing as the fireworks go off. I
wonder if he's thinking about me. He's a kid and sometimes
it's easier to talk to them because their world-view isn't set
hard, like concrete, it's still kind of fluid, and I know he
probably felt the glitch when the world shifted course. But
he doesn't speak a word of English. Well, he can sing the
"Teenage Mutant Ninja Turtles" theme song. Big deal. But
he's like five years old, so his mind is wide open; he doesn't
wear the blinkers of adulthood or even of first-grade-hood.
Maybe I can use him as a conduit to my father.

Yeah. And as these thoughts are racing through my mind
I'm still plummeting down the dream-esophagus of King
Strang . . . whizzing past suns and moons and gods and
goddesses and through the hearts of dusty nebulae. But I
have to concentrate on the universe inside my marble . . .
the microcosm. I close my eyes tight but I can still see the
strands of the River . . . or rather I can feel them, I can reach
my hand inside and grasp them, squeeze them, the way you
might put your hand into a nest of wriggling snakes. It's
got to be done though. Yeah.

—*Jesus*—

Can he hear me?

—*Hay-fucking-soooos!*—*Listen to me, you dadburned
varmint!* (he hears me as kind of spectral Yosemite Sam)—
Jesus!

I think he hears something. He looks up. A firework
bursts out up there, green, red, and white, the colors of
Mexico.

"*¿Teodoro?*" he whispers. It's like he's seen a ghost. My
image flickers in the candlelight. Shit, I *am* a ghost to him.
I'm dead in this new version of reality. Figures. Should've
known. "*¡Pero eres muerto!*"

"I know I'm dead," I tell him. He hears me in the whine
of the wind. He shivers. I speak to him in images, not

words. Today is the Day of the Dead and it's all right for you to hear me. I'm not going to hurt you. I need your help. Go to my father. I know you can't understand the words, but I will whisper the sounds in your ears and you'll be able to make him listen. Go, Jesus. A plan is forming in my mind. I've got to communicate with them or we'll never see each other again, and Joshua will be dead for ever.

Jesus looks for his mother at first. He's frightened now. He sees his mother by the grave of his little sister. She's rocking another little sister—the twin that lived—in her arms. I guess he realizes that she's preoccupied because he looks away now, looks at where my Dad and Serena are sitting, staring out to sea. I try to touch across the gulf. All he feels is a chill nothingness that creeps up his spine. "It's okay, Jesus," I say, and I start humming the "Turtles" theme song to him. And he's not scared anymore when he hears that silly ditty in the air, because I guess he realizes it's actually me and not some evil demon released by the dark magic of the *Día de los Muertos*.

Laughing, he toddles over to where my father is sitting . . . and I go on falling, falling, falling into an emptiness I dare not name.

chapter five

Armorica

Phil Etchison

And that, to me, was the moment of epiphany.

At once I remembered it all with the crystalline immediacy of an MTV montage: the brochures about the Day of the Dead. The cross-country drive, down the 79 through West Virginia and Kentucky, then cutting a swath west, a piece of Louisiana, a chunk of Texas, New Mexico, the Arizona desert, then turning south . . . I remembered it all. The dust. The bus popping up at the hillcrest, the station wagon huffing and puffing, the big blue crowded bus with flying streamers and horn playing the opening of Beethoven's Fifth Symphony again and again, tatata-TAH, tatata-TAH, as it caromed off the side rail and into us and then Mary's frayed seat belt breaking and the windshield shattering and the two boys, bouncing downhill like bloody logs, rolling into oncoming traffic and—

The bus bursting into flames. The Mexican police. The hospital. The morgue. A town called Todos Santos. It was as though I'd dammed up the memories and the sight of the headstone had broken the wall and now I was experiencing this collage of pain for the first time.

And then there was the other set of memories. The Chinese restaurant on Route 10 just outside Tucson. The man with the slate-colored eyes. My wife dying of cancer. The smell of a dying woman couldn't easily be dislodged. Mystic journeys and fantastical beasts and flying cities—memories that could not, logically, have any truth to them—memories that warred with these new memories of terror and loss—and clamored to be recognized as truths.

There were more fireworks. I read the two smaller headstones that flanked my wife's. I understood now why this section of the graveyard wasn't decorated with flowers and candles. The markers read:

in memoriam
Joshua Etchison

and:

in loving memory of
Theo Etchison

It was the gringo section of the cemetery.

"Why aren't they buried back home, in Virginia?" Serena said. "And how did they die?"

"There was an accident. It happened . . . um . . . a year ago," I said, seeing images of the funeral for the first time. "I couldn't face going back. I was . . . on the verge of bankruptcy. I wouldn't have been able to afford the funerals back in the States. And anyway I didn't want to see any of our old friends. I didn't know how I could face *you*." Suddenly I realized that, in *this* universe, I knew exactly who Serena was. But why couldn't I go back and face her? Oh yes. I had let Josh drive. Impetuous Josh, Josh-without-a-license. I had done it because I was all wrapped up in the opening lines of a new poem I was writing.

In the poem, a young man in a fantasy kingdom takes leave of his mother to go out into the world and seek his fortune. She admonishes him never to forget his name. But that is the first thing he forgets, and his adventures turn out to have been illusions. In the forest where things have no names, only illusions can exist. I was working on the poem or I could have warned Joshua or grabbed the steering wheel or . . . (No! screamed another part of my mind. You yourself have wandered into the forest where things have no names . . . you yourself have fallen prey to illusion . . .)

I could tell that Serena had not known that, in this world, her boyfriend and his brother and my wife were all dead. She'd been relatively calm up to that point, methodically explicating the implausible sequence of events that had brought us to this juncture, but now she was starting to cry. "Mrs. E. wasn't supposed to be *dead*," she said. "Just . . . you know, like in a psychiatric ward or something—so we could rescue her like we did before. I can't take this, I can't see a way out of this mess."

"There now," I said. "There now."

I embraced her. We sat down at the edge of the cliff. We looked out over the sea. I thought of the flaming angel. Serena sobbed like a child. I remembered how plucky she had been when she rescued Mary from the asylum and—

But that was another memory, from another universe.

We sat for a long time, not talking. In the cemetery, a strolling band strummed and sang love songs to the dead. A kid—it was one I'd noticed earlier, belting down a bottle of beer—came up to us and offered us some tamales from a basket.

"Thanks a lot, kid," I said, and fished in my wallet for a couple of bucks.

"Hey, no money, Felipe," he said. And when I looked at him blankly, he said, "You don't recognize me? You think we all looking alike, maybe? I'm Jesus Ortega, you know, the one who play with your son."

"But my son is dead."

Jesus laughed. "You silly man," he said, "your son dead, yes. I play with him." He cackled and did a little dance around Theo's gravestone. Chasing the wind. "Cowabunga, dude," he shrieked. He listened to the wind and answered it with a string of lilting Spanglish.

"Theo . . . he's your imaginary companion?" I asked him. I had to shout because the wind had begun to whine as soon as Jesus started dancing . . . almost as though it were reacting to the boy.

"You silly old man," said the boy, "you know Theo he is the wind. He is the wind and he talk to me, very clear, in the laughing."

For a moment I heard the laughter of my son. Serena must have heard it too, because she stiffened in shock. She was shaking. I could feel the warmth drain from her hands, her cheeks.

"Theo's talking to us," she said. "That's *his* voice. Listen."

I hear the clink of beer bottles, the silvery tinkle of children's laughter.

"It *is* Theo," Serena said. "The kid, he's like *channeling* him or something. I bet Jesus doesn't even speak English. He looks . . . um, the way I look when I'm in Spanish class and Professor Schmitz makes me read aloud from, you know, *Don Quijote* or something—and I'm just sounding it out, one syllable at a time, not getting any of it."

There he was, holding out his basket of tamales and smiling. He had the kind of large, liquidescing eyes that you see on those Sally Struthers late night sponsor-a-starving-child telethons. I took a tamale and peeled the husk and wolfed it down even though it was really drink I craved, not food.

"Stone," said the boy.

I look around. He's talking about the headstones maybe.

> *in memory of my beloved son*
> **JOSHUA EMERSON ETCHISON**
> *1975–1992*

But wait a minute . . . hadn't it said "in memoriam" before? And "Emerson" wasn't my son's middle name.

I was certain of that, as certain as I'd been only a few hours before that I had no son named Joshua at all.

"Stone," the boy said.

What went through my mind was a welter of free association: stone stone stone we are all stone *tu es petrus* and here was Jesus telling me *stone stone stone* and what kind of rock am I to build on when the foundations of the world are sinking sinking like a stone, stone?

But it was Serena who said, "He's talking about *Milt* Stone, you know, Detective Stone, back in Tucson . . . the Navajo guy who took us across the River last time? We have to go to him and—"

All I remembered was a man who could turn into a woman at will, who danced on the mesa in the sunset, who made us a big pot of peyote tea and shot us full of arrows and—

(Jesus is Greek for Joshua, I remembered suddenly.)

"Thank God. You *are* remembering," said Serena. "The kid's telling us we have to find Mr. Stone. In Tucson, I guess. We're going to have to make the crossing again. Theo pushed us back into the world so that we wouldn't have to get involved, but now he realizes this isn't the right world . . . that there's no turning back. Maybe the right world doesn't exist at all anymore. Or it's about ready to get zapped into the phantom zone."

"How can we get to Tucson?" I said. A vivid memory came to me: I'd sold my car to pay for the funerals. I wasn't due to get a royalty check from my agent for another three months. The university had fired me. I'd been living a hand-to-mouth existence, giving poetry readings on the beach to aging hippies passing through Baja, gathering a few pesos here and there, getting smashed every night . . . what a tawdry lifeline, I thought. I was glad I hadn't physically lived through it. But *someone* had. Whenever reality did one of these elastic snaps, it always seemed to invent the most cliché-ridden of possible pasts. Perhaps there was some kind of law of conservation of banality at work. Musing over these philosophical complexities, I found I had consumed two tamales, and Jesus' basket was empty.

"You go stone," he said, "you go stone, you go through stone, make stone flesh, make stoned flesh live." Which was about as clear as the Book of Revelation.

"Don't worry, Mr. E.," Serena said. "We can hitch a ride on Congressman Karpovsky's campaign bus. We're leaving here at midnight . . . He was really only down here for the Day of the Dead photo-op, and he's due to speak at the Phoenix Convention Center tomorrow night . . . come on, the congressman won't mind; he wants to be seen with poets, you know; it boosts his image with the space cadet contingent. Come on, Mr. E., we gotta get on the road!"

"Maybe the congressman won't even *be* here in this reality."

"We won't know until we walk down to the Hyatt, will we?" She was jumpy now, pulling me up from the graveside, dancing around me. "Come *on!*"

"*Hasta la vista, Señor Etchison,*" said Jesus, waving, as Serena yanked me by the hand and we made our way out of the cemetery . . . we ran downhill toward where the Hyatt stood, gleaming against the cliffscape like a glass cathedral.

Inside the lobby, a couple of young women, college age like Serena, manned a reception desk beneath a huge *Karpovsky* banner. There were plenty of tourists still awake, and a twenty-foot ice sculpture in the shape of a skeleton—the Hyatt's contribution to the festive atmosphere—dominated the bar area. Serena went over to the desk and returned with a badge imprinted with the legend PRESS CORPS. "It's totally easy to get things done," she said, "when you're a jeans-and-lumberjack-shirts type of campaign. No paperwork. No bodyguards. No fear of assassination." She pinned the badge on me. "Just look as though you belong," she said. "After all, Karpovsky will probably vouch for you anyway . . . he doesn't have any idea who's on the staff and who's not . . . you know how congressmen are." She smiled wryly and pointed with her chin.

Karpovsky was seated at a Steinway grand in the middle

of the lobby bar, pounding away at the keys and singing a
Tom Lehrer song—"The Masochism Tango"—at the top of
his lungs. Tourists were laughing and singing and thrusting
little pieces of paper toward him to autograph.

"You don't have a prayer," one of the tourists was shouting, as he took a deep slug from a coconut that had been
sculpted into a crude skull. "And I ain't just saying that
because I'm a libertarian."

At the word prayer, Karpovsky changed key abruptly and
switched to a rousing rendition of "The Vatican Rag."

"Congressman, Congressman . . ." Serena was leading
me toward him by the hand. "Isn't it just wonderful that
Phil Etchison has joined us?"

The congressman stopped singing, but so many people
were singing along that it made little difference.

"Hi, Phil," he said, and Serena mouthed the word *poet* to
him. "You're the poet, aren't you?" he said, not at all fazed
at her ersatz teleprompter. She mouthed something else to
him—I had the presence of mind to pretend not to notice—
and then he added, "Oh, yeah . . . the Washington Post cafeteria . . . met you there. Your assistance to my campaign
is something to be treasured, Phil, profoundly treasured."

I said, "Aren't you worried about the Catholic vote? I
mean, singing that Tom Lehrer song in public."

"Catholics?" he said blankly. The room became fuzzy.
The piano changed color . . . going from black to white to
crystal to a wild spectrum of color. The crowd was swimming before my eyes, faces melting, merging, melding . . .
Suddenly I realized that I was being hit by a bad case of
disjunctive fugue. The piano was metamorphosing into the
snout of a whale. The people were like barnacles. The air
reeked of salt and seaweed.

"Where am I? . . . Where am I going to? . . ." I said.
"Serena!" and Serena extended her arms to me, but her
arms were the fins of a leaping marlin . . . A kingfisher
hovered in the air above her head. Serena's hair was changing into a shock of wind-whipped kelp . . . and her tongue
flicked in and out like an eel . . . and then, at the far end of

the atrium, where the scenic elevator once was, there was a huge tree that had thrust through the floor of the hotel and burst through the glass roof toward the sun.

"Run to the Joshua tree," Serena cried, in a voice that sounded like the shattering sea, and in the background a band of angels sang "The Vatican Rag," kicking their legs like Vegas showgirls.

I ran—leaped through a hoop of fire—faded out.

—and—in a dream I suppose—I was falling, falling, falling, down the well, down the wrong end of a telescope, with the tangled skein of the River twisting and turning around me and I was falling, falling, falling until I saw the eyes of a flaming angel leaping in the sea and I cried out no, no, no, and tried to grasp a thread of the River but the water slipped through my hands and—

—flaming—

When I woke up I was on a bus and we were pulling up to a border crossing. It didn't look familiar, but there was the Rio Grande and a narrow bridge and, here and there, barbed wire.

"Need a shower," I groaned. I had no idea how I had gotten onto this bus or whether I even had my passport and my credit cards on me anymore. I suppose that it was silly to worry about passports when I had already leapt several tall universes in a single bound, but there are times when a little anal-retentiveness can get one through a lot of chaos.

"Wake up, Mr. E.," Serena was saying, shaking me as I wiped the crusts from my eyes. "World's gone haywire."

I found my wallet and my passport. I pulled them out and rubbed my eyes. Something didn't look right about the passport. I looked out at where the immigration officer stood and I saw a great blue sign above the road:

**WELCOME
TO THE UNITED STATES OF
ARMORICA**

I looked down at my passport. It read:

Passport
United States of Armorica

And between the two legends was blazoned a dragon swallowing its own tail, crushing a griffin in its coils; the griffin, facing left, gripped three broken arrows in its claws. "This isn't home," I said. I looked around me and saw the congressman at the back of the bus, orating enthusiastically while a news team videotaped.

"I know," Serena said. "This time the world has *totally* shifted . . . but I don't think anyone knows about it except us." She pulled me to my feet. "Let's get off the bus and look around. These immigration formalities always take hours. In fact, they seem to be searching one of our buses for illegals; it's like they've never heard of congressional privilege."

I staggered after her and she led me down the two steps to terra firma. I ached all over. I had no memory of the ride, but it must have been a bumpy one. The world must have shifted while I slept. And yet my memories hadn't changed . . . They were there, all of them and all the alternate memories also.

Outside, a desertscape stretched out in every direction, broken only by the river. The sky was a deep blue, almost indigo, and the river—the merest trickle—was the color of mud. The bank was steep and shored up with concrete in places. We walked along the edge for about a quarter of a mile, not talking, each of us, no doubt, wondering how we had managed to lose ourselves in this no-man's-universe. Here we were, crossing the river into America to find a shaman to lead us to Theo . . . and it wasn't even America anymore. Although some things were still the same. For instance, we could make out a stream of people in the distance, running across the stream toward a barbed-wire barricade on the other side. A patrol car raced alongside the fence, lights flashing.

El Norte was still the land of opportunity, to be attained by stealth and conquered by cunning. We watched the line of immigrants. Sometimes they popped out of bushes or crawled out from behind rocks ... sometimes a pickup truck would drive up, disgorge a load of people, then roar away. The border patrol didn't seem to be catching anyone.

Then, suddenly, we heard machine-gun fire.

I whipped around to see that Congressman Karpovsky's entire retinue had come out of the buses, and that men in neo-Nazi uniforms were mowing them down. No, they were not even men; the soldiers had the faces of pigs and lizards. It was shocking, unconscionable, but I had no sense of reality. I felt no outrage and no terror. I could only feel despair. Not only because I no longer knew what or where anything was; it was because I no longer knew myself. I turned my gaze away from the massacre, but I could still hear the rat-tat-tat of the guns and the thud of flesh on sand.

"Jesus," Serena said. "Let's make a run for it."

"What's the point?" I said. "What can we achieve? We're not truthsayers ... we have no role to play in these wars ... we don't even really exist here ... isn't that true, Serena? The only reason we're still here at all is to balance a few cosmic equations ..."

"Come on, Mr. E., it's lame of you to philosophize now; this is a crisis." She started down the riverbank. I followed her. The machine-gun fire went on. I realized that no one on that bus belonged to this universe and that the massacre was some kind of nightmarish attempt on the part of nature to straighten out the paradoxes. The bank was steep and I stumbled and finally our descent was more like a crawl. There was mud in my clothes, in my hair. I was breathing mud. But Serena was ahead of me. She was already into the water and running. I dragged myself to the edge. Though the water was barely ankle-deep, the current was swift. I tried to stand up and it knocked me facedown into the water. I coughed up mud and phlegm. I looked up at the sun through the watery blur and saw Jesus.

Haysoos, that is. He was hovering in the air above me. "Come on, Señor Etchison," he was shrieking. His hands were folded in prayer and he was nude, like a Renaissance *putto*. I heard the flutter of his wings.

"What are you doing here, Jesus?" I said.

"In Armorica, anything can happen," he said. He giggled. The sun streamed from his eyes. Serena was already racing to the other side, her feet barely skimming the water. The *putto* did a somersault and laughed, hung downward by his knees from an imaginary bar. "Run, Señor Etchison." And in the rustle of his feathers there was the voice of my son, crying out, "Cling to the truth, Dad."

"Theo!" I screamed. Because I could see him suddenly, pulling the puppet strings of this angelic apparition, his puffed cheeks whistling the desert wind, the gold dust falling from his fingertips. In this universe my son was God, but he was still my son.

And so, clinging to Theo's image in my heart, I sprinted across the water to Armorica.

book two

the forest of arden

. . . these trees shall be my books,
And in their barks my thoughts I'll character
That every eye which in this forest looks
Shall see thy virtue witnessed everywhere.

—*As You Like It*

TALES OF THE WANDERING HERO
by PHILIP ETCHISON

2: IN THE FOREST OF SEXUAL AMBIGUITY

Sometimes (my mother told me as I lay
Encradled, swaddled, diapered and squalling)
You'll only think you've reached the Tum-Tum tree
(Or Bodhi tree, depending on your mythos);
For there are other arbors of enlightenment.
Sometimes you'd think that all trees came equipped
With gateways into other worlds; that you,
Observing each new-minted microcosm,
Could always know the difference between lost
And found. But that, my child, ain't so.

Imprimis: found: the ancient Aztec priest
Who, flaying a virgin, honored mother earth
By dancing in her skin. Next: witness: lost:
Ed Gein, alone in the Wisconsin forest,
Straps on the mounted breasts of a dead woman
And dances, also honoring the mother.
Both celebrate the mysteries. Both elevate
The hostess-flesh, Jocasta, and transform.
Odin and Oedipus both traded eyes for knowledge.

One day, my son:
I'll send you forth into the wide wide world
With nothing save a loaf of bread, a sword,
A condom, and a kiss. So listen well,
As you lie cradled, squalling, diapered.

You don't need speech to know these truths are true.
I made you. One day you will kill me,
Flay me, wear my skin. And I shall speak
Anew through my insensate sluicing wounds,
And speaking, live. The river of life is blood.

O my son:
A lullaby I sing, knowing you too
Shall one day dance in the forest of transforming;
You too shall lose and find yourself; you too
Shall wear an alien skin. The shaman and the madman
Are the same person; only the watchers' eyes
Are different. So if thine eye offend thee,
Pluck it out. Blinded, you still shall dance.
The hungry mother shall devour her sons.
Within each tree there beats a human heart.
Don't be afraid, son. Dance. Dance. Dance
Till the heart grows still, and the river runs aground.

chapter six

In a Deserted Gas Station

Phil Etchison

And as we reached the far shore, Jesus the Cupid darted up—the wings invisible-fast, like hummingbirds'—into the sunlight, and was lost to view.

"Don't look back!" came the *putto*'s voice in the shimmering air.

I knew that he wanted to spare me the sight of any more carnage. I could still hear it though . . . tinny thudlets over the ripple of the river, video game rifle reports. I wanted to thank him, but all that was left of him was a shower of tinkerbell sparks. I decided to obey his admonition, especially since, being an educated man, I knew what had happened to Orpheus. It was just as well, for I heard a final, earth-shattering blast, smelled burning flesh in the air, felt the heat wave, saw the sky go blinding-bright for a moment before I closed my eyes.

And when I opened them again, it was as if none of it had happened.

The air was clean and dry. The desert vista stretched into the distance, where, at the horizon, a jagged band of mountains divided the blue from the yellow.

"Are you all right, Mr. E.?" Serena said. She held out a can of diet soda. I touched it; jabbed my fingers into cold. "Piece of the Arctic," she said, laughing.

"Where'd it come from?"

"Machine," she said, pointing up ahead with her thumb. "Our money still works here."

There was a gas station where she pointed. I was sure I hadn't seen it before. It was as though it came into existence at the very moment I chose to perceive it. It was a rather literary sort of a gas station . . . the pumps half-buried in sand, the mangy dog coiled by the garage door, the soda machine sweating fresh dew . . . the weatherbeaten old man on the rocking chair, shotgun in one hand, Stetson over his eyes . . . a battered Cadillac with its hood popped . . . an old newspaper blowing in the wind.

By literary, I mean that this was a gas-station-in-the-desert of the Ray Bradbury school of writing, poetic and atmospheric and yet somehow a plot device. Especially since there was no road, and even the rust on the pumps and the sores on the dog looked freshly minted.

Still, I wanted to know where we were, and to have some general notion of what kind of universe we were trapped in. Serena had already tested out the coinage, and I still had money and credit cards. We couldn't get far without a car, but perhaps the old man had a phone. With a phone, I could rent a car. We could get to civilization. Maybe.

"Sir? Sir?"

I tapped the old man on the shoulder. As he leaned back, the Stetson slowly slid up to his forehead. He peered at me and said, "Howdy, pardner. Welcome to the gas station of no return."

Serena and I looked at each other in alarm.

"Don't you worry, mister!" said the old man. "Had you right scared, didn't I? Some folks think I'm some kind of psychotic or even—" he rolled his eyes and raised his eyebrows so taut the Stetson popped right off his head "—some kind of serial killer!" He guffawed. "You'll never get out of here alive," he added. "The Texas chainsaw massacre don't got nothing on this place."

"I see," I said. "But would you mind telling me exactly where *this place* is?"

He only laughed. "This place," he said, "is what you make of it. It ain't nothing but what you see in it. Most people, they only see sand and cactus and the old gas station and the dog, and me, sitting here, born old. But then there's some that look out over that sand and they see, oh, wonderful things. To everything there is a season, you know. Pity that season's always dry around here."

"My name is Phil," I said, offering to shake his hand.

"Caleb Cadwallader," said the old man. The name, like his manner of speaking, had a rough poetry to it. I found him engaging, though I could not quite dispel the notion that he was somehow artificial, put on this desert to complete the fantastical illusion, like Adam's navel.

"Caleb," I said. His handshake was as salt-of-the-earth as I imagined it would be.

"Mr. E.!" Serena was saying. She'd gathered up the flying newspapers and was waving the front page at me. I took it from her and read:

Two Sun Gazette

KARPOVSKY IMPOSTOR SLAIN IN SHOOTOUT

A con artist purporting to be Congressman Oren Karpovsky (D-Philanderphia), together with an entourage of androids, was the victim of a terrorist bomb attack intended for the congressman himself. The man has been identified as Laurence Tremaine, sometime freak show impresario and snake oil vendor, who, disguising himself as the presidential candidate, had been stealing money

from American tourists under the guise of taking
campaign contributions. The shootout occurred
just a few feet from the Armorican border,
and Azteca patrolmen watched helplessly as
the bomb, an Atlantean model, went off. The
real Karpovsky will speak this evening at a
fundraiser at the Goldwater Auditorium at the
University of Two Sun. Once derided as a "New
Age monstrosity" by William F. Buckley, it is now
thought that Karpovsky has a strong chance of an
upset in the Platinum State primaries on Super
Baldursday.

At first I was convinced the whole thing was a hoax—
right down to the dangling modifier in the last sentence. I
had seen Karpovsky, seen the campaign workers, watched
him work the tourists. Then it occurred to me that the universe into which we had now been catapulted was certainly
bizarre enough to encompass such a scenario, even though it
didn't jibe with many of the details I remembered. There'd
never been anything like this in any other reality shift; gen-
erally the world had been the same, and only one or two
details altered—big details as far as my life was concerned,
to be sure, but of little consequence to most other people.

This new shift was of several orders of magnitude. It's
not just a bunch of weird spellings, I thought, as a second
sun, small and reddish, began to rise in what appeared to
be the northeast. Conflicting theories jostled in my mind.
Perhaps there was another Karpovsky in this universe—
somehow we had all gone through the interface together—
and the resultant paradox was so untenable that nature
had contrived this esoteric plot development to eliminate
the redundancy. and so, zap! Karpovsky had become an
impostor, and his entire retinue a passel of androids, and
as for Serena and me—nature had contrived to have us
slip quietly away. This was an impressive theory, except
that it endowed nature with purpose, foresight, and an
understanding of television-style plotting. And I did not

believe in nature as a sentient force. It was not my style.

I read the article over once more. Then I let it drop, and it was carried away by the wind.

"Is there somewhere we can rent a car around here?" I asked the old man.

"You're welcome to take the Cadillac," Caleb said. "It was left here by the last people who stopped here, ooh, five, ten years ago. Name of Etchison. Soft-spoken, all-Armorican family. Liked them a lot. The lady was dying of cancer, as I recall; she had them chemotherapy bald patches. Ain't nobody been here since. I've been a-sitting here, and a-rocking back and forth, for all this time, waiting for someone to give it to. I say, you look a lot like him. Don't recognize the young lady though."

"We had a station wagon before," I said, wondering what had happened to these otherworldly analogues of my family.

"Oh, that's here too," he said, pointing vaguely out toward the mountains. I thought I could make out a car's hood, complete with hood ornament, poking up out of the sand. "That's always been there, long as I've been. At first it was just a smudge, but the outline of the car gets more and more clear every year. I'd give it another couple of years before it pops."

"Pops?" I said.

"Things is always popping in this desert," Caleb said. "It's because it ain't real."

"What's not real?"

"Why, all of it, of course," said the old man. "You must not be from around these parts."

"We're from Virginia," Serena said, and the man nodded as though that explained everything. "I don't think 'popping' has reached our neck of the woods yet." She was as mystified as me, but she was a lot smoother about demystifying herself. "Could you, I mean, like, explain it to us?"

"Sure. I ain't got nothing better to do." He settled back in the rocking chair, which launched into a brief flurry of rocking, offered us both a chaw of tobacco, which we declined, and said, "Oftentimes, the future haunts the past. Around here, if something is for sure going to happen some-day, we sees an afterimage of it . . . okay, a *before*image is more like it . . . in the sand, you see. Now sometimes the future ain't so certain, and the beforeimage is noth-ing more than a bit of a glow, or what they calls an aura. Other times, this beforeimage, it just gets clearer and clearer, until, in the end, it *is* reality. You follering me?"

"I think so," I said.

"Sometimes this beforeimage is so powerful, it's even realer than the image which it's *before*. Like the Etchisons, for instance—"

"You met us before," I said, "and they gave you a message for ourselves? They projected themselves into the past, something like that?"

"Nah, you ain't the Etchisons," said Caleb, "because there was four of them. You look like him, though. I'd know him anywhere. He's a famous poet."

That was good to know. In the world I came from, I was, to be sure, a poet of sorts, but I could hardly be considered famous . . . not in a world where kitsch was king . . . but if Phil Etchison was a famous poet here, how could I be sure that he and I were the same person? Perhaps I was like the pseudo-Karpovsky, an impostor, soon to be mown down by Mexican machine guns.

"Like I was saying," Caleb said, "the Etchisons came here once. Or they will come. I forget. Things haven't been the same since time went through that Möbius strip . . . you know, after the big recession set in. And they said, if a middleaged man with a sad face, and a pretty college girl, was to come for help, looking lost and forlorn, I was to give them the Cadillac. You see. Everything works out in the end. Or beginning. I forget which."

"Is there a yellow brick road?" Serena said, and she was only half joking.

"There used to be," said Caleb. "They tore it up when they extended Route 10."

"So this *is* Arizona?" I asked. I was suffering from déjà vu, even though it was clear that the events I was living through had never happened before, although they might conceivably happen in the future, whereas, in the cyclical view of time, they might already have happened anyway, except that, if there really had been a Möbius strip that time had twisted through, then we were all inside out, although since existence is subjective there would be no way of verifying our inside-outness, and—

"Mr. E.?" Serena was saying. She touched me lightly on the elbow. "You're totally zoning out."

I blinked. The Cadillac had been moved. It gleamed in the harsh light of the two suns. It was no longer a wreck; it had been waxed, polished, burnished until it shone like bronze. How long had my mind been going around in circles? Long enough for them to have fixed up the car? Or had I been the victim of a bait-and-switch routine?

Caleb Cadwallader was handing me the keys. Abstractedly I took them. "I was trying to think all of this through. I mean, the philosophical implications," I said, though attempts to think things through had succeeded only in entangling me further. I was a mouse in an *n*-dimensional maze.

"Maybe I should drive," Serena said.

Gently, she pried the keys from my hand. She climbed in and I got in beside her. The car purred. The air-conditioning cut on and blasted my face. I realized that I had been sweating like a pig. I probably smelled like one too. The last time I'd shaved had been about twenty-nine universes back, and I'd spent the night on a moving bus. I sank back into the leather upholstery . . . It was soft and smelled brand-new.

"Let's go," Serena said.

"Where?" I murmured.

"Oh, you're hopeless, Mr. E.," she said. "We'll go to Tucson, or Two Sun, as they call it here. That's where Mr. Stone was when we left him."

"Mr. Stone? Oh, the Indian shaman. Right?"

"Really, Mr. E.," she said. "You're not seeing things *mythically*, that's your problem."

"You, my dear, are scolding me with the self-righteousness of a coed who's just had her first encounter with Joseph Campbell 101. I know all that stuff. I had *lunch* with Campbell, for God's sake!" Suddenly I wondered whether that was true.

"Okay. Well, maybe you're not seeing them *trilogistically*," she said, "or you'd know that we've reached Stage Two of the hero's quest—where the plot thickens, where everything seems hopeless—where the grail is impossibly out of reach—where the lady is unattainable—and we're proceeding right on course toward the encounter with the Ultimate Darkness after which—if we win—we go on the Ultimate Redemption."

"I see. But we might *not* win."

"In which case we'll all go home with the board game, the T-shirts, and the gift certificates, but someone else will go on to the grand prize."

If this was a hero's quest, I thought—but did not dare say it aloud, because Serena seemed so delighted with her specious undergrad conceit—there was something dreadfully wrong with the picture—me. I'm not a hero, I thought. Everyone in my family is more heroic than me. Joshua, with his raging hormones, charging into the void on the back of the dragon lady. Theo, uttering the truth no matter what the pain. And Mary, who is pain personified.

Oh yes. I knew who my family was now. The fact that the world had dissolved into a maelstrom of unreality had sharpened the focus on those whom I loved. I had plucked the images of my wife and sons out of the thousands of convergent memory lines, and I saw them clearly for the first time.

We drove on. There was, indeed, a yellow brick road; here and there, you could see a stretch of it alongside the freeway, threading through the thickening saguaro forest. Both suns had climbed up to the zenith, and the air-conditioning was beginning to wheeze. Serena drove on. The signs were in a kind of dream-English—they said things a preliterate child might think a grownup was saying:

JILTED ONCOMING TERRIFIC
PEDESTRIAN CRUCIFIXION
SPEED CRAP

I wondered whether God was a child in this universe.

It was at that moment that the air freshener spoke to me.

"We meet again, Señor Etchison," it said.

It was one of those dangling air fresheners. It gave off a nostril-clenching scent of baby powder. It was, indeed, in the shape of a baby, or rather a young boy, with delicately fluttering eyelashes and wings.

"Jesus," I said.

Jesus the Mexican street kid—first transmogrified into a Renaissance *putto*, then into this cardboard Cupid— was once more leading the way. "Did you hear what the air freshener just said to me?" I said to Serena, but her eyes were on the freeway, and she didn't turn to look at me. In fact, it seemed that I had been plucked out of the timestream altogether. Because the car had slowed down to an infinitesimal crawl . . . and it wasn't that we were moving slowly, it was that I was caught up in some real-life video effect. The vision was for me alone, I realized, yet another solipsistic experience I would never be able to share.

"Do you have a message from Theo?" I said.

In the wind from the air conditioner, the air freshener flapped back and forth against the rearview mirror.

"Si, señor." Then came a second voice, the voice of my son . . . "Dad. Come quickly. I'm afraid."

"But I don't know where you are. We're probably not even in the same—reality, universe, whatever." Again, the inadequacy of my role as hero was hammered home to me.

"Doesn't matter anymore. They're all starting to run together. The universes. The walls are breaking down. If I don't fix it, there's gonna be like one big goulash. The Great Unmaking. Chaos. Oh God, Dad, I'm so scared."

"Where are you, son?"

"A dark place."

"Tell me how to find you."

"I don't know, I don't know! The darkest place there is. The bottom of the abyss. Shit, shit, shit I'm scared and I just want to cry."

"Don't be scared. I'm coming. It's going to be all right." Jesus, I was weeping as I spoke those words of comfort to a fragrant piece of cardboard.

"Hasta la vista, Señor Etchison," said Jesus, and then the air freshener was just an air freshener again. Time sped up and the car was racing down the freeway.

A sign read:

TWO SUN—SMILES

Saguaros everywhere. Jagged mountains in the distance. A dust storm whirled, far off, against the deep blue sky. Oh, the place had an aching familiarity to it, though it was light-years from the world I knew. I'd been through an entire "Twilight Zone" season's worth of weirdness in the past twenty-four hours. I was worn-out. I started to drift off again.

Time for dreamland.

Time to prepare myself for another day of fantasy and dark magic in the good old U.S. of Armorica.

chapter seven

The Bottomless Pit

Theo Etchison

I've reached the bottom of the bottomless pit. I can tell because I'm not moving any more. I don't know if I'm still in the belly of King Strang. I guess not. That was just an illusion.

The only light is the vague blue glowing from the cosmic marble in my hand. I'm walking now, one palm up with the pale blue radiance streaming. I can make out shapes: here a statue with three eyes, here a stalactite. I can hear water dripping. I'm near one of the tributaries of the River.

I've just lost contact with Dad. He's on a freeway somewhere heading toward Tucson. I can almost hear the air conditioner squeal as he strains uphill. I'm almost there with him, but he can't feel my presence anymore.

Even while I'm standing in the darkness gazing in the marble I can see the filaments of the River coil and uncoil and I know what's happening and I know time is running out. The barriers between the worlds are all dissolving and pretty soon there's only going to be one big crazy goulash of a universe where everything is true at the same time which means chaos. It's all I can do to hold back the waters . . .

and I can't really do it all because my mind can't process all of it at once. I can carve out a kingdom where things aren't going crazy quite as fast. I can center that island of stability around where my Dad's car is hurtling up the freeway toward Tucson. But I don't know how long it will last.

I reach out with my mind and wrench the rivulets apart as best I can. I'm not able to reach my Dad anymore but I can still feel him and he's like a pinprick of a consciousness battling upstream against the flow of reality . . . the freeway itself is a kind of river . . . no, a thread . . . suturing the wounded world. I hope. God, I hope.

So I close my eyes and drift into an amniotic sleep. I don't dream because I can't.

It's morning and I'm in a forest.

I know it's a forest even before I'm awake. I've been in a forest before, at my grandparents' place in Spotsylvania County. A forest at dawn is all dampness and birdcalls and leafy-earth-sweet-rotten-smelling. I can hear the ripple of a nearby brook. It must be part of the River because beneath the babbling I hear the echo of the music of the dawn time.

I rub my eyes. I've been sleeping against the trunk of a Joshua tree. Two squirrels skitter up my arm and disappear. I listen for the ancient music which only I can hear. It's faint, but it's still here. I sit up and that's when I hear the bells. I reach up and touch my head and I pull down a jester's cap, you know, the kind the Joker wears . . . not the *Batman* Joker, the one in the pack of cards. I look down at myself and I see that my clothes are gone and I'm clutching a kind of a baton in my hand. It's a stick with a Joker's head on the tip with the same kind of cap and bells. There's clothes hanging on a line that goes from the nearest branch of the tree across to somewhere near where the water's whispering to me. They're pied clothes, half-green, half-red. If I put them on, I'm going to look like the court jester. Not cool.

But the morning air is nippy. I'm shivering. I spring up, jump up and down a couple of times to like get the circulation going, then I get into the dweebish threads. They're warm, but the sleeves are all big and they swish around when I move my arms. I stick the cap back on my head. I feel like a fool. Well, I guess that only makes sense.

I shake the stick. Somewhere, a cuckoo cuckoos.

"Okay," I say to no one, "Someone's decided to make me the court jester. But I don't know any jokes. I mean, why did the dead baby cross the road? Because it was stapled to the chicken."

I think I hear a laugh, but maybe it's the chittering of some forest animal.

I work my way toward the brook. It's farther than I realize, but that only makes sense, too. We're in topsy-turvy country and nothing feels right. In fact, it's only when I stop listening to the rippling, when I close my eyes completely and make myself still, and then I take one step forward, I discover that I'm suddenly there. By the water's edge. I've almost stepped too far, down among the rushes. I squat at the bank. I can see myself in the water. Underneath the circus outfit it's still me, Theo Etchison, a sad case of delayed puberty. I've got the same dirty blond hair and blue-green eyes. I shake the stick and try to think of a joke.

What happens next is that this little reed basket floats by, and there's a baby inside, and it's coughing and sneezing. I'm all, "Holy Moses!" and I reach out to maybe grab the basket, but I can't get it in time, I mean it slips from my fingers before I can get a grip on it. I wonder if it really *is* Moses, because, since the universe has just been radically reshuffled, almost any fragment of our history or mythology could be thrown up against any other fragment. Okay, so I don't want it to just drift out of sight, I mean the baby's squalling now, and maybe someone should be taking care of it. So I get up and I start following alongside the bank. The current's amazingly fast and next to the brook is all brambles and maybe even poison ivy because it only takes a few minutes before I feel itchy all over and I have to stop. There's a bend in the stream . . . it's wider now . . . and the baby in the basket rounds the corner and vanishes from my sight. But then I see that there's something else coming my way, bobbing up and down in the current, and it's like a big wooden chest, painted in blue and gold paint with a design of waves and dolphins . . . The lid's wide open and I see there's a baby there too, with a circlet of gold leaves around its head . . . one of those Greek hero dudes, Perseus maybe . . . wasn't he sent out to sea in a wooden chest? . . . and no sooner does that chest go sailing around the bend when there's something else . . . it looks kind of like half of a giant peach, and there's a baby all curled up inside the peach, too, swimming in peach juice. Not a clue who it might be, but it's Oriental-looking I guess. It must be some other classic hero from some culture I'm not familiar with. I don't know what to make of it, especially when more baby containers come drifting past me . . . There's a miniature Viking ship . . . there's a humongous lotus pad and the baby is sitting upright, cross-legged, meditating, with a pale yellow halo around his head . . . It's getting weird, I tell myself.

There's a lot of rushes now and I have to half wade out to follow where the babies are floating to. The water gets surprisingly deep all of a sudden and I see that, upstream, there's a lot more objects floating toward the bend in the creek. On the other bank, the trees go and on and on, so dark and thick that there's barely any light except for the rising sun skimming the water. Well, I think to myself, this must be the place where heroes come from. Dad's always telling me about how in mythology the hero tends to have an unknown origin . . . some king or princess finds him floating down the stream in a little raft made of rushes . . . and he turns out to be the child of a god. I've stumbled on hero central here, the lost-and-found department for the dudes who are going to save the universe. I guess it makes sense that this place would be at the bottom of the bottomless pit, the beginning at the ending.

But what am I doing here? I'm not really here to save universes, only to find my brother and bring him back to the world, my world. I don't really give a flying fuck about the rest of the world. I just want my family back and I don't want my mother to be dying of cancer anymore.

Well so anyway I'm standing knee deep in water watching the future saviors of the world go past in a solemn procession of miniature boats, rafts, treasure chests, and vehicles of the future. And then I see one that's not on a boat or a lotus pad or anything like that. There's like this three-ring binder, open to about halfway through, drifting downstream alongside the other mythology paraphernalia, and on it there's a baby with closed eyes, and he's not screaming or whimpering like the other babies, he's just lying there, and he's all purple-blue, like he's having trouble staying alive.

Somehow this has got something to do with me. It's the three-ring binder. I'd know it anywhere. I try to wade out farther but all of a sudden there's like this gully in the stream bed and I'm way in, up to my neck, and the water's ice-cold and soaking into my Joker threads. I'm not that great at swimming and the current's pretty strong but I push back against the riverbed and try to propel myself toward the binder and the baby. And all the while I'm remembering what's in the binder, the words I wrote myself, scribbling down my crazy dreams all the way from Virginia to Mexico not knowing that they weren't dreams at all . . . I can see the writing, uneven felt-tip scrawlings, the immature handwriting of a fourteen-year-old kid, and I know that if I don't catch the book soon the water's going to seep into those cheap college-ruled pages and the writing's not waterproof and even if it were how could it withstand the water of making and unmaking? . . . and I know I've got to save the notebook, save the child too, or the things in the notebook are going to be flushed down the toilet bowl of eternity.

So I try to grab hold of the book and I try to hold it and the baby above the water. I can see words here and there like *the King sitting on the* and *lizard skittering up the limbs of the Joshua tree* and *dragon woman screeching in the sky*. But the sentences are dissolving. Changing. The baby's not completely dead but I don't know how to wake it up. I know the baby's not me but I have a feeling it's part of me, that I'm responsible for it. The pages are getting soggy. I can't do any more than steer the book and the child towards a shallower part of the shore and so that's what I do. I give it a little push and there it goes. I can't tread water any more and I feel myself submerging and the icy water flood my nostrils. I grab on to some rushes and drag myself toward the bank. When I pull myself out, the book and its cargo are already rounding the bend. I can't lose that book! My whole world is in that book. I'm pretty frantic I guess and I'm thrashing around, not really getting anywhere. I make it back to shore, but it's not the same shore I left behind . . . because here there are these twisted rocks that jag up out of the soil and they're shaped almost like beasts . . . and then I see an old man, leaning against one of the rocks, fishing.

"Help me," I gasp.

He doesn't look up and I'm crawling and staggering toward him, shaking the wet from my carnival costume like a dog.

"You gotta help me, dude," I say. "Out there . . . there's something that belongs to me. If I don't fish it out of the water—"

He doesn't say much. But he casts his line way out over the stream with a sudden flick of his wrist and then he starts reeling like crazy. And pretty soon there's my dream book, hooked by one of the rings, zeroing in on us. And the baby along with it. He pulls it in and I pick the binder gingerly out of the water. I don't really know what to do with the baby. It seems smaller than it was before . . . and dry, like a mummy almost.

"Is it dead?" I ask the old man.

He snorts.

I cradle the child in the crook of my arm and it seems to stir a little, but it's even smaller than it was before. It's shrinking . . . shrinking . . . Presently it's almost like a little axolotl, wriggling in the palm of my hand.

"Quick!" the old man says. "Swallow it before it regresses into nothingness! Or else it'll never be reborn."

He turns to me and looks at me with such commanding urgency that I believe him. I open my mouth and gulp it down. It's the size of a tadpole but it burns the roof of my mouth and it sears my throat as it goes down, like acid.

The old man looks at me, nods curtly. "Good."

"What was it I just did?"

"Not for you to know yet. But you're going to be glad you did it. When the right time comes, that is." He throws the fishing line out once more, and stares at the water dourly. There are no more babies floating by. The forest has thickened still more. The air is misty and still.

I take my notebook and leaf through it. Most of it still seems to be there. "You can dry the pages over yonder fire," the old man says, "and your clothes too, I daresay." He points behind with his thumb, and creeping behind the massive rock he's leaning against, I see there's a fire—the wood is damp and green and there's a lot of smoke—and an unidentifiable animal, a rabbit or lizard, spitted above it. I place the open book against some warm stones and I shuck my jester's outfit and spread it out on the rocks. There's a pile of blankets, and I wrap myself in one of them and try to warm myself. My stomach is still queasy from swallowing whatever it was, the distilled quintessence of hero I guess. I keep thinking a monster's going to burst out of my stomach like in the movie *Alien*. Presently I hear the old man cry out: "Boy! Boy!" and I scurry to his side. I get the distinct impression that he's used to being obeyed.

I just sit there, watching him as he fishes. I've got the blanket wound round and round my thin shoulders. I'm holding on to the jester-headed stick, listening to the wind toy with the bells on its hat.

Now and then the old man turns to look at me. His eyes are sunken in a field of crosshatched wrinkles. He wants to say something, I'm sure, but he can't get it all out for some reason. So he turns back and stares at the tip of his fishing pole.

"Who are you?" I ask him a last.

"It is not for you to question," the old man says. But I don't feel I'm in danger, so I know he's not working for Thorn or Katastrofa. "Perhaps I should start by testing you, child. Do you know what this place is?"

"The bottom of the abyss," I say. "And I guess right here is like, the birthplace of heroes, judging by the little boats that go floating by. I've recognized Moses, and Perseus, and the little dude in the peach, he's from some Japanese fairy tale, isn't he?"

"Momotaro," says the old man. "There is also Karna, son of the sun. And half a dozen others you can look up in any good dictionary of mythology."

"But what about the hero I—I swallowed?"

"Oh, that's the best one of all . . . the hero with no name . . . the one who is to come." And the old man smiles for a moment before the sadness sucks him up again. "Do you know who I am, boy? Perhaps we have met before."

"I think you are a king," I say, "even though you're not dressed like one, I mean, you're not wearing a crown or any of that shit."

"So you can identify me even through my disguise. Wait! I think there's a nibble."

The fishing line snaps.

"Got away," the king says sadly.

I know where I've seen him before now. "You have my father's eyes," I say, "but you're not my Dad. The last time I saw you was beside another shore, and you were at the head of an army, and you were all covered in gold and jewels. Today you're dressed in rags, but I still know that you're King Strang."

"Good for you. A good fool always tells the truth. He is the only person at court who can get away with it. Know any good jokes?"

"Well, I *do* know a few dead baby jokes, but maybe this isn't the right time to tell them."

The King laughs. "A nibble!"

"You're not using any bait."

He laughs again. Then he reels in the line, peers at the hook, and murmurs, "You're right." He pulls up his tunic. There's a wound in his side that oozes pus and dark rheum. There's like worms crawling in and out of it. It's totally gross-looking but I can't help staring at it. They're not maggots; these worms are *big* motherfuckers, with armored segments and fangs, and they're all dripping slime, and they're a silvery black color. Vomitous. I wonder why someone like King Strang would have a festering wound and not get it treated. After all, even though he's precipitated the present cosmic crisis by stupidly dividing up his kingdom between his quarreling children, he's got to have *some* resources, I mean, he's an ex-emperor of the universe for God's sake.

"Are you okay?" I say. "That thing looks like it needs stitches."

"Oh, it's not a wound that can be healed by any ordinary means," says the king. "In fact, you're the only one who is even capable of seeing it." He picks out a nice fat worm and threads it carefully onto his fishhook.

"Why?" But I already know the answer to that question. I am Theo Truthsayer, and I see the truth however great the pain. That's the job description. That's what I do. The wound in the king's side is an old wound and there is no mortal means of healing it. I feel the pain too. I can't help feeling it, it's almost as though it belongs to me too, to everyone. He doesn't answer me, but as he pulls his tunic back over the wound, the pain recedes into a dull ache, just gnawing at the threshold of pain.

"So, fool," the king says, "make me laugh."

"Why did the dead baby cross the road?" I say.

"It was stapled to the chicken," says old King Strang. He laughs again. "No, child, you don't need to tell me jokes. Your very presence lightens the sadness in my heart. I once had children of my own."

"And they are all betraying you. All except Ash."

"Don't mention Ash to me!" says the king, and he stares steadfastly at the stream.

The day goes on; my clothes dry; my notebook remains more or less intact; I get over my nausea at having swallowed the future savior of the universe. I eat the tender flesh of a brook trout. The king holds court in the ballroom of the forest, in a clearing in the light of the rising moon. The constellations are all new, and they dance across the sky. I'm the king's fool, and I dance and sing in front of him and sometimes I elicit a faint smile, as when I attempt to act out the music videos of Right Said Fred and Nirvana, music from a lost world.

Then, as the moon begins to set, as the fire dies down, I tell King Strang this isn't where I belong. "I didn't come here to make you laugh," I say, "although God knows you need someone to cheer you up after all that you've suffered. I didn't come here to heal your wound—you've told me it can't be healed. I came to find my brother. I've gotta bring him back to my world before it's too late, because I think he's got this love-death thing real bad."

King Strang has started to snore, his hands folded across his lap, leaning against a rock that's shaped like a human face. He doesn't seem to be listening to me. I think, well, shit, I guess I should start on my quest now. I know that Joshua has to be with Katastrofa, because that's where he was bound when he leaped into the sea.

I get up and get ready to steal away.

But King Strang tugs at my elbow and whispers to me, "You're wrong. You *are* here to heal and to make laughter." I jerk my arm away and look down at him. He's been talking in his sleep, I'm sure of it, because his eyes are still closed and he's started to snore again.

I move away. Twigs snap on my sneakers.

The king stirs again, and he cries out, "My son, my son," in a voice so hurting that I'm tempted to stay with him after all. But I can't.

I want to say to the unhearing air, "I'm *not* your son, I'm Theo Etchison and my real Dad is a middleaged poet

from planet Earth." Somehow it won't come out. I'm a
Truthsayer and it feels untrue to say that I am not his son.

So I just slip from the clearing and move deeper into the
darkness. I keep within earshot the sound of the River. I
stare into the marble, trying to get a fix on Katastrofa.

King Strang may be right about a lot of what he's telling
me. I mean, he's been around. He's ruled the universe
before, though now he's an old mad king who only wants
to go fishing. But even if he *is* right about my real purpose,
I still have to find it out for myself. I'm young, but not too
young to have a sense of destiny.

chapter eight

In a Love Motel

Serena Somers

TWO SUN—SMILES

was what the sign had said, and it wasn't kidding. *Smiles*, as every second-grader knows, is the longest word in the dictionary because there's a whole mile in between—yeah. We'd been driving down that freeway and every road sign had this quality of being plucked from the mind of a kindergarten prankster. From where we were into Tucson was about the longest mile I've even driven. It took like *hours*. But the universe sort of "grew up" as we drove, after a few hours there were fewer and fewer of the signs with stupid puns, and it was almost as if the cosmos had like lost consciousness or something and it was rapidly clawing its way up through the chaos of infancy and settling down into the world we all knew. In fact, about early evening, there was only one sun setting behind the jagged blue mountains, and the forest of saguaro that stretched out on either side of the highway seemed almost the way I remembered it.

71

"I think things are getting, you know, more normal, Mr. E.," I said. Mr. E. kept on silently driving, but at least he wasn't talking to the air freshener any more. "Look!"

I pointed to a sign that read: *Tucson—25 miles.* The spelling, along with the number of suns, was back to the old way. "Theo's been working on the universe," I said. "Pounding in a few nails, plugging up the leaks."

"My son is an unlikely demiurge," said Mr. E., "but better him than me."

I thought of the massacre on the Mexican border and shuddered. "We're not home yet, are we?" I said. That would be too much to hope for. "Maybe Theo's patched up the whole works, and Josh and Mrs. E. are waiting for you back in Virginia."

"No," said Mr. E., sighing. "My passport still says *Armorica.*"

We pulled into Tucson long after midnight and there wasn't anywhere else to go. Chowed down at the Pack-'em-Inn Steak House—no kidding! The place was still there even though we'd shifted sidewise down a zillion universes—and ended up sleeping in a cheap motel on Oracle, one of those twenty-two-dollar-a-night places where the cowboys go to cheat on their wives. It was a dingy fleabag and there was only one queen-sized bed in the room, but I really didn't think Mr. E. was about to molest me, so I just fell asleep on the window side of the bed, fully clothed, watching Mr. E. pacing back and forth, fiddling with the TV, which only had like two channels—CNN and a hard-core porno channel. On CNN, Congressman Karpovsky was being creamed on "Crossfire," and on the porno station two lesbians were eating each other out and looking so bored doing it that I wondered how anyone could get excited watching it.

Drifting off, I heard the congressman say: "And I think it's about time all these *National Enquirer*-type scandals were laid to rest. Yes, I've had my share of amours, but you know, nobody's perfect . . . Give me a break—Jack

Kennedy used to have women delivered to the Oval Office by a secret back door, at least so the rumor goes . . . why don't you guys stop policing my bedroom and start examining my policies?"

I drifted and dreamed.

First off, in the dream, there was Joshua and the sea. A shimmering Joshua, walking to me across the water. I guess I was maybe on a boat. I could feel the rocking, hear the creaking of rope and wood, taste the salt water on my lips. The Joshua I remembered so vividly even though I was in a world where he had never existed. Sullen Joshua, glaring slitty-eyed at the sea, avoiding my gaze, Joshua whose proximate maleness was so threatening I'd hidden my real self behind folds of lard, Joshua I'd loved in secret until, grudgingly, we'd sought each other out; Joshua of the excruciating wordless evenings at the drive-in with his little brother as our reluctant chaperone; so what if he didn't say anything, I could always fantasize about him being the strong, silent type, couldn't I, and not face the fact that his silence was his own way of hiding from himself, as palpable as my obesity? and this was all racing through my mind as I watched him walk toward me on the water with his hands outstretched like one of those kitschy paintings of Jesus and all of a sudden I realize this is going to be one of those sex dreams or maybe a religious dream I'm not sure, sex and religion all squished together like one of those Madonna music videos I guess but that's like totally trivial and so fucking adolescent turning your innermost longing and anguish into images from MTV damn it Serena, you're a college girl now, this is bullshit, bullshit, but (I love the way Joshua smells, not a harsh male odor=malodor [did God intend that pun?] but kind of a faint muskiness lacing the tang of the salt sea) there's something about MTV, when you grow up on it you can't stop seeing the world that way, a jigsaw of bit-sized images set to the pounding beat of teenaged loins, oh *Josh Josh Josh* was what I—

—I cried out, woke up a little I think, thought I still smelled that fragrance of his in the air above the Pine-Sol

rodent-dropping blend of the motel room. Then I heard Mr.
E. snoring beside me. He was cocooned in the bedspread.
The television was still on and the moonlight was streaming
in through the open window, and I was shivering because
like, in Tucson, the nights can be freezing sometimes. I
staggered out of the bed so I could shut the window.

At the window:

A lone neon sign flickered, on-off, on-off, an electric
pink wolf next to a cactus. I lowered the shades. Now
the only light was from the television set. I sat against
the headboard and stared at the screen thinking maybe I
could hypnotize myself back to sleep. I wondered what
was going on at Karpovsky headquarters and whether—
since this Karpovsky was not the same Karpovsky I'd left
Mexico with—whether I'd even be expected to turn up for
work there . . . or whether I'd find another Serena Somers.

On TV, Larry King was interviewing Congressman
Karpovsky.

"Congressman—I know you probably don't want to hear
this, but all the pundits are saying you don't have a chance.
Why?"

"Well, Larry, I think that people need a little dose of
reality now and then. The world needs a Truthsayer. Only
a Truthsayer can show people the way toward healing. Only
a Truthsayer can save the universe."

"But how are you going to answer the charges of sexual
harassment that the young woman has brought forward?"

Congressman Karpovsky looked straight out of the television set, straight into my eyes. I knew I wasn't just watching
television anymore. Shit, maybe this was still part of the
dream. I almost got the feeling that his hands were going
to reach right out of the CRT and touch my face. "Serena,"
said Karpovsky in a husky parody of a sexy voice, "if
you're out there listening, remember that I still love you."

"You're lying!" I said, thinking, I'm talking back to the
television, this is like, stage one of paranoid schizophrenia,
maybe it's time to see a shrink and have him write up a
prescription.

"Oh, Serena," And his face *is* coming out of the screen now, it's a big distended face with a slobbering tongue. "It wasn't rape! You asked for it! You were wearing that titillating halter top—and I'm just your average red-blooded American male with a libido the size of Vesuvius.—Oh, don't worry, I'm not saying any of this on national television, it's just our minds talking, telepathically linking through the crystal energy of the television set, bet you didn't realize there was anything to all that New Age bullshit, did you?—oh, I'm here on Larry King mouthing an endless string of platitudes, but my soul, my soul is in that fleabag with you and your boyfriend's father, maybe we should wake him up for a threesome, eh, wouldn't you like to get it up the ass as well as in that moist and quivering mouth of yours, baby, yeah."

And I suddenly had a memory, fleeting but crystal-clear—the memory unraveled and it was like watching a fast-forward videotape and I was watching it like it hadn't really happened to me and maybe it *really* hadn't happened to me, maybe it was a memory from some other reality, some other me, but if it hadn't really happened why was it so vivid, so compelling?

I think it's the congressman's office. It's a cluttered place—books, papers, a great bronze eagle perched on the desk peering at a crystal whale, a trophy from an environmental organization. And it's me, seventeen, a summer or two back, an age ago.

I'm shaking Karpovsky's hand across the wide mahogany desk (how many acres of obliterated rain forest goes to find one mahogany tree, one desk? but I live with the contradiction, tell myself Karpovsky didn't buy that desk, it was always there, like the glass-eyed eagle and the Colonial-style filing cabinet and the sofas upholstered in red leather and) *Why do you want to work for me, Serena?* His eyes are fixed, hard, emotionless. *I believe in your message. And anyway, Congressman, you're kind of cute.* Why had I said that? I don't know why, it's like the time I played with matches when I was little right after they told me not to and I made the big bonfire in the backyard and the neighbors' treehouse caught fire, but it served them right, too, because they wouldn't let me up in there because there was a big sign that said NO GIRLS ALLOWED and that was B.J., you know, Before Joshua. But the words had come out and what happened next was like, you slip at the top of the stairwell and in the split second before you fall you see the whole thing, your mind draws a chart of your trajectory, and it's all cold and logical and scientific and then, well, you fall (the plush pile carpeting and row upon row of leatherbound tomes all meticulously dusted but never opened) *I'm glad you believe in my message, Serena. Love one another. Would you care for a joint?* (I don't do anything like that, sir.) *You don't do anything like that?* But my eyes betray me because in a moment his hands have reached for me across the burnt-out rain forest and pulled me between the eagle and the leaping whale and all I can think about is Joshua, if you could only see me now, my blubber cushioning me against the bronze beak and the crystal snout and the congressman's breath smells of old wine and tobacco.

No! No! I don't remember this, it's false, it's invasive, it's been planted here, it never happened to *me*, not, not, not *me*.

Then why am I crying?

CNN cut to a commercial now. It was a personal-injury lawyer telling me I could sue, put a dollar value on pain and suffering. Mr. E. continued to snore.

I've got to know if this is all true. Even if it's a false memory that's been tacked onto my mind because of one of the laws of conservation of reality, it hurts too much. I get up. Somewhere in one of my pockets there's a phone number. A secret number.

You see, Serena, I'm a very big man. An important man. A man who's going to change the way the world thinks. I have inside me this huge and overwhelming compassion for all who suffer. But I also have a tragic flaw, oh, can you

*understand that, Serena? I'm a lonely man, and I never
had a childhood . . . and here we are, you and me, you're
so fresh and young, like an unplucked flower, and I am old
and weary and withered, a great man with a tragic flaw,
an uncontrollable libido.*

Yeah. Scrawled on the back of my driver's license. The
secret number of the cellular phone that rings everywhere
the congressman is, because the little sucker is always
tucked in the back pocket of his pants and he *always*
answers it.

I looked back at Mr. E., who's moaning a little in his
sleep. Maybe he's dreaming about his sons. I hope so. Our
dreams are the only things that keep things real sometimes.
I picked up the phone, dialed the number, charged it to my
parents' credit card.

Déjà vu. The last time I tried the phone in an alternate
universe I'd ended up talking to myself.

"Serena!"

"Serena. I figured you'd call."

"Serena. What are you doing over there? You're here,
not there."

"Aren't you the least bit surprised there's two of you?"

"No." There was a lot of giggling in the background. I
heard a man snoring. "Why should I be? I always have these
dreams. You're my shadow or my alter ego or something.
You're always flitting through my life and you're always
on some life-and-death mission and shit."

"Karpovsky's asleep? And you're—"

"In bed with him. Along with half the staff!" Serena's
laugh was as familiar to me as my own. "Our beloved idol's
just getting a little relaxation in—you know he has a big
press conference tomorrow, and Larry King really raked
him over the coals this evening. It wouldn't have been so
bad *in person*, but this interview-by-remote business sucks,
like, it's totally hard to act like a human being when all you
have to react to is a talking head on a monitor upbraiding
you from Washington."

"You gotta help me, Serena," I said.

"No problemo, sis," she said. "I know why you're here. You're looking for Mrs. E. and for that Navajo police detective."

"How'd you—"

"You leave clues. I leave clues to myself maybe. I find them scribbled on Post-its and while-you-were-outs. They're in my own handwriting. Maybe I'm one of those automatic writing people, they had a bunch of them on Oprah last month."

"Well, so what do I do next?" It looked like I'd been through this universe many times before. Maybe I'd planted clues on every pass.

"I'm not sure, but I'd recommend the madhouse first. According to these notes, you busted Mary Etchison from there once. Maybe, now that you've jumped worlds again, she's back inside and hallucinating up a storm."

"How much do you know about all this?" I said.

"As little as I can help. Do you think it's fun having a multiple personality? Only reason Karpovsky keeps me on staff is to fend off the folks from the equal-opportunity-for-the-handicapped league. Yeah, and I keep my mouth shut about the orgies. Unlike some other people I could name."

I'd gathered that some tabloid sex scandal thing was in the works, but I knew no more about it than I'd glimpsed on CNN just now. I was more interested in whether I'd actually . . . well, how true that memory was. I owed it to Joshua to have been faithful to him, I guess. A strange feeling to have about someone who didn't exist. I didn't want it to be true. Yet, if it wasn't true, how come I had the secret phone number?

"I want to know something, Serena," I said. "I just arrived here. I was watching TV . . . and I had like, this flashback. About Congressman Karpovsky in his office and, you know, doing things to me."

She laughed. "Oh, he's in therapy now."

"But did it happen?"

"Oh, Serena, why torture yourself over it?" Serena said. "Getting thin, getting fat, yoyoing back and forth, you and

Oprah have a lot in common. At least you have someone
to love, you and your Joshua. There's no Joshua here. All I
know about him is from the little notes. I envy you, crossing
from world to world chasing after him, I mean it's like,
so romantic. My therapist says that's why I made you up,
because there's a big yawning hole in my life because of,
you know, the congressman, robbing me of my youth or
something . . . These therapists, they're so anxious to have
you fit into their theory, they like mythologize the shit out
of everything you tell them. Fucking idiots."

"Did I or didn't I?—"

"Funny, I was dreaming about Joshua just before you
called. About him walking on the water."

The Serena on the phone was me all right. No question
about it. She understood me to the core and I understood
her. But Joshua to her was just a dream-companion, a
mirage. This Serena had missed the boat. I knew how she'd
lain awake nights, thinking vague thoughts about sex, something that only happened to other people, or woke up in the
middle of a thunderstorm with a gnawing and unnameable
ache inside about something she only half understood. I'd
lain awake like that too. But of course I also had Ash, my
imaginary companion . . . the third Darkling.

"You're just a shell of a Serena," I said softly.

"You always end up telling me the same thing," she
replied. "I don't know how you can like say that, seeing you're nothing but a phantom, a secret shadow of
myself."

"Bullshit!" I said. "I dare you to come and meet me, and
then you'll know."

"I'd rather hear voices than see hallucinations. I mean
like, you can be a little bit crazy, and then you can be totally lock-'em-up-and-throw-away-the-key psychotic. I don't
mind having an imagination, but I don't want my imagination to run my life."

"You're *not* imagining me!"

"Sure. Say hi to Joshua for me." Serena hung up on
me.

It was maybe three in the morning or so, I guessed.

I switched channels. The hard-core channel was going full steam. I watched three people grunting and heaving to a New Age score for a while, hunched up in the sofa because Mr. E., sensing my absence, had spread out all over the bed and I didn't want to move him.

I'd go to the asylum tomorrow and see if Mary Etchison was there and if she remembered her two sons. I'd go to the police station and look for Officer Stone. But first I wanted to go down to Karpovsky HQ and give my alter ego the surprise of her life.

chapter nine

Another Serena Somers

Another Serena Somers

My therapist always told me not to block out these . . . imaginary friends. These voices that claimed to come from alternate realities and talked about things that were like just enough different from the real world to make me think I was going crazy.

When I was younger, I mean, the day I had my first period, I saw this man-woman hovering over my pillow and I couldn't exactly hear what he was whispering in my ear but anyway I got the feeling that his words weren't really for me, they were for another me that somehow occupied the same space and time as I did but wasn't the same person. Does this sound like multiple personality disorder? But no, I wasn't all the way crazy like that. My therapist called it a borderline case. She said, well, it could have gone all the way to dissociation if the trauma had been really bad, I mean like if my Dad had raped me when I was three and shut me up in a cage and stuff like that. Lots of people, their minds fragment because the things that happen to them are so intolerable they create other personalities . . . buffers between them and the pain of it. Luckily, nothing like that had ever happened to me.

Maybe to another me, but not *me* me.

I used to daydream a lot though. About the not-me mes. There was a me who lived on another planet, a kind of cosmic shopping mall where the meaning of life was for sale in every major department store. There was a me who was abused and abandoned and chained up inside a coffin by sadistic Satanist parents, forced to participate in weird ritual sacrifices, and yes, that me was an all-the-way multiple personality, naturally. There was a me who wasn't the slut of GW Junior High, but who kept herself pure and had been in love with one boy all her life, since childhood, a boy named Joshua, but that love was such a big and scary thing that she shielded herself from it by becoming a fat slob. This particular me was often visited by a creature from another dimension named Ash, a imaginary playmate who was sublimely beautiful and sexually nonthreatening. The man-woman hovering by my pillow. Yes, the things Ash whispered in my ear were intended for this particular me, a me who was intensely vivid to me, who was in many ways my ideal picture of myself, and yet was alien to me because she wasn't me.

One time I told all this to my therapist—well, she's not really *my* therapist, but you understand, we are in family therapy because of my parents not getting along and fucking up each other's personal space—and she said, "Honey," which I hate being called, "you are going through your changeling period."—"What's that?" I said, and she's all, "Why, everyone goes through that in their adolescence sometimes. You think that you're really someone else— maybe a faery child, come floating downstream in a basket— magically conceived, yes?"—and I'm, "I just wish I wasn't such a slut,"—and she sighed and said, "You need to get a firmer grip on your femininity, and that doesn't mean squatting on mirrors and fingering yourself; so maybe you are screwing around a lot, which is not a good thing and I hope at least you're practicing safe sex when it comes to that, but you see you're not giving your *self* away in those sex acts, you're not yielding your true self at all, because your true self belongs to this fantasy lover, this Joshua, you see; and I know you've thought this fantasy thoroughly through because the name you picked for your secret lover, Joshua, you know that was the given name of Jesus, and so you know that you are looking for redemption by saving your true self for this fantasy lover, that you can lose your virginity a million times but you become a born-again virgin in your imaginary landscape, you follow what I'm saying? and there's not much I can recommend for that except I could give you a pyramid to put under your bed."

"Sure," I said, "like, a pyramid. Totally fucking phallic." My therapist always made perfect sense up to a point, and then she'd spring some New Age bullshit on me like a pyramid or some crystal. It always amazed me that our insurance condescended to cover these wacky voodoo sessions.

That day in November, I still had the pyramid with me, and before I slid into Karpovsky's bed I also took the pyramid out of my sleeve and chucked in underneath the mattress. Another of the girls saw me do it and laughed. There were three of us who did these special "night duties" with the congressman—none of us really minded, you know, because we did really believe his message, and we did really believe him when he said that this thing of his was an addiction, he was in therapy, and that we weren't bimbos, we were his special girls. We believed he was a great man with a fatal flaw and that we were there to assuage that flaw so he could be great for the rest of the world. Tonight, it was me and Janelle Silverman on duty. She was a nice Jewish girl from North Arlington, ex–Yorktown High School, sophomore at Smith now, taking a year off, writing a children's book on her laptop PC in between the congressional perquisites.

The congressman was tired after his big speech. The university audience really used to get him fired up—those rows and rows of coeds with their ill-concealed beavers

beckoning to him as he stood on the pulpit and rhapso-
dized about his shining vision of a future where poverty
would be defeated, where the old would live out their
years with dignity and health benefits, where the young
would be better educated and know about safe sex (for
some reason he was particularly insistent, some might even
say strident, about this issue, and those of the retinue who
knew the dark secrets would glance demurely at the floor
whenever he touched on it), where women and children
and minorities were empowered (my parents used to shudder whenever they heard that word uttered; you'd think
it spelled the end of civilization; they were, of course,
Republicans), where, where, where—and he always did a
Jimmy Stewart–like stammer here as his passions hit fever
pitch (he practiced the stammer daily after brushing, before
flossing)—the human spirit could soar once again—like the
great eagle that once soared above the fruited plains, before
We came to dispossess Nature and Ourselves. God it was
moving. God I loved a good cry, and this audience loved the
speech. Truth, Justice, and the Armorican Way. Yeah, okay,
so he's tired, and he nods off after a single perfunctory hand
job from Janelle, while I watch television.

CNN—human interest story—*today marks the tenth anniversary of the suicide of Phil Etchison, the poet who was
to become the guru of the Me Generation.* (Sort of a
masturbatory Rod McKuen). Never read him, but I don't
know, I felt some kind of frisson watching a bunch of
ha-ha-twenty-nine-year-olds, wearing nouveau New Wave
duds—Jesus, I barely remembered those Michael Jackson
zippers—laying a wreath at his tomb because it was
back in Alexandria and against the backdrop of Virginia
green that I'd missed out here in desert country. Cut to
Tucson, where apparently his wife, in a loony bin here,
has come out of her padded cell for her one day a year
of semilucidity; she speaks to a group of earnest-looking
students, ironically enough, in the same building where
elsewhere my lord and master was addressing a packed
hall.

Oh yeah. The frisson. There's been a Post-it note stuck to my wallet earlier today. Found it when I was fishing out the credit card to pay for lunch. *Find Mrs. E.* Well, that was this woman, wasn't it? Of course.

Last month, in the toilet, scribbled on a tissue box: *bust her out of the madhouse.* In my handwriting, always in my handwriting.

I watched for a moment, and then there came a phone call on the secret number. Janelle giggled and I answered it.

It was one of the other Serenas, so I assumed that what was happening now had subsequently sprang out of my own imagination . . . my not-quite-insanity.

"Karpovsky's asleep?" she said. "And you're—"

"In bed with him. Along with half the staff!" This wasn't true, but I'm sure my alter ego got her kicks that way. After all, since she was only a figment, she couldn't know the reality of a man's tongue, slithering down your midriff like a prehensile snail. I cackled. (I can be wicked when I'm talking to my other selves, much more wicked than I ever am in my plain-jane reality.) Then I told her about looking for Mrs. E.—why not? I'd just seen that nut case on television. And the Navajo police detective was in another note to myself. Scrawled in lipstick in an old address book. (Actually, one time, the congressman had us tie him to the bedpost, and we, in full warpaint and loincloths, danced around him shaking baby rattles.)

Was I leading her on? What difference did it make? I looked around and now both Janelle and the congressman were fast asleep even though the lights were all on and the television and there was even music, a Tori Amos song leaking from the abandoned headphones of Janelle's Discman. Whenever I'd talked to myself in the past like this, I always ended up alone somehow, so I could never prove anything to anyone afterward. There'd be like this bubble of unreality that would descend on me. God it was weird.

So this alternate Serena seemed very concerned about whether I'd fucked the congressman or not. You know, the real answer to that was no, not exactly, not all the way, you could sort of sense the final scruples clattering around in his head like jawbreakers in a gumball machine. Congressman Karpovsky had, for reasons I couldn't totally fathom, stopped a couple of centimeters shy of the final insertion. Don't ask me why. I wouldn't have cared. I had been round the block a whole lot of times. In his own way, I guess, the congressman respected us. A complicated man. He wanted to *not* have his cake and *not* eat it too. Denial was fulfillment. Well, you know what they say—brought up by Jesuits.

Shit.

So I was talking to myself on the phone, making up some line about having dreamed about Joshua because I wanted to share some part of what I'd never experienced. But she knew I was lying. Because she said to me, "You're just a shell of a Serena," and she dared me to come and meet her.

How could I meet her, how could I like face myself and *know* that I was crazy, like that poor Mrs. Etchison? I suddenly remembered once, in Modern American Literature 101, they made us read one of Etchison's poems, one about his wife's madness and how she believed she had two sons.

She is walking away from the river's edge, sometimes
I know she will never come home,
Better I do not look at all; for in the momentary
  closure,
The blink's breadth between two truths, two truths can
  both be true.
When I close my eyes I have two sons, and each
Is the other's shadow; she is the two-breasted Madonna
Who suckles the dark and light, the quick and lifeless,
Red as blood, as desire, as disenchantment.

The oddest part was how these lines all came to me at once, a crystal-perfect memory, even though I was sure I had dozed through the class and I probably thought it was a total crock at the time. Now I remembered not only the poem but Professor Martindale's tortuous exegesis—myth and archetype, illusion and reality, love-death, madness, the Manichaean duality of existence, Etchison's obsession with the Gnostics, the place of neo-Hellenism in the classical revival of the early 1980s, oh, yeah, the whole lecture unfolded in my mind like the fucking Bayeux Tapestry.

There was a knock on the door.

A secret knock: three shorts and a long—Beethoven's "knock of fate." I was too scared to answer the door. I knew what was behind it and that it was now or never; either I was crazy or I was crazy.

Another knock: the old shave-and-a-haircut.

An agonizing wait for the "two bits" that never came.

Then Congressman Karpovsky murmured in his sleep: "The damn door. Shit. Didn't anyone do the damn do-not-disturb sign?"

I had to open it, but I made sure the chain was latched. Cautiously, I cracked it, just wide enough to prove to myself that I was looking straight into my own face. But thinner. I mean, this was a me that looked *good* when I knew I only looked average. Even though she clearly hadn't showered in a couple of days and her hair was all stringy.

"Can we talk?" she said.

"You can't come in," I said, panicking.

"Yeah, I know. Come down to the lobby or something."

"Okay." I didn't know why I was so quick to agree, but, now that I was certifiable, I guess I didn't like have much to lose. I went back inside and slipped into some clothes—actually it was one of the uniforms of us Karpovsky's cheer-leaders—short but unscandalworthy gray skirt, any color blouse, UAW jacket, little green button to show solidarity with the Greens. I went out into the hallway.

"You won't need that," Serena said, and I realized I was still clutching the secret-number cellular phone. "We're talking face-to-face now."

*   *   *

The lobby was a forbidding place at night. This was a faceless name-brand hotel with a lot of mirrors and a scenic elevator and a lot of fountains, conspicuous consumption in the middle of the desert. Tall columns of circular mirrors dwarfed us. They were hung with ferns. It was a kind of techno-redwood forest. A stream ran through the middle of the lobby and it was stocked with koi. There was no one else around. Once more, no alibis for my insanity.

"We don't have much time," Serena said, and she pushed me into the nearest sofa—plush, southwestern, pink and beige—"because one of us is going to cease to exist any minute."

"What are you talking about? Is this fusion?" Which was what was supposed to happen when multiple personalities started getting to know each other and the barriers broke down and they could become absorbed into one another.

"No, Serena. It's like, not what you think. You're not crazy."

"I'm glad we agree about *that*," I said, and neither of us laughed.

"This isn't the America you know anymore."

"America? What's that?"

"I mean, Armorica."

"Okay, so *I'm* not crazy, just everybody else in the world."

"Okay, this is gonna be hard to swallow, Serena, but you and I are equivalent people from like these parallel worlds, okay? And all the worlds are smooshing into each other, as in a multiuniverse pileup, because the River that connects all the universes is going through major turbulence because Josh went back through the barrier and Theo went after him and the Darklings are battling each other and—"

She looked at me in frustration. "I'll take that part as read," I said. "But what about us?"

"Well, I think there's really only supposed to be *one* of us here. When we crossed over, the universe did radical

surgery on itself to eliminate all the paradoxes as quickly
as it could. It killed off one complete busload of Karpovsky
followers and convinced everyone they were all impostors.
Then it shifted Mr. E. so that he's been dead for ten years,
so the Mr. E. I'm traveling with could be the only one. Josh
and Theo are gone anyway, so that just leaves you and me,
and one of us has got to go."

"So you're gonna blow me away with a .357 Magnum
now?"

"Oh, get real, girl." She gripped both of my hands in
hers and I saw, suddenly, that she really *was* me. The me
that would have been if I hadn't given up on myself when
I reached puberty. The me that had been kept strong, and
innocent, and wise, by a deep, unself-conscious love. Oh,
God, I envied her. Me. And when I looked into her eyes
I saw that this was a chance to become that me. To wash
the soiled laundry of my life. "I figure," Serena said, "if we
really concentrate hard on it, if we *both* agree to like, die,
maybe we can somehow connect, merge, reinvent ourselves
as a single person, bypass the dimensional paradox. Do you
understand what I mean?"

"You're talking suicide pact!" I said. But you know, I
wasn't shocked.

Because there had always been like, this unreality to
my life. Face it, dudette, I told myself, you've always
been the phantom of someone else's opera. If in dying
I could become more real, more fully myself, I couldn't
really refuse that, could I? And this was what my therapist called fusion. It was really death. It was transformation. Right? Right. I found myself gripping my alter
ego's hands so hard her palms were bleeding. Or were
they mine? I didn't know. The blood was swirling like
a miniature galaxy. No, the whole room was swirling.
The two of us were swirling. I was a woman with two
heads and four arms, one of those Hindu goddesses. We
got up from the sofa and then the sofa was the world
and we—I—was astride it, joyous, dancing to the hip-hop
of the cosmos. My four arms whirled like the spokes of

a wheel, they flamed, I was breaking the world on the catherinewheel of my passion, breaking and re-forming the world, and yawning the stars and moons from my lips, and the clouds wreathing my spinning feet, I juggled chaos and order in my lightning hands, and, and, and—

Everything became very still. The tempest had receded into a faint throbbing. Only my heartbeat.

I was the only person in the lobby of the campaign headquarters hotel. The alter ego was gone. "Serena?" I said. Then came the memories. They flooded me. They overwhelmed me. I could see the dragon woman screeching across an orange sky and I could feel dead Joshua coming back to life in my arms. Not just shards of a daydream. It was *real*. And I remembered a country called America, rock-solid, not a phantom.

Serena Somers

"Serena, Serena," I said—because I wasn't all used to not talking to a mirage of myself—"Serena, what if there are other mes out there, or if other mes are going to be hurled out because of all these cosmoses collapsing in on each other?"

I answered myself: "We'll draw them all into ourself. We're not going to be pieces of a person. We're going to heal."

I slipped into the congressman's suite and I called Mr. E. from the cellular phone even though it was like four A.M. He groaned. "Mr. E.!" I said. "Like, I died and came to earth."

"What are you talking about?" he mumbled. "Serena?"

"Wake up, Mr. E.—oh, wake up—something wonderful has happened. Let's go to the asylum and get your wife."

"Now?"

"Did you know it's the anniversary of your death?" CNN was broadcasting the news again. "Turn it on! But you know, we're still in the middle of the Days of the Dead, aren't we? And you're dead, but you're walking the earth again, aren't you? And I've just killed myself, but I'm alive, aren't I?"

"This is too much to take all at once," said Mr. E.

"No, you see, it all makes sense because on the anniversary of your death, she becomes lucid . . . *Two truths can both be true* . . . you said that. I learned it in school."

"Maybe I did," he said. "Maybe I did."

"Well like, now is the time when two truths are true. It's a window of opportunity. I know this because I have all my own memories and all my *other* memories too. I know this world as well as I know my own world. I mean, I belong to both now. So I'm telling you, we've gotta spring Mrs. E. from the madhouse before dawn. Do you think we can find Detective Stone too?"

"Yeah." He was coming to now.

"I'll meet you back at the hotel, outside. Look, I took the car, so don't panic. I had to drive down here to Karpovsky HQ on some personal business."

"Personal?"

"Integrating my soul," I said. "Can't get much more personal than that."

I slammed Karpovsky's door behind me and took the elevator back downstairs. The Tucson night was cold and I was glad of the UAW jacket (which had kind of materialized on my back after the two of us fused). I got back in the Cadillac and drove on back to Oracle.

Phil Etchison

I staggered to the lobby just as the Cadillac pulled up. The Serena who greeted me was the same and not the same. She wasn't as thin as when she'd left, but she wasn't fat either; for the first time, her proportions seemed to be right—she seemed to be comfortable with the way she looked as she hopped out of the car and waved at me to hurry up.

I had woken from a nightmare, was rubbing nightmare ectoplasm from my eyes. I staggered toward her. She supported me as I eased myself onto the seat. "I'll drive," she said, coolly in control. "I actually know where I'm going, for once."

We moved into the night. I was relieved that she was driving. The Cadillac's gearshift was labeled PRNDBQZLL. We were in the Q-gear at the moment, and the 7-Eleven was no longer at the corner. Disjunctive fugue was setting in again. Reality was in flux, had always been in flux, and it was all I could do to stay calm.

chapter ten

Yellow Brick Roads

Theo Etchison

I don't know how long I'm walking. The sound of the stream on my left is the only constant thing. The forest keeps shifting and transforming. Sometimes it's all cactus, sometimes it's redwood, sometimes it's a Tarzan-type jungle with swinging vines that might just be coiling anacondas. It's a scary place, but at least I have my Dream Book now, and I still have the marble . . . so I still have some idea of where I'm going as long as I don't look too hard at what's surrounding me, just walk straight ahead, straight through piles of decomposing leaves and branches, through twisted tree trunks that melt like mirages when I pass through them. The forest is full of sounds. Birds tweet and screech, rodents scurry, monkeys chitter, snakes slither. I'm afraid but I keep on walking. Walking. There's no breeze in this forest; it's as close and claustrophobic as a locked closet. I keep walking. I have the jester's bells tucked into my pants and my notebook under my arm and I keep walking.

I'm fixated on one thing: Joshua. I *know* I'm going in the right direction. I know with the certainty of Truthsaying that he's near me, but there's something missing from the picture, something I can't quite see.

I keep on walking.

It gets darker. And darker. And day never comes. Night deepens into mega-night. There's never going to be day in this forest, I think. I just keep walking. I'm exhausted and hungry. Have I been wandering around in circles? I don't think so. Hasn't the stream been at my left hand the whole time? Or is the stream a circle? I take the marble out and try to peer into its depths, but there is so little light that all I can make out is the writhing of the filaments. Why is that I wonder? Is there a truth so obscure that even a Truthsayer can't see it? Or am I losing my powers? I can't tell. I'm getting totally frustrated now.

I keep walking, I don't know for how long. It doesn't get any lighter and the air doesn't get more breathable. The vapors of night cling to me and I'm almost suffocating. The trees have started to come alive. The vines hiss and lash out at me. They rip at my face. I feel something clawing at my arm, turn to look, see only a pair of soulless eyes in the darkness. I have to keep moving even though my limbs are leaden. There are things pursuing me and if I stop they'll catch up with me and kill me. A tremor shakes the darkness, like the purring of a giant black cat against my body, I can feel the vibration in my guts . . . Oh God I'm frightened and I quicken my pace now, quicken, quicken, though I'm short of breath and every step is more agonizing than the one before . . . Faster. Faster. Faster.

There are creatures running behind me. Their paws pound the hard earth. Their spoor stinks up the air. I keep running. And a part of me says, *Stop, stop, turn to face the demon.* And another part says, *No, no, no, I'm scared, gotta keep running—*

Running.

Running.

But I'm too exhausted. I have to stop. And I do. I turn.

Eyes—hard—yellow—crystalline—a blur of mottled yellow and black fur—canines slicing the thick air and—

The jaguar pounces and I—

There's nothing to fight back with. Without thinking I pull the jester's bell's from my pants and I kind of brandish it and I hear the tinkling and see the silvery light that streaks against the forest canopy and—

The jaguar's at my feet, purring softly. Soft light emanates from the bells in my hand. I shake them again. The tinkling . . . the jaguar's fascinated by it. The jaguar's hypnotized by the dancing light. The birds' harsh screeches turn to delicate twittering. I hear the whisper of the nearby stream.

I shake the bells. Music pours from them. It's sort of a New Age sound, hardly anything to get up and slamdance to, but around here it seems to have magic. I don't feel the magic. I'm immune to it, I guess. But the forest is bewitched. Animals crawl out of the undergrowth—rabbits and fawns and porcupines. A vulture settles on the jaguar's back and tilts its head back and forth in time to the music. A snake unreels from a nearby branch and hovers over me but somehow I don't feel threatened. The music continues even after I stop tinkling; the bells are on autopilot I guess, like one of those Christmas cards that play "Jingle Bells" when you open them up.

Finally I can take a breather. I sit down on spongy earth. All the animals' cries, purrs, and chatterings begin to blend together. Soon there's a wall of harmony around me. It's almost like one of the production numbers from the *Jungle Book* cartoon. I know it's supposed to make me feel like Orpheus charming the wild beasts, soothing the savage breasts and all that shit, but the music doesn't have any power over me at all, it's just like this cosmic Muzak I guess, transcendental elevator music. I lean against a tree trunk. I wish there was something to eat. Why can't there be fruit hanging on any of these trees? Oh, but there are—it's just that they're all glittery and jewel-like, they're decorator fruit, not nutrition. Like everything else here, an illusion.

I sit under the tree for a long time. Maybe I fall asleep.

I'm not sure. I'm so hungry now that my stomach's stopped hurting. I'm all stretched out thin, like air. The light radiates outward from the bells and forms a circle around me. The jaguar growls softly, paws the ground, worries at something. I have a feeling that I know him.

"Who are you?" I say.

He stares up into my eyes. His eyes aren't hard anymore. He is weeping. His tears are like drops of amber. I bend down and wipe one away with my finger. I have the feeling that he's very old.

"What are you crying about?" I ask him. It wouldn't surprise me if he could talk; I've run into talking animals and even plants in these strange worlds. But before he can answer me I see that there's a deep and festering wound in the jaguar's side. He licks at it and continues to weep.

"I think I know who you are now," I say. But it doesn't make sense to me.

And that's when I notice the trail of breadcrumbs, leading from where I'm sitting, away from the stream and into the thickest part of the forest, and, beneath the line of strewn crusts, beneath the undergrowth, the glint of metallic yellow . . .

Phil Etchison

Serena drove fast. I barely had a chance to compose myself when we found ourselves outside the Tucson police station.

"The place looks different," I said. I had begun to remember how I had come here with Joshua last year to look for Theo . . . and how Joshua had been captured by Katastrofa. "Are you sure it's the right place? I don't remember this art deco façade."

Serena double-parked—a foolhardy thing to do in front of a police station—and said, "Why don't you go inside, Mr. E., and find out if there's a Detective Stone here."

I must have looked worried, because she added, "Don't worry. Would you rather have me go?"

I said, "No, I'll do it. But leave the engine running; I don't want you to get a ticket. If there's a problem, go around the block or something."

I went up the steps. The reception area seemed familiar enough, the woman at the desk appropriately dour as she pecked at a manual typewriter, a faint whiff of death and stale tobacco in the air.

"Is there a Detective Stone here, ma'am?" I said.

She glanced up from her paperwork. "Stone?" she said. "Not on your life. He was—retired, you know, without pay. Unofficially. You should know that."

"I should?"

"You're not a reporter, are you? After they had my picture in the *Enquirer*, I almost got fired."

"I don't know what you mean."

"Well, it's not every day that a respected cop gets photographed trying on women's lingerie at Frederick's," she said. "Frankly, what they do when they're in Hollywood on vacation's not the department's business, but then when Action Against Defamation of Native Americans issued a statement saying that Milt was a *nadlé*, some kind of transvestite witch doctor, and then the ACLU put in their two cents, and someone dug up a photograph of Milt Stone in a tutu doing the pas de deux from Swan Lake with that defector from the Bolshoi Ballet . . . well . . . I'm sure you saw the whole thing on Sally Jessy Raphael last month."

"Ah . . . I've been in Mexico."

"He a relative of yours?"

"Not exactly. A . . . a friend."

"Oh, I see. A fellow fairy, huh. Not that I'm into queer bashing—against department policy anyway—but anyone who would hang out with Milt Stone is probably sort of a funny bunny himself."

"Milt Stone's not gay," I said, somewhat repelled by her prejudice and at the same time feeling a little awkward about having to defend Milt's honor against a creature such as this, "he really *is* a *nadlé*, a sacred man-woman of the Navajo people. Seriously. He can do amazing things

. . . walk between worlds . . . die and live again . . . things you couldn't possibly imagine."

"Yeah, right," she said. "I guess you're not one of his fag friends then. You're one of his fellow druggies. Peyote, shrooms, LSD, he did 'em all, according to the thing on Channel Six."

"Well, could you tell me where I might be able to find him?"

"Went back to the hogan," she said. "You want directions?" She fished in a drawer and pulled out a Xerox of a crudely drawn map. "Come to think of it, you're Etchison, aren't you?" she added. "He said you'd be coming by. There's some other stuff with the map." She handed me a Jiffy bag with lumpy contents. "That better not be drugs," she said. "Word of honor?"

I nodded, though I had no idea what the contents might be. I felt the Jiffy bag. It seemed to be full of rocks. "Thank you," I said, adding, as I read the nameplate by her typewriter, "Ms. Magdalen."

"Mariel," she said, and smiled at me for the first time. She rummaged in her drawer again and, after considerable pushing aside of papers, produced a battered, coffee-stained, coverless copy of *The Embrasure of Parched Lips.* "It really *is* you, isn't it, Mr. Etchison? I really didn't believe that a lowlife like Stone could actually know a *famous* poet—he never really knew any white people, socially that is. My heavens, I'm sorry about all the things I said. His friends that aren't actually Injuns are all white trash, you see. Milt told me you'd call me *Ms.*—because you got class, you know."

"I see," I said. It was hard to make sense of the map. It showed the freeway leading northeast out of Tucson. An exit (labeled "unmarked") led to a thread of a road that snaked up into mountainous terrain and wound in and out and up and down itself and tied itself into knots and ended up in a jumble of squiggles just past the Painted Desert. Tony Hillerman country, land of kachinas and gateways into other worlds. There was no rhyme or reason to the way it twisted. It obviously belonged to the "yellow brick" category of road . . . a concretization of the metaphoric journey of the soul . . . yet another "human condition" flag for the academic poetry professors who had been my most loyal and most pretentious audience for the entirety of my career.

I signed *The Embrasure of Parched Lips* with the felt-tip pen Mariel held out to me. Then, on a whim, I flipped through the pages, thinking at least to anchor myself to the remembrance of familiar words.

But it is a sea of words, a seething melee of letters running into one another with now and then a single significant word breaching the maelstrom like a singing whale:

*aghastaflamelove**seeking**jumpriverhigh**storm**bursting
leapriverleap**leap**fuckingcoprolalialexico**nameliaearhart**
oh   my**soul**
applejumpleapflame**seethe**lovetruthteethapple
good   and   evil
seepappleseepseekappleseepappleseekappleseekseepsikh
and ye shall **find***

What was I to make of these Joycean thunderclaps? I knew they were not my words. But my signature was now on the flyleaf, and my name was on the spine, and *Ms.* Magdalen was fixing me with a starry-eyed stare; I searched the cinema-multiplex of memory for some image of myself and these words and came up empty.

So I thanked her quickly, a tad brusquely, for her kind information, and left the police station with the road map in my pocket.

Theo Etchison

I'm amazed at how hungry I am. I keep picking up the crumbs and wolfing them down. I guess I must have been walking in circles for days because the hard crusts are sweet as candy. The jaguar follows me. I hold the bells in front of my face like a torch. I walk in a circle of light. The crumbs have a distinct flavor of gingerbread, and as I move farther from the River I get the feeling I'm being sucked into the story of Hansel and Gretel.

The light begins to spread and the trees thin out a little and pretty soon I see the outlines of the gingerbread house, which is not at all like the way it's usually illustrated in kids' books—it's big and ominous and many-gabled—more like the *Psycho* house at Universal Studios—looming up in the middle of a clearing. It's completely encircled by a row of like these twisted, rainbow-colored mushrooms—psychedelic shrooms maybe—and it has a chimney that spews out industrial-strength smoke. It's the gingerbread house from hell. It's a little bit like Auschwitz and a little bit like Pittsburgh. The jaguar growls and I pet him to make him calm down.

I'm scared to go inside even though I know the story says I have to end up going in there and doing battle with the witch, so I hang around on the porch. I'm still totally starving so I keep tearing off little strips from the wall and chewing on them. The gingerbread's rich and spicy and it makes me lightheaded because my mind begins to drift a little—I see an image of Serena Somers—a dozen Serena Somerses, fat, thin, and medium-sized, dancing in a ring, converging slowly into a kind of mega-Serena in the middle.

Then I hear a woman's voice: "Theo Truthsayer," she says, "you've gone and eaten my food, and that means you're my prisoner now; you have to stay in my kingdom forever."

I turn around and see her: she's tall, redhaired, with a sweeping cloak and the eyes of a serpent. "Katastrofa Darkling," I say softly.

I know this is the place I've been meaning to go all this time. I know that Katastrofa has my brother captive somewhere in this cannibal candy mansion.

"Theo," she says, "why do you hate me so much?"

"Because you killed my brother."

"Your brother chose to come back to me because he loves me. And he's not dead, not exactly." She smiles this cat-and-canary smile that tells me that tells me that she has me trapped. She strokes my cheek with the edge of a single fingernail. I blush in spite of myself. She's beautiful. She's all perfumed and licking her lips and I feel something unfamiliar, you know, down in my pants, and I'm thinking, O Jesus, don't tell me my hormones are finally kicking in, what a stupid time for this to happen, nobody ever told me it would be embarrassing like this . . . and I force myself not to think about her, to think only about Joshua and the things she's done to him . . .

"I want to see him!"

"Then you'll have to come inside, Theo Truthsayer. And perhaps you'll have to run me a few simple errands . . . simple enough, at least, for someone with your special gift."

"I'm not taking sides," I say, "in this big old war you've got going with your brothers. It's totally none of my business. I didn't ask to be a Truthsayer. I only came back here to get Joshua."

"Just park your jaguar outside and get in the goddamn house. If you want to see your brother alive you'd better be prepared to do something for me in exchange."

The jaguar has coiled up by the front door and seems to be dozing as I step over the threshold of Katastrofa's castle.

Phil Etchison

It was getting light when we reached the asylum. I wasn't entirely sure how I was going to manage the next stage of the plan, but, since I could come up with no Machiavellian ruse, I decided on the direct approach.

I pulled right up to the front of the building—which bore an incongruous resemblance to the Parthenon—and parked illegally in an ambulance space. Serena and I marched up the steps, attempting to appear as though we belonged.

A lone, corpulent nurse sat behind the reception desk. It looked as though a replay of the scene at the police station was about to occur: the only difference was the decor—art deco there, neoclassical here.

"Excuse me," I said.

She looked at me and screamed.

"What's the problem?" I said to Serena. "It's not as if she was seeing a ghost or something—"

"Actually," said Serena, "you *are* supposed to be dead in this universe. According to CNN."

"But the policewoman at the station didn't think so . . ."

"Probably just behind the times," she said. We watched the receptionist flailing in horror; I wondered when she would get around to calling the Ghostbusters. "Come on," said Serena. "While she's busy screaming, we can probably make it to Mrs. E.'s room."

She was already heading toward the elevators, and I realized that I, too, knew the way . . . as though we had trod through this segment of our lives a thousand times before, and would again a thousand times . . . I pushed the button, we negotiated the narrow corridors, turned left, left, right, right, found ourselves opening a familiar door, facing a familiar woman . . .

"Mary," I said.

And she was the way I remembered her before the cancer. Her hair hadn't been eaten away by chemotherapy. Her cheeks were full, her lips had the impertinent pout they'd had the first time we'd ever met. She stood there in her hospital gown in a darkened room framed by the severe metallic window sill against iron bars that gleamed in the soft moonlight. Oh, she was translucent, beautiful in an elfin way; and she was strangely young; and I remembered that, in this incarnation, having taken refuge in her madness at an early age, she had not lived through many of the apocalyptic events that had taken their toll on the Mary I'd lived with, the one who'd toiled beside me twenty years and more; no, this was a fresh Mary, in a very real sense a virgin Mary, a clear white parchment Mary.

"Philip," she said, "I've waited here so long. I thought I was doomed to die an unconsummated Rapunzel." She smiled. "I've always known you weren't really dead; that your death had been manufactured to prepare for this moment. Oh, come, come quickly, before the sun rises, because that's when I retreat into darkness for another year."

We embraced.

"Way to go, Mr. and Mrs. E.," said Serena.

We kissed, and in that kiss we mingled the disparate memories of our sundered selves; and oh, I knew then how much I loved her, and how much I needed to be whole.

chapter eleven

Katastrofa's Castle

Theo Etchison

Of course, the interior of the gingerbread house isn't what you'd expect from the outside. Because folded up inside it is the entire domain of Katastrofa, second child of King Strang, the dragon woman. Oh, when I step inside there's like the impression of a witch's hovel. There's an iron stove puffing away at one end of the chamber, and the floor is strewn with straw and bones, and there's beat-up leatherbound grimoires with human skulls holding up guttering candles, and a shelf full of alembics and retorts and crucibles with bubbling fluids in neon shades, and bats and rats dangling from the ceiling on ropes, and all the usual bullshit; but then, you look *past* these things, and *through* them, you look around corners, and you see there's much, much more. Behind the stove, there's a steep canyon, and a lake of fire, and a path that zigzags up a cliff to a mesa, and on that mesa is a Cadillac, upright, half-buried, its front end pointed at the moon; sometimes these vistas seem like wallpaper, sometimes they move. Wheeling over our heads are mist-creatures—fanged, clawed, winged, dissolving in and out of one another. It's a scary place. But I can feel

Joshua's presence. I guess I've felt him all along.

Katastrofa leads me by the hand . . . Her hand is almost scalding-hot but she won't let go of me. The heat seeps into my fingers, races through my veins, makes my heart beat faster, yeah, makes this demon inside me stir, this sex thing I've spent the last couple of years trying not to think about because it scares me.

"When am I going to see Josh?" I ask her.

"In time," she says. But she seems nervous.

"Show him to me now."

I'm losing my fear because I know she needs me to win her war, and I'm too valuable for her to harm. I've been through this bullshit before, and furthermore, this time, I came of my own free will, and I know the score.

"If you insist," says Katastrofa Darkling. "But first, the grand tour; I'm sure you feel like a grand tour, don't you?" And we start to descend.

I know from previous experience that the tour will only show me images plucked from my own childish fantasies; that the real world that these creatures inhabit is full of things I have no referents for; so the best I can do is construct these mirages around myself, pictures from pulp and celluloid, from comic books and my Dad's flights of poetry, from PBS specials and Bart Simpson cartoons . . . This is the only reality I know, but I'm the Truthsayer, not some brilliant visionary, not some transcendental world-builder, only me; and so this is the reality they're all stuck with. *I was a teenage demiurge*. Fuck, what a trip.

This place is nothing like Thornslaught. The castle of Katastrofa's brother is full of daunting endless spaces, vaulting ceilings, sweeping staircases. This is just as vast, but everything has a twisted, claustrophobic, tunnel-like feel to it. The giant vistas are there but they are all gorges and canyons with towering cliffs that hem us in. There's never a feeling of being outside even when we glimpse the sky through a lattice of thatch or a jungle canopy. Katastrofa doesn't let go of my hand.

Thorn had a lot of servants scurrying around, lackeys

fawning all over him the whole time. Ash had his minions too, although they weren't slavish like Thorn's. Katastrofa's not like that. She's a loner. As she drags me deeper and deeper down the dungeon steps, there's barely any people around. Oh, now and then, a gnomelike creature skulks past. Stairwells coil. Our footsteps ring against cold metal. Walls drip with blood and wet graffiti. Katastrofa doesn't say very much, but now and then she turns to glower at me, and sometimes she licks her lips with a forked tongue. She moves with a slithering motion; even in human form there's something of the dragon in her.

At last we seem to reach the lowest level of Katastrofa's castle. "Your room," she tells me, and points to a cell—one of those medieval dungeon-type things—iron bars, straw pallet, chains hanging on the wall. "Not exactly the Hyatt, but you can change it around any way you want."

"Jesus. At least Thorn tried to recreate my old room back in Virginia . . . tried to make me feel at home, in his own way."

"I'm not like Thorn," she says. "Thorn has illusions. He's the eldest, you know. He sucks his people's blood, but now and then the human condition gets to him a little, and he gets saddled with compassion."

"Didn't see too much of that."

"Oh, but you did." I guess I do remember a few vulnerable moments. "You won't find them with me. Do you know why I chose to become a weredragon?"

"I couldn't guess."

"Because I rage through the world, I am anger, I am vengeance."

"No, you're not," I say. Because I'm a Truthsayer, I can't help shattering her self-delusions. "You're just a typical middle kid, with a middle kid complex. You were jealous of Thorn's power; you couldn't stand it that Ash was the apple of Strang's eye. You chose the form of a beast because you hate yourself."

"That's ridiculous. Men fear me. And they love me. A glamour clings to me. Even through my human skin there's the shimmer of serpentine scales. I am sensuality as well as rage. I am the love that kills."

"You're only trying to convince yourself."

Sullen, she turns away from me. There's less glower in those glowing eyes. "Don't think you can subdue me with mindgames, Theo Truthsayer. You too are clinging to something you don't really have anymore—your childhood."

She kisses me. I can feel her tongue against my lips, pulsing, hot, trying to force them apart. Her arms entwine me like the coils of a boa constrictor. My dick is all straining, uncomfortable, it's not desire exactly, it's my body going through the mechanics of what it's just learning to do. I'm confused. It's like I'm losing my anchor on the truth. Quickly I pull away and say, "You don't dare seduce me. Maybe I'm like Peter Pan, you know; if I grow up and I feel real desires and come and all, I'll lose my powers." The minute I say this I wonder if it's true. It *feels* true. But I'm not sure, the way I'm always so sure of everything else. I want to change the subject.

"Joshua," I say. "Show me Joshua. Or you won't get any help from me."

"All right."

She claps her hands. Some of the prison walls kind of melt away and we're in like this torture chamber. There are cages hanging from the ceiling, dozens of them, and in each cage there's a naked man or a boy. They're all wasting away, skin and bones, most of them. They stare vacantly into the dimness. They were all beautiful once. Like my brother I guess; he was always the straight and tall one and I was always the creep. I follow Katastrofa as she works her way through the dangling cages. Now and then she stops in front of one of them and she reaches in and caresses the young man's thighs and he begins to sigh . . . It's like she's sucking out their youth . . . their manhood . . . yeah, and there's a faint odor in the air and I recognize the smell from the times I've gone to the bathroom after Joshua and he's kind of slinking past me on the landing with a

magazine wrapped up in his towel. The jacking-off smell.
Yeah. Katastrofa's a vampire too, a sex vampire . . . She's
everything that scares me about sex and about growing
up. The dudes in the cages are all whimpering, moaning,
they're all older than me, they've gone through puberty,
and now they're being drained, they're slaves of their own
desires . . . Jesus I sound like a fucking television minister
and I should know better but I'm scared, sex to me is a big
old dragon waiting in a cave and I'm a knight without a
sword standing outside pissing myself with terror. Actually
I think I might really piss myself and I tell myself no, it's
been too long since you wet the bed, you can't regress to
that anymore, you're the Truthsayer, you're supposed to be
in control.

And I can sense Joshua getting closer and closer; it's
almost like he's inside of me.

Katastrofa moves quickly, sometimes brushing past a
cage and making it swing back and forth; I watch the boy
inside, helpless, slide from side to side against the bars. At
last we reach the end of the hallway.

"My beloved," says Katastrofa. She whisks aside a cur-
tain and that's when I see Joshua, in his own chamber, in
his own coffin.

There's like an altar rail in front of the coffin. In a way
it reminds me of the shrine where my mother, the statue,
was being worshiped. There are votive candles and, on the
wall, where his head is pointed, there's an icon of the One
Mother, her hands outstretched, weeping tears of blood; at
Joshua's feet there's a stone Cupid, and it too is weeping.

It's a glass coffin. But he's no Snow White. He's not a
perfect creature in a dreamless sleep; he's a corpse. The
coffin is filled with seawater and you can hear the wind
howling through high, barred, glassless windows, and outside the windows you can see the cliffside bungalow by
the laetrile clinic and there are gulls screeching and a faint
murmur of a festive crowd and, fainter still, the salsa music;
out there, the Day of the Dead is still going on.

Katastrofa laughs. "You think he's dead, don't you?"

"Yeah." I don't feel Joshua's presence at all, even though I know he's here, right here, in the decomposing flesh. That feeling of him close by, crying out to me, I left that feeling behind as soon as I stepped into this little room. "You've drained him. You can't keep me here because you've killed him."

"I did not kill him. I gave him love."

"It wasn't love. It was a kind of craziness." It has to be craziness. I know that no human woman's ever made me feel the way she does just by touching me. "It was Serena who loved him. And me."

Katastrofa bends over my brother's face. The salt water's been eating at him; some of the skin is peeling; the complexion is green; the eyes are jellied; a crab skitters across his lips. "Look at his eyes," she says. "Pearls; they catch the light; see, see." She flicks the crab out of the way and kisses him.

Joshua stirs. I feel a tugging in my heart.

His eyes seem to flash for a moment. "Joshua," I say softly.

Katastrofa reaches into the crystal sarcophagus and puts her arms around him, draws him into a sitting position, hugs him hard; a sulphurous mist exudes from her nostrils; her dragon nature is trying to burst through her human shape. And Joshua begins to move. His arms slowly animate themselves in zombielike, stop-motion little jerks. The fingers begin mechanically to knead Katastrofa's back. And Joshua speaks: "*Ka . . . ta . . . stro . . . fa . . .*" God, I'm going to cry. I can't stand to see him this way. I'm scared and enraged and full of grief, all at once. I sort of tackle Katastrofa and try to push her off of Joshua and I'm screaming, "No, you don't, no, he's my brother, you can't do that to him, you can't, you can't—"

She lets go of him all of a sudden and he collapses back into the brine and she's totally laughing at me, doing the whole wicked witch thing, and I see the twitching pseudolife go out of Joshua and he's just like a rag doll again, limp, dull-eyed, dead.

But the moment he goes completely lifeless is also the moment that I feel, once again, the glimmer of his presence within me.

I don't know what it means. I know there's a chance of bringing my brother back. I know I have to stay here until I figure out how. I know Katastrofa's castle is an even more terrifying place to be than Thornslaught, because when Katastrofa comes close to me she somehow puts me at war with myself. God, I hope I lose my powers one day. I just want to be normal. I don't want to see anymore.

I turn my back on the dragon woman and on my undead brother in his glass sarcophagus. Oh, God, I'm drowning. I want out. I hate myself and I hate my life.

"Don't you dare turn your back on me," says Katastrofa. "Don't you understand, little man, that I have the key to your salvation?"

"Leave me alone! I wish I'd been an ordinary kid, I wish I'd spent my life ditching school and tagging the bus and shoplifting instead of having these dreams that aren't dreams . . . I want to forget everything. Take away my gift, take away my knowledge."

"Take it away!" She laughs. "There are those who'd give their right eye for such knowledge . . . and not just humans . . . even the gods themselves."

So what? I'm thinking. I'm not Odin or any of that crowd, and I never asked to me.

"We're just talking a simple bargain," Katastrofa says. "My brother for your brother. You help me kill mine, I help you bring yours back to life."

I don't look back at her. But she comes close to me and she puts her arms around me as I stare at the dungeon floor, and she kisses the crown of my head, and I think: I hated Thorn. I love Joshua. Why shouldn't I kill one and save the other? What fucking difference does it make to me whether Thorn or Katastrofa inherits the kingdom of the fisher king?

Somewhere, a jaguar growls.

chapter twelve

The Dancing Woman

Serena Somers

I was still the designated driver because Mr. and Mrs. E. were lost in a private reverie. It was maybe an hour before dawn and I knew they needed to talk about a lot of things before the Day of the Dead came to an end; afterwards, who knew what Mrs. E. would know, or whether her sickness would be of the soul or of the flesh. I let them both sit in the back and I tried to be a good chauffeur, not eavesdropping too much. I had the map spread out on the passenger seat, and the dome light on, trying to make head or tail out of it.

"I turn into a pumpkin at dawn," Mrs. E. said. "But for now, I see everything so clearly . . . I mean our lives. The poetry readings by the fireplace, you telling the kids that poetry *is* the best kind of Sunday school; and the weekends in Spotsylvania County with the grandparents; and in Colorado, Theo swinging across the creek scrunched into an old tire that hung from a cottonwood tree; and in Alexandria, me getting the test results from Dr. Schmitz, knowing there wasn't any more hope; oh, God, you don't know what it was like in the madhouse, with all the wrong memories, sometimes not knowing my own name; and the

111

voices telling me my illness was the price of the world's
salvation . . . delusions of grandeur."

She was talking mostly to herself, and Mr. E. was listening; sometimes, looking up in the rearview mirror, I
saw him with his eyes closed, knew he was drinking in the
things she said, the confirmation of his own confounded
memories. And sometimes he'd just say, "Yes, Mary, oh,
God, yes, I remember now."

Mary said, "Please don't let me forget again. It's like
being blind and not even being able to remember what it
was like to see. They used to Thorazine me when I heard
voices."

"No, Mary, you're not going to forget everything when
the sun comes up. Because we're with you now, and we're
from the real world, your world."

It wasn't that bad going up through Pinal and Gila Coun-
ties but after that, going in to Navajo County, was when
the map started getting weird. For one thing, it should have
been day a long time ago, but the sun stayed beneath the
horizon; we were stuck in a twilight that never wanted to
become dawn. On the map, the road we were on ran straight
only a little while longer, then became as involuted as a ball
of yarn. I was all trying to follow, wrenching the wheel hard
left and hard right, scraping the bottom of the car when the
road dipped or swerved abruptly. The terrain was barren and
repetitive, and there were these monster rock formations,
sandstone dinosaurs that seemed to totally lumber over the
sea of sagebrush.

"I'm starting to feel dizzy," Mrs. E. said. And for the first
time since we'd rescued her I started to smell a sick-sweet
odor, like the smell of old oranges . . . that was how she
used to smell when she was dying of cancer. Even the
Cupid-shaped air freshener couldn't withstand the odor.

"Oh, Mrs. E.," I said, "oh, Jesus." But I had to concentrate on the road because now it was like one of those racing
car video games, up and down and around and around, and
the smell of the dying was heavier now, cloying, suffocating, and I had to concentrate hard on keeping my eyes on

the road, and the desert was shifting too, I could see shapes
and patterns in the sand and it was like a landscape-sized
animated sand painting with bands of colors rippling and
stick-figure kachinas dancing up and down and . . . the car
careened and Mr. E. shouted "Jesus!" and the cherubic air-
freshener began to sway, I thought it would come to life
like it did before and tell us what to do but no, it just
dangled and swung and finally got entangled in the rearview
mirror . . . and the clouds were gathering now, sweeping us
up, a dust storm was pelting the windshield, the car was
spinning in the air as though we'd been picked up by a
tornado and . . .

"I don't know where I'm going anymore!" I screamed,
and it was true, I was flooring the gas and the car flew of
its own free will, the wheel was steering itself, the gearshift
was stuck on the letter *Q*, whatever the fuck that meant, and
then, all of sudden, I saw we were hurtling toward the edge
of a precipice a chasm a canyon and we were off the edge
now and below us a lake of fire yawned spitting up sulphur
fumes and . . .

*The far edge of the canyon: on the plateau: a woman
dancing.*

. . . the Cadillac was in free fall! And the Etchisons
weren't wearing their seat belts, and they were in each
other's arms, a ball of arms and legs clambering over
the seat back and . . . I heard something pounding . . . my
heartbeat . . . the drumbeat of an Indian song.

I saw a woman dancing.

Blackout.

Phil Etchison

When we came to, the Cadillac was buried, nose-down,
in a sand dune of some kind. The door swung open and fell
off and skidded off the ledge and I could see it plummeting
down, down, down into a fiery river far below us. The
wind was sandy and raucous. We tumbled out of the car
but were not blown over the edge; we fell into soft sand.

The sun was edging up over distant, toothy peaks. Clouds roiled in a thousand shades of mauve, vermilion, crimson, rust, maroon.

A woman was dancing against the rising sun.

The three of us stood there, me flanked by the two women, holding hands. The woman danced in a circle marked by stones. She sang in a highpitched, ululating voice, and outside her feet a small nude boy crouched, beating on a drum. The boy had a pair of feathery wings, their whiteness in sharp contrast to his mestizo complexion. The boy was Jesus Ortega, and he looked up and cried, "Oh, you come now, take too long, time almost running out."

The woman was garbed in a buckskin dress. Her hair was long and it streamed in the wind as she danced. Her face was painted white, with a streak of yellow lightning down the middle, and one eye was the sun and the other the moon, and her arms were covered in crisscross patterns, and she moved in a slow and stately motion around the sacred circle, her hands, holding sheaves of corn, upraised in a gesture of invocation. Around where we stood a dust storm was raging, but we did not feel the wind and the sand in our faces. It was as though we were inside a glass bubble, and inside the bubble there was only the heartbeat of the music and the adagio movements of the dance.

"I think we've found our woman," I whispered—one did not feel that one could speak too loudly, for fear of profaning this music—to Serena.

"Yes," she said.

We stood still, the three of us still holding hands, until the music ceased.

The woman laid down her sheaves.

"Señor Etchison," said Jesus Ortega, "you come a long way in twenty-four hours, no? But I am good boy. I show you the way all the time."

The woman stepped over the circle of stones and immediately became a man. The change was as smooth as it was rapid, like a high-tech computer-generated special effect. She had not changed her clothes or removed her makeup, but his every movement was different now, less fluid, and when he spoke to me it was in the deep, familiar voice of Detective Milt Stone: "*Ya'at'eeh, shiyaazh,*" he said: *greetings, my son.*

Then he greeted Mary and Serena also.

Mary said, "Who is this man?" and I knew the past was slipping through the sieve of her memory like river-water.

"It's Detective Stone, Mrs. E.," Serena said, "the man who took us over to the other side, last year; he stuffed us to the gills with peyote tea and shot us full of arrows and carried us across the river of no return. Don't you remember?"

"Not . . . really," said Mary.

"It is well," said Milt. "In time you will remember everything, my twice-born friends."

Serena said, "Detective Stone . . . are we going to have to . . . die again?"

"No," said Milt. "Fact is, as the saying goes, there ain't no way to cross the same river twice. When you died and crossed over to the other side and had your grand old adventure, maybe you thought that, after the climax of the story, you got right back on that horse, turned toward the sunset, and rode right back into the real world; you thought that, didn't you? But it ain't true."

I thought about what he said and it implied. A year ago we had come to the top of a mesa, come to a kiva, a sacred Navajo place, entered a magic circle. We'd drunk the peyote tea and our souls had left our bodies and then we'd crossed over into a crazy country where all the rules were askew. We'd brought back Mary and Josh and Theo, and then we'd driven south, down to the laetrile clinic; wasn't that all true? It had taken me two days of sorting out my memories to get this version of the truth straight in my mind, and now Milt was telling us that we'd *never* gone back to reality . . . that we were still inside the topsy-turvy dreamtime . . . that somewhere, on the other side of the river, on a different mesa in a different Arizona in a different Armorica in a different universe, our vacant bodies still waited for our souls to repossess them . . . might wait, in fact, for all eternity . . . He was telling us there is no going home, no matter that homecoming is as basic a human desire as love, as hunger.

"I can see," said Milt, "that the truth hits you hard, Phil Etchison."

"Yeah," I said.

"Oh, you old fools," Jesus said, "enough of this bullshit philosophizing. Can't you see we don't got no more time?" He jumped up and began to pound on his drum, his wings flapping. All at once there came a fluting from the air itself. "While we are sitting around here, señores, worlds are falling into ruin."

He laughed; he capered; sand, catching the sunrise, flurried about his head like pixie dust.

I could feel Mary's hand stiffening as I held it. Was she becoming stone again? But still she stepped forward, as did I, as did Serena, toward Milt, toward the magic circle.

"I'll tell you a secret," said Milt. "Not only have you never returned home; you've never even left the circle that you entered the other world through; you've been within that magic circle all this time, and everything you've seen since that moment has been part of your vision."

"You mean . . . it wasn't real?" Serena said. "I haven't graduated high school yet, I never went to college, never worked for Congressman Karpovsky's campaign, never was seduced by him on the mahogany desktop on the Hill?"

"Maybe not," Milt said. "But don't make the mistake of thinking that the vision ain't reality. Because reality itself is an illusion. It's the fabric that we weave around ourselves to shield our senses from the overloading sensations of a billion, billion, billion, billion, *billion* realities . . . ."

And he was chanting that word *billion, billion, BILLION* like Carl Sagan on speed. Chanting it in time to the beating drum. At each repetition of the word it was as if another layer of fabric had been stripped away from our eyes and now we were seeing far, far out over the world, over other worlds, we were seeing canyons and jungles and pyramids and cityscapes and dinosaurs and starships and aliens and exploding suns and temples and we were surfing on blood corpuscles through the veins of God and still came the chanting *billion billion billion* and below us the lake of fire was rising, rising, rising until the plateau we were standing on was an island buffeted by flames, and the Cadillac was bucking and buckling and sprouting metallic pseudopods and Rube Goldberg appendages like a robotic version of *Alien*.

"What the fuck's going on?" I shouted, but Milt seized hold of my arm and pushed me into the stone circle. We landed in a heap, me, Mary, Jesus, and Serena. The mother of all tornadoes was billowing around the circle and bobbing up and down in the wind was all the débris of my life, pages from poetry books, the house in Virginia, my dead dog Rover from my childhood, my grandfather's coffin, my baby sister's training bra, the wicked witch of the West . . .

"Be still, Phil!" Milt cried. "Your life's not passing before your eyes. Get a grip on yourself."

"What can you see, Mr. E.?" Serena said, her face rapt and beatific. "I'm seeing the day in the drive-in when me and Josh were pretending to have sex in the back seat to convince Theo we were cool, and I'm seeing the time we found you in your study by yourself and you were drunk and you started rambling about the sixties and then you read to us from the *Kama Sutra*—"

"Never happened," I said, laughing.

"Sure it did!" she said, giggling as if stoned.

Mary sat crosslegged at the center of the circle. She was becoming very still, Buddhalike almost. She was withdrawing into stone. Slowly her features were becoming set, immovable. It didn't dismay me as much this time. I had seen her turn to stone before. And I understood now that the other things that had happened to her—her madness, her cancer—they too had been ways of turning to stone, metaphors for the One Mother's sorrow over the wounded earth.

The storm raged around us; the storm raged within us; but in the circle there was tranquillity. Presently, the Cadillac metamorphosed into the towers of a great city, and our circle into the central hall of a great temple, where Mary was enthroned beneath a crystal dome; and around us, past rows and rows of Ionian columns, we could see the plateau-cum-island, flying now, over a lurid and desolate terrain.

"We're back in Caliosper," I said softly. The wind screamed; above the screaming came the keening of choristers as they praised the name of the One Mother, my wife and my creator.

"You've never left," said Milt, and I saw that the boy Jesus was now perched on his shoulder, and their wings were beating the incense-rich air in alternating strokes, causing the smoke to curlicue around their heads.

It was all very well for him to say that we had never left, and that our lives between then and now had been a dream within a dream; but that was like saying all places are one places, all gods one god, all heroes one hero, all myths one myth. I half expected Joseph Campbell to form out of the swirling incense and command me to follow my bliss. But I had lived those dreams within dreams, and I was no cookie-cutter hero; I was no hero at all; in this story things happened *to* me; I did not make them happen. Once again I felt helpless, adrift.

"Don't feel that way," said Corvus—his speech was now interspersed with fragments of birdsong—"It takes all kinds of messiahs to save the world—there's the fighting messiah, the seeing messiah, and the passive messiah."

I knew that *passive* comes from a Latin word meaning *to suffer*, so I was prepared to believe him.

Serena said, "Where's Ash?"

A flurry of activity: storm troopers in Trekkie outfits, bearing phallic weapons, were running around, their boots clanging on the temple's marble floors. There was a burst of turbulence—it was difficult to ignore the fact that the entire flying citadel was zooming through space at the speed of thought—and the choral antiphonies were cut off in mid-phrase.

"Ash," said Corvus-Stone.

And there he was. Of all the Darklings, the most serene and the most ambiguous, Ash (and not, as I had feared, Joseph Campbell) was forming out of the cloud of incense. He shimmered; cold blue radiance haloed his preternaturally beautiful features; he was clad in a cloak of light.

"Ash," said Serena, and the two of them embraced. I stood agape, always the last to understand anything.

Caliosper sped up, banked right, causing Corvus to trip and land on his ass while Jesus fluttered up toward the dome.

"As you can see," Ash said, "things are tough right now. We're in a hurry. We have to try to stop a full-scale war."

"Between Thorn and Katastrofa," I said.

"Yes."

"But . . . wasn't there some kind of game they played, a surrogate for actual warfare . . . wasn't that one of the things they were using Josh and Theo for?" I said.

"They can't play *shenjesh* anymore," Serena said, grasping the situation more rapidly than I. "It's because reality is breaking down, isn't it? And—"

"There is only one Truthsayer in the whole cosmos," Ash said. "The other one was rendered . . . inoperative."

"Josh—is he—" said Serena.

"He's not entirely dead—and not entirely alive."

"And Theo—?" I said.

"In Katastrofa's clutches. She seems to have some kind of hold over him. Perhaps she's told him she'll bring Joshua back to life if he cooperates with her. Even though that's not really in her power at all."

"We have to get him back," I said.

"Not yet," said Ash. "there's something we have to do first—if we can."

"Where are we going now?" I said, despairing of ever seeing my sons again.

"To the battlefield."

At that moment, the city of Caliosper began to rise, steeply and swiftly, and presently we were leaving behind

even the semblance of a recognizable terrain; we burst
through the cloudbanks and thrust into the ionosphere of
this unknown planet; we soared into regions where nebulae
wheeled and planets whirled and light went wild; we saw
colors too strange for psychedelia; and even when I closed
my eyes the lights still danced, because we did not see our
way with our eyes alone.

   God, I wanted a drink. I wanted a drink so badly I could
have killed someone for one.

book three

the elven forest

"Mein Vater, mein Vater, und hörest du nicht,
Was Erlenkönig mir leise verspricht!?"
"Sei ruhig, bleibe ruhig, mein Kind;
In dürren Blättern säuselt der Wind."

"My father, my father, oh can't you hear
What the Elf-King's whispers are promising me?"
"Be still, child, be still; it's only the wind
As it wuthers through withered dead leaves."

—Goethe, *Erlkönig*

TALES OF THE WANDERING HERO
by PHILIP ETCHISON

3: IN THE FOREST OF ADOLESCENT ANGST

And as I trekked the sylvan labyrinth,
I came upon a sage, who said: "My son:
The hero's burden is a two-edged sword.
I speak not of the object of the quest,
Not of the grail, but of the journeying.
The slaying of fierce dragons is one aspect;
The other, the seduction of fair maidens.
Do not confuse the two, until the moment
They demand to be confused."

　　　　　　　　　　　"What do you mean?"
I said. "How can a woman be a serpent?
Is good then evil? What, if so, is truth?"

I shared my loaf with him, because I saw
That he had trod the path that I now trod,
And paid for all his wisdom with an eye.

"There is in the dark forest of the soul
A certain leakage of identities.
You have come far; seven leagues you have traversed
With but a kiss, a condom, and a loaf;
But now you must embrace the two-tongued truth,
Twin-breasted Madonna: dragon, mother;
Lover, constrictor; beauty, beast; betrayer
And redeemer. So unsheathe your sword,
Risk all; trust all; win all; or pay the price."

chapter thirteen

A New Kind of Dreaming

Theo Etchison

I hear the growling of a jaguar.

Punting along the River I pass under the bridge of sighs. The River's all thick and oozy almost like it's made of styling gel or something, just inching its way along, slow and sticky and the sun beating down as I lie in the snake-shaped boat against the rock-hard stern and the sun's driving the sweat out of my pores and the sweat's pouring down my face making my whole body slick and sticky like the water of the River and I'm all naked and clutching the stiff wood and the sweat licks the firm stern and my pliant body and the sweat dissolves me and I'm melting in the sun into the viscous flow into the River that reeks like one of Mom's old maxi pads like the time the dog came into my room and she'd rooted the pad out of the trash and was wearing it on her snout and she leaped into my arms and . . . like when we're real little and me and Josh are in the tub together smashing our GI Joes into each other and like wrestling and the soapy water's all slipping and sliding and slithering and I'm all jeeze Josh your weewee got all big and he laughs and empties the Johnson's Baby

Shampoo over my head and I saw the commercial that says it doesn't hurt your eyes but I start bawling anyway just to attract Mom's attention but she doesn't come and I'm screaming at the top of my lungs and once I heard Mom scream that way and she was all don't don't don't *and I thought he was going to kill her and I was in their bed because I'd just had a nightmare and I thought I was still in the nightmare so I shut my eyes real tight and prayed for it to end but the screaming had a tinge of laughter in it and I didn't understand so I counted sheep but the sheep were bleeding the wool was all soggy and sticky and I was like five years old maybe and the shampoo running down my face and running and running and all of a sudden the dragon has reared up out of the water and she grins at me and her teeth catch the sunlight and I glimpse the forest where she's plucking an apple from the nearest branch and I say* no no no *and the current's deeper now and the water's gathering and swirling eddying as we pass the bridge of sighs and oh God the water's streaming now and the mist is rising and the stern of the ship's all moving, bending, pulsating, and I can feel something stirring between my legs and I'm scared and I want to wake up I want to wake up wake up wake up—*

I open my eyes.

Slowly. One—two—three—be awake.

I'm lying in my bed. It's Virginia. An Arnold Schwarzenegger poster is peeling from the back of the door. I've pissed myself. No it's not piss. No. Daylight is shining in through the slatted window. I get out of bed and peel off the BVDs and toss them in the hamper and hope that no one will notice.

The room: piles of dirty clothing, a baseball bat, a photograph of Mom and Dad in a cracked frame, my Dream Book open next to my computer.

I pull on my blue terrycloth robe with the big gash on my ass where I snagged it against a nail one time. I walk over to the door, and when I open it I realize that this isn't Virginia.

"Josh?" I whisper past the half-cracked bedroom door. I want to ask him about the dream. It's a sex thing, I know it. It's big and it's frightening. I don't want to be ready for it yet. I want to be a kid. I want to sit in the tree fort of my childhood and watch the world and never have to climb down. Because there's a dragon coiled around the trunk and I can't come down without dealing with the dragon. Up here I can see across the universe and that's all I need. Down there I'll see the universe too, but only a piece at a time.

This isn't my bedroom. It's another of those illusions I can manufacture around myself when the world becomes too wild to understand. It's here because it's familiar and because I don't want to face what's beyond the bedroom.

The stick with its bells that bewitch wild animals is lying on my desk along with my jester's cap. I think it's pretty fucking stupid to be trapped in this alien world and have to dress up like a sausage vendor at the Renaissance fair, so I look in the closet for something I wouldn't be embarrassed to wear. There's a shitload of clothes here—everything from a medieval executioner's uniform to the threads of a "Star Trek" science officer—but it takes me a while to find something normal-looking, and when I do find it it's exactly the clothes I was wearing the very first time I got sucked into this alien universe—the too-long Redskins T-shirt and the shorts—and I've kind of outgrown the shorts, but I find another pair of pants that kind of fit—they're like sci-fi pants, with silver-lamé trimming, which could either look cool or faggy, depending on where you go—and then like I put on the shirt which is still thank God too long and it covers up the pockets where most of the obnoxious glitter is. And now I'm ready for the next adventure and I go back toward the bedroom door, but I don't forget to take the tinklestick and I remember to stuff the marble in my back pocket, because it's the one thing that can tell me where I'm going in this crazy world.

Where the landing should be there's that corridor with the cages full of adolescent boys, the boys that stare listlessly and shake their heads from side to side and rattle their thin arms against the bars, that squat in their own shit, too dazed to move . . . and I know that at the end of that hall there's the room where my brother lies in his glass coffin like a sleeping prince whose princess will never come . . . only the wicked witch.

I close my bedroom door and start up the dungeon stairwell. I'm thinking about the dream I had about the river and the dragon and the sunlight and the sweat. I know that no matter what my quest is, there's going to be a dragon guarding the threshold. I've just got to grit my teeth and deal with it one way or another, or there won't be any quest.

I hear the growling of a jaguar.

It's morning in a galaxy far far away and I've awoken from a wet dream.

I've been climbing the dungeon steps for a totally long time. In fact it's been kind of like an M. C. Escher stair climbing; I've been going up and down at the same time, depending on how you look at it, and I've never gotten anywhere. It's only when I stop looking at anything and reach out toward my destination with my mind that I start moving, and then it's like when I was falling down the dark well, only in reverse. I'm chuting upward through dark tunnels with only an image of Katastrofa to guide me, a dragon that coils and coils and coils around the tree of the forbidden apples.

Katastrofa's lair: well you kind of expect to see this big old cavern strewn with human skeletons and piles of putrid fewmets, and that's exactly what there is, except bigger and twistier than any dragon's cave in Tolkien. There are stalactites and stalagmites and trails of sulphurous smoke. The cave is an illusion, of course, just like the witch's oven in the gingerbread house; but the River, which trickles along a channel gouged from the limestone floor, is real enough; I know, as soon as I hear it rippling, that it sings the true music of making.

Katastrofa's been waiting for me. She's sitting on a throne made entirely of human bones. Her hands are resting on two skulls, her head against a mandala-pattern of spoked thighbones. Although she is in human form her eyes remain the eyes of a serpent.

"Took you long enough," she says. "You spent forever in the sleep of changing."

"It didn't work," I tell her. "I haven't changed." But now, looking at her, I can feel the dream I had last night come over me in all its brutal power. I *am* changing. In a way that I don't dare name.

"Oh, Theo," she says, and the underlying meaning is *Don't you lie to me; a Truthsayer can't lie anyway*.

And it's true that I don't sound convincing. I can't convince myself and I can't convince anyone else. I'm scared of Katastrofa in a way I never was with Thorn.

"Are you ready to go into battle now?" she says. "That jester's costume my father made you wear seems somehow inappropriate."

"I don't have any other clothes anymore. Maybe like after the battle, we'll go down to the mall and pick up something a little less dorky," I say. I'm getting tired of being a part of all these other people's role-playing games.

I remember those battles from the last adventure—when I was fighting on the other side. There was like this totally big arena and in it there was a holographic starfield that represented the whole of the known universe. Thorn made me leap into the starfield and then it was as though I were a character in a real-live Nintendo action game, slugging whole solar systems out of my way, juggling galaxies, that kind of thing. I had really gotten into it until I came to know that everything I did was real . . . that worlds went under . . . that planets fell into the void . . . and the fates of races were determined by the outcome of the game. And then again, I found out that my arch-rival in the mega-videogame of death was Joshua, my flesh and blood. Fucking Jesus It sucked.

Seeming to read my mind, Katastrofa says, "There won't

be any video games anymore. You want to know why?"

She doesn't pause to hear my reply but goes on, "Come on. We're burning daylight here." She gets up out of the *Texas Chainsaw Massacre* chair and comes toward me, and she's already beginning to transform.

By transform I mean the whole Animatronic® shebang. Appendages shooting out, tendrils of flesh whipping at the air, claws sprouting, scales flowering out of the smooth skin, her hair receding into her scalp and her forehead becoming all bony and green and her torso flattening and lengthening and she's all the time screeching like Godzilla. Her jaw begins to broaden and lengthen and her teeth start to multiply and sharpen. She's getting so big that I'm scared she's going to bust right out of the cave.

"Get up on my back," she hollers (her voice now has a metallic ring to it, and the echo of the cavern makes it huge) "and start navigating!"

I have to obey her and so I start to climb up. It's difficult to get a foothold because she keeps growing and she's not all firm like she'd be if she was a dragon ride at an amusement park—she's living flesh, quivering all over, burning my hands when I reach out to steady myself. And being this close to her, to be honest, it keeps bringing back the dream and it keeps making me pop a boner which I keep trying to will away.

I'm perched on the dragon's neck now. I ask her where we're going, and she says only, "You are the Truthsayer . . . take me to where my brother is."

But before I can even start to put out a mental feeler for the vampire Darkling she's already moving toward the water. And then she plunges in. It's cold. I hold on. I think she's trying to drown me, but she thrusts one finny wing across her back so that it partly shields me from the water. It's not watertight and so I squat, shivering, against one scaly wall. The water splashes me and has a bitter, mineral water taste.

I sit huddled and wet and holding the marble in my hand. I'm gazing into it now, trying to feel my way along its convoluted pathways. But it's not as easy as it used to be. I feel resistance. I'm not as sure of where I'm going. I'm certain now that my powers are slipping away from me. Somehow I'm no longer pure. It has something to do with the dream. It has something to do with the dragon's embrace.

The dragon moves with the speed of thought, my thought that is. Somehow we're linking and somehow she senses the direction I'm thinking of as I try to focus in on the idea of Thorn. But for now all I see is a swirling, hungry dark, like he's drawn a cloak of obscurity around himself. It's taking all my Truthsaying powers even to see this much. It's black and red and coagulating. It's a whirlwind of blood.

I concentrate harder. But now I'm losing that fix and I can't conjure up an image of Thorn at all. My mind is on war. I know that there's a tremendous battle looming ahead where hundreds of worlds are going to be tossed aside so that Thorn and Katastrofa can rule over what's left, assuming there *is* something left. I know that Strang, in his madness, has closed off many of the gateways between the worlds, and that any path to anywhere must probably be forged anew by me. I think of the last time we battled . . . in that arena of mega-virtual-reality that turned out not be to be so virtual after all . . . and I think maybe if I go in that direction I can reorient myself to the River's uncountable streams. I close my eyes and try to recall that place. I see myself dancing among points of light . . . I feel myself stretched thin, thinner than vacuum, straddling whole galaxies, filling the emptiness between the stars, between subatomic particles, threading the superspace between the black holes and the white. It all comes back to me now. Me and Josh as pixels on the infinite CRT of the cosmos, me and Josh slugging it out, surrogates for the Darklings' sibling rivalry, working through our own rivalry too; I remember thinking *Jesus Josh I fucking hate you sometimes. All the time.*

No sooner thought than done. We're breaching the dank dark depths of the River, thrusting up through icy water,

and then the wing-fin-canopy is whisked aside and I see
the foam recede on either side of me. I'm standing on
the dragon's back and the water's drying off and I can't
see the River at all now because what's happened is that I
visualized the place and called to it in the secret language
of Truthsaying and the River thrust out a temporary tendril
toward it and now the River's gushing back where it came
from through the vortex between the spaces and leaving us
ashore, except that ashore is the middle of the grand hallway
of the gaming arena on the island where a thousand streams
meet, where the last great game was fought. I know that,
stretching around the building I'm standing in, there's a
Blade Runner–looking city crisscrossed with rivulets from
the River. I know that it's a teeming city on neutral turf in
a quadrant of the many worlds as yet unclaimed by any of
the scions of Darkling. But as I look around the arena I
realize that it's a lot different now. There used to be like
tiers upon tiers which made the place look like the inside
of a mega-Colosseum. Now the tiers are still there but the
teeming crowds that filled them are gone. There used to
be aliens of every description: octopoids and plantoids and
sauroids and jellyoids and tornadooids and cloudoids, aliens
in bottles and aliens in chariots and aliens in tuxedos, and
now, yeah, there's a couple of aliens here and there, but at
least one of them seems to be a corpse.

But one thing is just the same as I remembered it: the
starstream-hologram that erupts out of the floor of the arena
and goes all the way up as far as the eye can see. It's like
a stretched-out representation of what's in my marble. It's
virtual reality and it's hyperreality at the same time because
from inside of it you can reach out and change reality. When
I look at that thing it brings back the memories and I start to
get scared. I don't want to go in there. I know that I've been
inside before and that I've innocently flung star systems
into each other and hurled planets around like baseballs.
That was before I realized I was killing people—millions
of people—by people I'm saying aliens as well as human
beings, creatures with souls.

Katastrofa is rapidly changing back into a woman. Now she's wearing like this glittery Saran Wrap, and her hair is all flaming and changing color, but her eyes are still the same; I'd know her eyes even if she transformed herself into something totally different, like a toad or a tablecloth.

Her eyes are the one thing about her that never change.

"Why did you bring us to this place?" she says. "You know that the wars are no longer fought here." She kicks a used candy wrapper out of the way and I realize that the level we're standing on bears a real resemblance to a beat-up movie theater in the wrong part of town.

"I can't control my Truthsaying. If I could, it wouldn't *be* Truthsaying. There's gotta be a reason why we're here."

"True," Katastrofa murmurs, closing her gold-lidded eyes in thought.

The reason becomes obvious when Thorn emerges from the stellar vortex. He's wearing a cloak of darkness and his dark hair frames his face so that mostly you see the slate-colored eyes glaring out of a tempest of shadows.

"Give the child back to me," Thorn says.

His herald, the sometime Mr. Cornelius Huang, restaurateur and conch-blowing virtuoso, steps out from behind his master. He's scary and cadaverous as ever. He lifts the conch to his lips and blasts us—it's a deep, bloodcurdling noise that makes even the dead alien twitch and causes Katastrofa to look away from her brother's eyes.

Oh, and the Cerberus-thing—the three-headed dog. I can't forget that. Thorn's pet appears behind Cornelius Huang, yapping at all our heels at once.

"I want the child back," says Thorn. "It's not fair, I captured him first, you got the other one, you screwed him up, you've only yourself to blame for killing him in the process."

I shudder. Am I wrong to think that Joshua will come back to me? Am I too late? I think of Joshua and think great big clouds of blackness but then, through the blackness, I can hear a voice, a child's cry. I know that there is still a way for me to bring him back; I know that Thorn is wrong.

It gives me courage although I still don't understand how I'm going to achieve this impossible, the resurrection of the dead, even though, according to some people, I am God.

"Bullshit," Katastrofa says, though she still doesn't meet her brother's gaze. "You captured him, brother, but you lost him. He was up for grabs."

"Bullshit," I say myself, "none of you owns me. I'm me, I own myself, and it looks like I'm the only game in town. And I don't want to help either of you because neither of you has any business ruling the universe when you can't even make peace inside your own family." Just like my family, I'm thinking, and I know I shouldn't speak so boldly because there's Joshua, in his glass coffin, still waiting for me to call him out from the bowels of Katastrofa's dungeon.

I hear the growling of a jaguar.

But I can't stop to think about what that means.

Katastrofa's looking up again, and I can see the hate flashing in her eyes. Her hate is not for me but for her brother. "I wish we had never shared a womb," she says. "I wish I'd killed you before you were born. I wish that you'd choked on your own phlegm while you were clawing your way out of our mother's womb . . ." I hadn't known before that they were twins.

"What would you have preferred, little sister?" Thorn says. "That we'd stayed inside forever? That we'd grown old and died and putrefied within those fleshy walls?"

"There was no need to kill our mother," says Katastrofa.

"I didn't kill her," says Thorn. "Her death was an inevitable consequence of our birth—you know that as well as I do."

"You could have thought of something. You're so ingenous, so full of new ideas. At least you never tired of telling me so. And everyone else who will listen . . . and in *your* kingdom, they'd better listen or they get eaten up."

These dudes must have a different gestation period than humans or something. I don't understand what they're trying to say and I don't like the pictures it conjures up in my mind—images of siblings, wet and bloody, scratching and biting each other inside their mother's body—screaming their anger at each other—that woman's womb must have felt like a living drumkit.

"Just hand over the goddamned child," says Thorn.

"I told you I'm not gonna get tossed around like a ball," I say, but they continue to ignore me.

"No!" Katastrofa screams. And then the two of them are rushing each other, fangs droolings, talons outstretched, she's a blur of scales and claws and he's a whirlwind of leather and fur, they're wrestling each other and it's like a fight in a comic book, a swirling cloud of dust where you can see now and then an arm or a wing or a tail or a spurt of blood.

"Kids, kids," I say. I feel like a hall monitor in a kindergarten. The cloud disperses and the siblings separate, panting, glaring. This isn't how you expect godlike superbeings to behave. Somehow you think they should be above this pettiness. But they're worse than me and Josh. Or are they? I know that even when I hated my brother more than anything in the world, even when I wished him dead, even when he was beating me up for no reason except for maybe some sexual frustration thing I couldn't even understand . . . even then I knew there was love there, somewhere, frail and hidden. Did Thorn and Katastrofa have love, a love that had gone so sour that they couldn't live in peace unless one of them killed the other? Did Cain love Abel? I bet you anything he did.

Wasn't that part of why he killed him?

So here I am playing referee between two of the most powerful beings in the universe, who could crush *me* much more easily than they could ever destroy each other, and somehow I find the nerve to like lecture them on sibling rivalry. Fucking Jesus I'm stupid. But I mean well.

"Okay," I say, "isn't there some way this can be settled without taking the whole universe along with you? Isn't there some kind of way you can withdraw, retrench, stay within the boundaries Strang drew for you?"

"No," they both say at the same time.

And they laugh, knowing how much alike they are, and then they both stifle their laughter at the same time and I see that yes, there is a love there, buried so deep that not even I, the Truthsayer, may be able to coax it out.

"Isn't there like, some game or something you can play? Winner take all, you know, poker or . . . or chess?" I persist, thinking maybe it can all come out kind of like *The Seventh Seal*, you know, where the knight plays chess with Death. But that, of course, was only a movie, and it wasn't even in English.

"Strip poker," Thorn says, and there's another grim laugh, a meeting of gazes; maybe he's talking about something in their youth, some secret, I think, something shameful; but then, I think, they were in the womb together, and conscious, so they must have shared many secrets. The love between them is a dark and twisty thing, and it's laced with guilt and disillusion. Oh God, their love is a scary thing and it's more comfortable to think about their hate, pure and black and elemental.

"War," Katastrofa says, "let's play war."

"Yes," says Thorn, the final *sssss* turning serpentine. And then they leap into the vortex, the two of them, deadly and playful at the same time.

"Stop!" I shout. "You don't know where you're going . . . you don't know the way in there because you're not Truthsayers. You'll smash the universe to smithereens before you're through!"

And well, there comes Thorn's voice, mocking me: "Who gives a shit, little one? And this was your idea."

Okay. So I'm standing there alone now, not working for either side. I can just stand there and let them blow each other apart, and that's just what they'll do. My dad once told me that, in the Roman arena, the lowest class of gladiators were called *andabatae*. They had no skills. They were common criminals. They fought in helmets that completely covered their faces. They were blind. They wielded clunky, rusty swords and thrust unseeing at each other.

They fought with savage desperation because they'd had everything taken away from them, even their faces, their identities . . . They smashed, they bashed, they swung, they didn't care about anything anymore . . . and they always died. An *andabata* didn't live to fight another day. If they happened to survive, they'd be thrown to the lions or whatever the next act was.

Well like, that's how Thorn and Katastrofa are, the way they hate each other; inside the vortex that is both an analog of reality and reality itself, collapsed a jillionfold into itself so that a Truthsayer like me can grasp it in my hands, they will be blind, and their blindness will make them strike out at everything; and this is how the world is going to end; not with a bang, not with a whimper, but with the petty bickering of a dysfunctional family.

I know I have to stop this.

I'm a Truthsayer and a Truthsayer only sees, he doesn't do. But I'm also growing older and I'm starting to feel the changes in my body and I'm starting to feel something awesomely grownup, like, some kind of responsibility or something. I know that as I try to stop this war I'm going to age a little more, and aging is going to slowly close the inner eye through which I see the cosmos. Oh, fucking Jesus I am scared. I stare for a long moment at the starstream. Around me, the arena seems to be decaying second by second, crumbling into the primal dust we all spring from. The darkness beckons. I sense the two of them inside, and I too leap into the eternal cold of the space between the spaces.

chapter fourteen

Pizza in Caliosper

Serena Somers

Ash had come. I was feeling better already even though I wasn't totally sure where we were going.

He and Corvus led me and Mr. E. out of the nave of Mrs. E.'s cathedral and into a little chapel that also served as the main control room for the flying city. There were painted icons of all four Etchisons on one wall, and a reproduction of the weeping Madonna we'd seen in Baja California in the place of honor behind an altar railing with a dense fog of incense dancing all around it. Facing the wall of Etchisons was like this huge portrait of the Darkling family, but it must have been during better days. It was by like one of those Renaissance artists, Michelangelo or someone, and it showed King Strang sitting on a throne with a scepter in his hand that even in the painting seemed to catch the light and sparkle, and his long white hair flowed all the way to the ground, I guess that's why it reminded me of Michelangelo, that sculpture of Moses with the wild hair, so thick and convoluted that some people say there's like this self-portrait of the artist hidden somewhere in the hair, you know . . . And Thorn and Katastrofa were standing on either side of him, Thorn with his Dracula cape billowing and Katastrofa, a dragon's head on the body of a nude woman with her arms outstretched and with leathern wings that stretched way up and ended in vestigial claws; yeah, they were monstrous in a way, but they were also all smiling and gazing fondly at their father, and King Strang was beaming as if they'd just presented him with straight-A report cards; and in front was Ash, no more than a boy (or girl because you couldn't really tell, neither then nor now) clothed in a few wisps of mist, the only one not smiling but looking off into some far horizon, an otherworldly kid who somehow didn't partake of the family dynamics. The picture was framed in gold, you know one of those frames that's full of all curls and swirls and squiggles.

Next to this picture was a painting in a lead frame, and it showed the same family many years later. I knew the story that the painting depicted—it was the old *King Lear* story as it applied to the Darkling family. It showed an enraged King Strang, ugly now, his face devoured by the pestilence that consumed his kingdom. It showed Ash, grown now, weeping as an angel with a flaming sword banished him from the gates of paradise. It showed Thorn and Katastrofa, still standing on either flank of their deranged father, their expressions transformed into masks of consummate fury.

In both these paintings there was also Mary Etchison, a wraithlike creature hovering above King Strang in a halo of pale blue fire.

Mrs. E. was the link between our world and the world beyond; a dying woman from Virginia in ours, the Great Mother, lady of perpetual tears, in the world of the Darklings.

The oddest thing about this whole chapel was that there was a dinette table set up in the middle of it, one of those IKEA specials, with four chairs; in the center of the people there was a statue of a jaguar rampant, clawing the air; and a man in a blue and orange uniform was bringing in a stack of pizzas.

As he set them down, he intoned, like a priest, "Pepperoni, avocado, sausage and shrimp. Pineapple, gingko nuts, relish and crabmeat. Sweet-and-sour duck, sour cream, ginger root, and eye of newt. Double cheese plain." Then he put out a pitcher of beer and a pitcher of soda and slid away so smoothly he might as well have been on roller skates.

"Eat now," said Ash, "while you can. Soon there's going to be too much excitement for us to be able to order out for pizza."

We ate in silence for a while. There wasn't much I could say really, and Mr. E. was even more overwhelmed than I was. When conversation finally began, it was all trivial because no one could bring themselves to talk about the really important stuff.

For instance, Mr. E. began by like, commenting on the pizza. "The only time I ever saw pizza like this," he said, "was in California . . . at a New Age pizza place in Topanga Canyon."

"Oh, yeah," I said. "I hear they have things like, Peking duck pizza, pizza with Thai barbecued chicken . . . I read about it in Congressman Karpovsky's campaign guide book where it talks about American culinary habits, you know, so you won't make a fool of yourself on the campaign trail by thinking that chicken fried steak has chicken in it . . . and . . . oh, you know, insulting some poor redneck who's just donated his life's savings to—oh, I don't mean that perjoratively, I'm just quoting what the congressman said the night we all got stoned and—oh shit, putting my foot in my mouth again—that was supposed to be a secret."

I was dying of embarrassment, even though, with the fate of the universe at stake, I should have known better. To be honest, it was like the time that had elapsed between the last adventure and this one—leaving high school and going to college and taking the time off college to work on the campaign and growing up and all that shit—it was like it had all been shrunk down to nothing. I felt like a know-nothing teenager with a tenth-grade vocabulary and a Valley girl sensibility. Especially when Mr. E. went on, "Yes," without even seeming to have heard me, "one of the most unusual things about these transdimensional crossings is the food, isn't it? I mean, that's what Alice said in *Through the Looking-Glass*; she seemed to be constantly obsessed by fish; but then you could see a lot of Freudian undertones in that if you wanted to, I mean, what with the phallic symbolism of fish, the fishy odor of the female pudenda, and that's not even getting into the Christian symbolism; I mean, it's a semiotician's paradise and—"

Then Mr. E. began to weep. Not just a teardrop or two. He was bawling his guts out.

I said, "Mr. E. . . . I know how you feel."

"No you don't," he said. "Nobody knows how I feel. I've been a blind man in a sighted family . . . Theo and Josh and Mary all have these gifts . . . and even you do, Serena . . . seeing hidden truths or whatever . . . I don't even have a way to describe these fucking talents of yours . . . God, you don't understand how helpless I feel . . . You don't understand a goddamn thing."

And maybe he was right about that. Mr. E. was like Joseph after the angel told him his wife was going to have God's kid, and there were going to be like all these cosmic events, and the world getting redeemed, and the great big eternal war between good and evil, and millions called to judgment, and on and on and all he was going to get to do was kind of be the stepfather of the universe—and it was all going to happen whether he wanted it to or not.

Bummer.

Mr. E. wept like there was no tomorrow.

Phil Etchison

It was at that moment, chattering inanely about semiotics while trying to eat pizza in the side chapel of my wife's cathedral in a flying citadel that was streaking through the starstream at warp factor seven, that I realized that I had completely lost control of my life. There was, indeed, a cosmic drama unfolding all around me—not just *a* cosmic drama—indeed, *every* cosmic drama from every mythos of every human and nonhuman culture was hurtling toward simultaneous climax. I had always dreamt of being a part of history ... of being more than myself ... but I felt less myself than I had ever been. It isn't easy for me to cry despite the fact that I am immersed in the literature of crying men. Losing my sons, my wife, had not caused me to break down this way, but now I realized I had also lost myself. Even as I wept I was thinking about how selfish my weeping was, how it was improper for me to weep for such solipsistic motives. And the most appalling thing of all was how solicitous they all seemed to be. Serena kept assuring me she understood—I knew well that she did not— and Ash put his arm around my shoulder, but I would not be comforted.

But presently the tears ceased flowing and the pizza was all devoured, and the flying city continued to smash through the transdimensional void. Most of the others had all gone up to some viewing pavilion to see the dancing lights of hyperspace. Only Corvus, the astrogator, remained, and he seemed preoccupied, humming into a handheld device that was to a "Star Trek" tricorder as a computer is to an abacus.

I sat at the table, looking at the icons of Darkling mythology and of my own family. I stared for a long time at the jaguar centerpiece of the dinner table, stared so hard that I seemed to catch a flickering in its eyes. It too could have been alive, like the many statues of the One Mother in this land, I supposed; it would not have surprised me. At length, Corvus-Stone said to me, looking up from his instrument: "You find it fascinating, the *nagual*."

"Is that what it is?" I said, remembering the word only vaguely from some decades-past college lecture on pre-Columbian art. "A *nagual* is some kind of were-jaguar, isn't it? Let me guess ... the Aztecs ... No, the Toltecs."

"Such a learned man," Corvus said, laughing. "You forget who you are, you forget the names of your children, but the intellect stays with you forever."

"But that's about the limit of my knowledge on the matter."

"And about the limit of everyone else's too," said Corvus.

The bird-man was, it must be said, wavering a little in his shape; he seemed to be turning back into the familiar Detective Stone; perhaps, with only me in the room, there was no need for him to assume the guise of the city's navigator. But then again—because I could not help thinking up new theories, even in the direst of circumstances—it also occurred to me that, if reality was somehow the sum, the intersection, of the perceptual universes of each person present, then it stood to reason that the Milt Stone I saw when I was alone in the room would have to be different from the Stone I saw when many others, who saw him as an entirely alien being, were present; perhaps the bird-man image was merely the average of all our disparate perceptions. If I actually saw Milt Stone through Ash's eyes—if Ash had eyes, granted— would it drive me mad, or even burn me to a cinder, like an unmasked view of God? Though I was consumed with grief and helplessness, a part of me viewed all this with a certain detachment, analyzing data, toying with structures of ideas; my second-rate academician's intellect may have been a house of cards, but it was the only roof over my head.

So preoccupied was I by Corvus' seeming metamorphosis and remetamorphosis that I missed half of his explication of the *nagual* myth, and zoned back in only toward the end of it: "You see, the *nagual* is in a perpetual state of *becoming*; that's the main thing. And it comes from the Toltecs, the oldest civilization in the New World, and that makes it also the oldest symbol of *my* people; my people back home. You know." His voice, too, wavered between the crisp enunciation of Corvus and the down-home twang of Milt Stone. "The elder Darkling, you know, the man who started it all, he likes to think of himself as a *nagual* sometimes, you see, because he came up from nothing, on account of his pact with the River's dark side."

"The River has a dark side?" I said, although my nodding acquaintance with Carl Jung suggested that a mythological Manichaeanism was almost mandatory.

"At the source of the River," said Stone, "which, as you know, has flowed up from the first world, the perfect country, Elysium, Paradise, all the way up to this imperfect world of the bereaved, the disconsolate . . . well, you got good and evil both, you see. Potential. Embryonic. It takes both good and evil to create *hozhoni* . . ."

"Which is some kind of untranslatable Navajo concept of balance . . ."

"Nah, Phil, sometimes we Injuns overestimate our uniqueness. It's natural in an oppressed people. A good translation might be *chi*. Or is it *wa*? But you're right, those are both brownskinned words, and some say that our people is just the Asian people, displaced across a narrow little strait. Or was it the lost tribes of Israel?"

"You archetypes can never get each other straight," I said, laughing despite my desolation.

Milt said (a hint of wings rustling about his form) "That's a wiser observation than you might think, Phil. There's got to be a fatal flaw to set the story rolling, you see. Without Adam and the apple there's no Bible because they never get out of paradise, never burst out of the womb, never fulfill their destiny as humans. Without Prometheus stealing fire from the gods, without Pandora blowing the lid off that primal box of tricks, there ain't no human story—there's just a bunch of gods, living high on the hog in Olympus, screwing around now and then, hurling a few thunderbolts, but they're boring thunderbolts because the drama hasn't begun, the Big hasn't Banged, you know what I mean? And that's how it was with Strang. He struck the bargain, took the scepter that steals men's souls, forged structure out of chaos—yes! what would these myriad worlds have been without the ordering of Strang's will? The universe became a poem. To be a work of art it had to have light and darkness, and it had to encompass both love and death. And like every work of art, like every enforced reversal of entropy in creation, it had to contain the seeds of its own destruction. To be or not to be are not the only choices. There's also to have been. To be about to be. What's more, there's being and there's *being*. When you choose *being*— you also choose death."

"You're saying that to be *is* not to be." I had to admire the casuistry. Milt's words had started off by being playful, but gradually he had become more impassioned. It was more than just a word game to him. It was a central truth of his view of the world, and it had the pellucid obscurity of a Zen *koan*. I had to admit that I loved to watch him juggle those ideas; back at the college I'd often participated in Dean Reinman's heated cocktail party arguments, but they *were* only games; sitting around deconstructing the universe over a martini was a way of thinking out loud about how to word the next grant proposal; no, this was real. And it was like the proverbial Chinese food, too; I had been lost in the elegance of Milt's logic, but no sooner had he finished speaking than I was hungry again.

"But you look bored, Phil," said Milt, slowly turning back into Corvus, "and we really should join the others."

He started to leave; I turned to kiss the weeping statue of my wife.

Serena Somers

The observatory of the palace of Caliosper was an amazing place because once you went into it it was like you became physically adrift. It was kind of a ballroom-sized bubble and what was around us wasn't the city of Caliosper with its avenues and gardens and shopping malls and minarets and all those things that cities of fantasy and science fiction always have to have, but a deep black nothing. In the nothing, stars zoomed past—stars and galaxies and planets with rings and ghostly nebulae—but each image was fringed with rainbow, as though the whole observatory were a great big prism and the starstream was a cosmic hologram.

Ash and I had abandoned Mr. E. to his sorrow because, I guess, we felt we were intruding on him. We didn't talk much; Ash kept pacing up and down . . . It looked as though he was walking on air, because the floor of the observatory was a kind of Möbius-stripping forcefield that allowed you access to any part of the spherical image, and the direction your feet pointed always felt like *down* which was totally confusing when I saw Ash striding upside-down toward me and then reverse himself without me catching the moment he had reversed . . . well, as I say, he paced. And the mist he was draped in paced along with him, tendriling around his private parts the way wisps of cloud drape nudes in a Renaissance painting.

"I wish Corvus would hurry up," Ash said. "He's probably started expounding philosophy to your friend . . . the more mystical he gets, the more diffusely he navigates . . . I've known him to steer us into seventeen realities at the same time . . . it's the peyote that does it to him."

"Do all pilots take hallucinogenic drugs?" I asked him, trying to get him to stand still for a moment.

"Of course they do! They can't all be Truthsayers. And even after they drink the water of transformation they can only perceive a faint echo of what bombards a Truthsayer's mind, day in, day out; they're all mad, you see."

"But I don't understand . . . where are we? Are we still in the River?"

"Yes, yes; it's not exactly an underwater view of things but, in the River, you see what the River wants you to see. Usually I don't spend much time in the observatory, frankly, or I have some homely image projected so I don't feel as disoriented."

I stopped paying attention because, suddenly, as the stars went whizzing by, I thought I saw Theo.

Theo was a tiny spot in the distance and then, almost instantaneously, he zoomed in for a closeup. He was bigger than the whole city. He held a marble in his hand and the marble was brighter than a sun. Theo's outline was wavery, insubstantial, and before I could cry out his name he had dwindled back to a blip among the clouds of stardust.

"Oh, Jesus, that was—" I saw that Mr. E. had come in. He was staring at that blip, watching it go out, *poof*, like a candle flame.

"Yeah, Mr. E.," I said. "It was Theo."

"In that case," said Corvus, who was now stalking around and flapping like a mutant ostrich, "we are going in the right direction; you can stop panicking, Prince Ash."

Then came the dragon, zooming like Theo out of nowhere, thrashing and coiling and clawing, wrapping herself around our sphere of darkness like a serpent about to devour an egg; fire flashed in her eyes, and her claws glittered like diamonds, and then, like Theo, all of a sudden she was gone too. And before I could say anything there was a bat-thing leering down at us with slate-colored eyes and beating black leathern wings against the barrier of force, and it too disappeared.

"Is that Katastrofa and Thorn?"

"They are nearby," Ash said. "We tracked them all down. They're about to have some kind of battle . . . with luck we may be able to slip in, spirit Theo away, leave the two of them at each other's throats. . . ."

"Time to breach the River now," said Corvus. "This is where they're going to fight."

"What kind of a place is it?" said Mr. E.

"Well," Corvus said, "it depends on your private mythology, Phil; some will see it as a *Star Wars* kind of deal; some will see it taking place in a dark forest, the forest of the soul, whatever . . . I think some might even see it as a forest of their own traumatic relationships with friends and family . . . when we all look upon it at once, we'll all see the same thing, more or less, but if we get separated, well then it's private epiphany time. . . ."

I felt like this distant thrumming, as though the whole city were changing gears. Those prismlike fringes around the stellar objects were starting to dim and I realized we were slowly making our way to the surface of the River and were soon going to reappear in what passed for reality around here. Before we blinked back out, there was a final image . . . it was almost transparent against the starfield . . . it was the image of an immense child, you know, like the star-child in *2001—A Space Odyssey* I guess, but this neonate was in the middle of a transformation scene right out of *American Werewolf in London*, but it was turning into a kind of a cat—a jaguar maybe—with glittering emerald eyes.

"It's Father," Ash said. He didn't seem as self-confident as he had a moment ago. "Is he getting involved too?"

"Well, Prince Ash," Corvus said, "it is true, there is something you must confront, somehow, before this story can resolve itself."

I remembered how Ash had been the one child of Strang who had dared tell the truth to his father; how he had been banished from his inheritance for his pains; how his father, in his pride, hadn't spoken a word to him since then, leaving his only loyal child to wander the universes master of a single citadel with no fixed resting place. Jesus, how must it feel? I thought, and I wanted so much to make him feel better, but I didn't know how. Because for all of my life it had been Ash's job to make me feel good about myself, and not the other way round. He was the visiting angel and I was the frustrated fat girl who dreamed of love and ate away her sorrows. How do you console a fallen angel? The thing that he's lost, you know, it's so big that you can't even imagine what it must have been like to have it, let alone losing it. It made me and my own sufferings seem pretty damn small . . . a little teenage crush, a little sexual harassment, a couple of bouts of eating disorders . . . How could I know what it was like to lose the world when I didn't know what it was like to *have* the world? All right, so I went up to Ash and tried to hold his hand; he squeezed mine, and I think he even felt a little comforted maybe; then again, maybe he was just making me feel good by making me feel useful.

"Jesus, Ash, you drive me crazy sometimes," I said.

"What am I to do? Corvus is right. I've got to come to terms with Dad somehow."

Ash's Dad—whom once, in an ecstasy of teenage rage, I had called a *mega-dweeb*—wasn't worth coming to terms with as far as I was concerned. "Let him go," I said.

"I can't," he said. "But thanks for the therapy anyway."

"No problemo," I said.

Then the war began.

chapter fifteen

A Page of Memory

Theo Etchison

The war's about to begin. I'm flung through the star-spangled night. I stretch. I grow. I thin myself out so that the galaxies pass through me unaffected. I'm hearing the echo of a billion Big Bangs. I look down and I see Thorn and Katastrofa locked in each other's arms in a way that looks like hatred and looks like lust. They're intertwined and whirling through the darkness. I grow, I flatten, I wrap myself around the universe, I become the sentient fabric of space.

That's the easy part.

The hard part is to follow them through the vortex, to see where they will emerge, always knowing that they're still inside the arena inside the city on the junction of the River's tributaries which is maybe all inside someone's mind, maybe my own. I follow them. I'm smaller than an electron and whizzing down the tangled light-threads inside the marble in my hand. I'm a white blood corpuscle racing through the pumping bloodstream of the universe on a speed chase after a pair of crazed bacteria. They don't know where they're going, they don't understand the twists and turns of reality, don't understand that they can't lose me because I *am* the way. I start to relax. I ride the River like I've seen surfers do, giving in to the arc and swell of the wave and making it part of me. There they are—just up ahead—wrestling the water and each other. Destruction follows them. I feel the stilling of millions of heartbeats as they travel the stream, lashing out, cutting off worlds forever, severing the arteries that connect one cosmos with another. They love pain, they're wallowing in it, others' and their own. I hate them. But I'm trying to push that hate aside, trying to focus.

Yeah.

I can feel others too now. Dad and Serena are lost in this maze too, somehow. In the labyrinth of star systems there's a faint whiff of pepperoni pizza and that's so out-of-place, so homely in the midst of all this alienness that it would bring tears to my eyes if I had eyes, if I had tears, if I wasn't Theo Truthsayer.

Okay. They're about to breach. I follow them and we—

—break out of the River into a lush green place bursting out of a creek that winds its way round back of my grandparents' place in Spotsylvania County. It's a page of memory. I can see Joshua there only he's much younger. I can see me too and I can't believe I'm so fucking tiny I guess I'm maybe six years old and it's summer I mean hot fierce fiery steamy summer with a storm maybe about to break.

I see me and Josh (I guess he's like ten years old) and we're playing tag or something, just running in and out of the trees by the side of the stream. And Josh is screaming, "I'm gonna kill you, I'm gonna fucking kill you," I don't know why, I think it's because I decapitated one of his action figures. So I'm running and he's pursuing and hollering and he's a lot faster than I am so that's how I know his anger is just pretend because otherwise he'd have beaten me up by now. But still I'm running as hard as I can because I'm just in to running with the hard sun against my skin brushing laughing and—

Joshua catches me and wrestles me to the ground. He punches me a couple of times but it's kind of just pretend hard and he punches the ground more than me; the sun is behind him and he's dark, a raven, a black dragon.

"Lemme go."

"I'll teach you to cut off Commander Salamander's head, I'll cut off your dick, then you'll never be able to grow up."

"I hate you! I hate you! I hate you!" I'm laughing and laughing because this is how you tell someone you love him when he's bigger and more powerful and too young to appreciate the word love.

"I hate you too," Josh says, laughing too. He's beautiful and I'm awkward and I like to linger in the shadows and I can already read Shakespeare, kind of, one word at a time, the shiny syllables dancing before my eyes one at a time, so many colors, so many senses; Joshua can't. He prefers the Teenage Mutant Ninja Turtles. We both think each other's stupid.

But too I'm thinking with the sun in my eyes and the swell of my brother's sweat and fabric softener in my nostrils, I don't want to grow up anyways, why would I grow up, why would I want to be like *them?*

And that's when we hear them.

Joshua looks up. I'm still pinned down but I don't struggle to get out of his careless hold because I'm kind of enjoying the sensation of being pushed around by my big brother.

I don't want to grow up.

This is what we hear coming out of our grandparents' house:

"*I hate you!*"

"*I hate you!*"

But not the same way that me and Josh were saying it. It sounds like they mean it. So well we creep up to the house. We know the grandparents have gone to the store or something or my parents wouldn't fight like this; they came down here to escape fighting after all.

We go inside, leaving our Chucks by the door so we won't make the floorboards creak. We slip upstairs. They're getting louder.

—*You just refuse to understand. It's a fucking midlife crisis or something and I'm scared and all you want to talk about is yourself.*

—*I'm not talking about myself, Phil. I'm talking about the future.*

—*My poetry's not the future, I know that.*

"He's pissed off because of the review in the *Post*," Josh whispers to me as we crouch beside the door. The grandfather clock in the hall goes *bong* and startles us. I gasp. I'm sure they've heard me, but they're too involved in the screaming match to be aware of us, two small slivers of shadow, two right ears plastered to the hinges of a scarred oak door.

—*I don't know why Dirda allowed that to get printed. He's a friend of yours, isn't he?*

—*That's not fair. You know it's not personal, Mary.*

—*You and your friends.*

—*If you're going to tell me I've ruined your life again, if you're going to tell me I stole away your future on the day we met, I—*

—*I hate you.*

"What are they arguing about, Josh?"

"Nothing. Fucking nothing."

Josh gets up and stalks away, confident now that they won't hear. He stomps across the landing toward our bedroom which is also the TV room although there's no cable out here so we never watch it and we didn't bring down the Nintendo either so all we ever do there is sleep or sulk.

But I stay in the shadow of the doorway because I think sooner or later I'll hear something that'll explain why it is they're so angry at each other. I mean, the things they're saying, I really don't understand them. Not that well.

Then I hear this:

—*You don't even spend time with the kids.*

—You don't either. You're lost in your own narcissistic navel-gazing.

—It's a low blow to use the kids.

—I'm the only one who ever—

—If you're going to throw some kind of martyr thing at me, I don't buy it. I didn't choose to be what I am.

—Martyr? So you're the fucking martyr around here? I'd like to drive in the nails myself.

What does it mean? I don't even know who's saying what, they've become so shrill that it all seems to be the same voice, yes, it's just one long loud monotonous roar of rage and I'm sitting in my corner, shriveled into that little piece of shadow, wanting to cry but not wanting my sniveling to distract them and make them turn on me. Is part of what they're saying that they don't love us anymore?

Suddenly I notice the muddy handprints on the doorjamb next to the hinges and I wonder if I'm going to get into trouble, because now they'll know there was a small person squatting here, spying on them, like the time they thought me and Josh overheard them having sex and they became all weird, withdrawn, not speaking to us for days, though it was before we knew what sex was, and I still don't really know even though we read through the big book about it together, the four of us.

And then I hear, I don't know, it sounds like a struggle. Are they going to hit each other? Oh Jesus they've never hit each other before. I can't stand it, I get up and shove the door all the way open and I'm standing there I catch them in this like embrace of hate or maybe love. And maybe Dad's about to punch Mom out or something, I don't know, because they're in a jumble together on the bed and it's stifling hot in the room, there's no airconditioning out here, the window fan is blasting my face with burning air.

And so I scream, "Don't you hit her!" at my father, and they turn toward me.

They see me standing there. And suddenly the tableau of violence breaks up and they're both all smiling at me.

"Theo," Dad says, and he gives a half-hearted laugh, "I didn't see you there."

"Hello, honey," Mom says.

I don't buy it. There's no joy in their smile, and there's even a hint of fear. Did *I* cause them to fear this much? I see it all because of who I am, though I don't know it yet, of course: I'm a Truthsayer and I can see the churning beneath the surface, and I run to my mother and she takes me in her arms and I can smell beneath the sun-ripened smell of sweat a trace of old perfume; I snuggle my head between the breasts that sag, braless, under the cotton print summer dress and I don't look at Dad at all and I say, "Mommy, Mommy, maybe you should have married me instead of Daddy."

Daddy rails against the window: "My life's going to pieces and here I am witnessing some cliché-ridden Oedipal drama in my own household—what a disaster." He leaves me alone with my mother. I hear his footsteps down the stairs and hear him yelling, "Josh! Josh!" which means maybe Josh will get someone to play baseball with for a while, even if it's only that Dad needs to be distracted.

"Stop, stop, stop, stop, stop," I scream at the top of my lungs, not at anyone in particular just because I desperately want the storm to die down.

"I meant it when I said I should have married you," I tell my mother.

She puts her arms around me. She enfolds me in herself. It is now, for the first time, that I feel an alien thing inside her, a sickness; it's years before anyone will diagnose it; what I feel is a kind of ooze that is seeping through her body, dissolving atom by atom into her bloodstream; when I look up at her face I know she doesn't know, because she's only half-smiling and staring far off, through the window, toward the sun that's glaring through the windless treetops.

She says, softly, "My little knight, my little husband," and kisses me gently on the lips, and I'm filled with confusion and I'm all warm from the suffocating sunlight and the rushing of my blood. I twist away and my mother laughs again. "What would I do without you, Theodore Theophilus Theomancer?" None of which are my names because I'm just plain Theo, rhymes with Geo.

"I love you too," I say. Mostly because she wants to hear it. And because she's crying now. And because I feel the illness working its way from cell to cell inside her, and I know that I'm going to be the only one who will know for a long time, for years to come maybe.

Then I step back and it's me watching myself, me out of the macrocosm gazing down at little me and little Mother. All of sudden the room is shaking. The windows shatter. My mother's skin peels away and I see Katastrofa inside her flesh. The dragon's claws rend flesh and Katastrofa's standing there now, with the tatters of my mother's body dissolving into the hot moist air from the fan.

"How dare you pretend to be my flesh and blood?" I shriek, and I'm rushing at Katastrofa, pounding at her with my puny fists, but her scales are hard as iron and my fists start bleeding and with each blow I feel a more than mortal pain not in my hands but in my heart.

"Oh," Katastrofa says, "but I'm not pretending, am I?"

I whip around to see Dad. He's being sawed in half, from top to bottom, by an invisible buzzsaw, and his two pieces fall to the left and right and inside him is Katastrofa's vampire brother.

"Tsk, tsk, little brother," he says to me, "you almost fucked your mother!" Then there's a sound like a beat-up record player being started up and then I hear this old Tom Lehrer record with a song about Oedipus Rex which Dad used to play sometimes and it's stuck on the words *I'd rather marry a duckbilled platypus* and it plays those words again and again and again.

Outside, a shadow crosses the sun. Darkness falls. There's a sudden chill. It's an eclipse. My arms are prickling with tension.

I see my six-year-old self trapped between the warring demons. The baby-me sees Dad in the doorway and Mom on the bed, crying, and only dimly senses that they've become monsters. I can't remember if the eclipse is real or if it's just a projection of my childish terror.

My older self is in a forest clearing. We've never left the forest of the night, the place I plunged to when they came for me in Mexico. The two are circling me and I'm in the middle. They're almost dancing, you know like in those old westerns, me tied to the stake and them capering and pounding on their drums and yelling for my blood. And yes, the whole of my grandparents' house is a house of cards that collapses like the cards at the end of *Alice in Wonderland,* cards flying every which way blowing in my eyes slicing my cheeks with papercuts.

No, I scream *no, get me out of here—*

And I seem to hear a voice: a grating, steam-driven voice: it says: *The trap is of your own devising; to escape you must think the unthinkable; you must undo the unchangeable; you must unkill the forever-dead.*

And I'm thinking, you can never get a straight answer around here, every riddle is answered with another riddle. The dragon and the vampire circle me, breathing fire, spitting blood. I hear the Indian drumbeats too, *POM-pom-pom-pom POM-pom-pom-pom,* and the war whoops and the weird, winding melody of their song . . .

And at the same time that we're in my house, trapped in my memories, and we're in the forest of confusion, at the same time as all this we're also out there in the middle of a space battle of some kind—Thorn and Katastrofa and their storm troopers and their planet-long spaceships and their star-destroying weapons. The ships are whooshing and roaring the vacuum of space and that's how I know they're ships of fantasy and not science fiction and that even this macrocosmic spectacle is still taking place within the jungle of the soul.

How can I break free? By solving a few simple riddles? *What has four legs in the morning, two at noon, and three in the evening,* cornball enigmas like the one Oedipus guessed, and so he slew the monster but ended up marrying his mother and plucking out his eyes?

*   *   *

And then all of a sudden I'm back inside my memory
again . . . inside it and outside it at the same time . . . I'm on
Mom's lap again . . . I don't know that there are monsters
hiding inside her flesh. She's kissing me and then she sets
me down on their bed. I lick the curious taste from off my
lips, part cinnamon, part alcohol, part blood.

I have a dream in which I see my parents making love,
only I don't know that's what it is. My parents have become
like dolphins, and they're riding each other and swimming
through the moonlight ocean at top speed. I wake up and I
expect to see that my Mom has come in to look in on me
because that's what always happens when I cry out in my
sleep. But instead it's only Josh. We're even younger now,
I'm maybe four years old, I sleep with two stuffed animals,
a Tasmanian Devil and a Pink Panther.

Josh says, "Shut up, you little fuck."

I say, "What's a little fuck?"

He says, "You stick your weenie into a girl and she has
a baby, that's what a little fuck is."

And the dream comes back to me in all its liquidescent
terror.

"Josh, I had a dream, I'm scared."

"Okay, little brother," Josh says. He sits beside my bed
and he strokes my brow, softly, left to right, until I begin
to drift again.

Josh is melting away. I grip his hand. His hand comes off
and it's just wood, like Pinocchio's. Josh is grinning away
and his teeth are chattering and he's like a ventriloquist's
dummy or a marionette and—

I'm looking up and I see dark creatures in the ceiling
pulling my brother's strings and making him flop this way
and that way and—

Joshua's a corpse, the skin's peeling from his face, a
maggot works its way out through the edge of his lower lip,
Joshua's eyes are dead white like my mother's opals and—

It's years later and I'm sitting in Mommy's lap and
feeling the sickness trickling through her veins and she

kisses me and my lips tingle and her kiss confuses me like the kiss of a serpent and—

Mom's head goes round and round like *The Exorcist* head with a *ratchet-ratchet-ratchet* sound and she's all, "Fuck me! Fuck me!" in a deep bass devil voice, and—

Space! The starfleets smash into one another like coalescing nebulae.

Someone help me.

The open sea! The ships are ramming each other and catapulting fire onto each other's decks and the galley slaves' oars are snapping like matchsticks and—

Help me.

Joshua lies in his coffin. My mother has turned to stone. There's only one person left in my family and that's my father, the only one who doesn't have a single spark of Truthsaying in him. Where are you, Dad? Oh, Dad, we're all inside one another, lost in the labyrinth of our own nightmares.

chapter sixteen

An Encounter with the Deity

Phil Etchison

I asked Ash how he was going to go about confronting his father at this stage, when all hell was in the middle of breaking loose. "I don't know," he told me. He looked lost.

Everything started happening at once. I mean, first all these people in silver-lamé spacesuits came charging into the observatory and they were speaking into communicators, juggling orbs of colored light, scribbling notes in the air, and doing all kinds of other incomprehensible things. They bustled about and they elbowed us this way and that; not that they were being rude, really, they were just so preoccupied that Serena and I didn't seem to be there for them. Ash was preoccupied too; he was soon having a heated conversation with two of the paramilitary-looking people, and Corvus took me aside and said, "Perhaps we should go on a secret mission of our own."

"What do you mean?" I said.

"Ash is never going to seek out King Strang on his own. They're very much alike, you know; their pride is a fearsome thing. But it must happen or we'll all be left hanging. You understand, don't you?"

"But what can I do?"

"Phil," he said, putting his arm over my shoulder, "you've been feeling useless, haven't you?"

"Yes," I said softly. It was hard not to, when every person one ran into was either a marvel of super-science, gifted with psychic powers, or king of the universe. "But I guess I'll get over it. I've been known to feel useless before. You wouldn't have anything to drink, would you? Alcoholic, I mean."

"Oh, Phil, Phil, Phil," Corvus said, and he led me by the arm away from where Ash's minions clustered. Serena was busy with Ash; she didn't seem to have as hard a time fitting in as I did; perhaps it was because she had known Ash since childhood. "Come," said Corvus, and as we moved away from the others, it seemed to be that his demeanor was once more becoming far less avian, far closer to my friend Milt Stone's. "We're going to go on a little quest of our own."

"To find Theo?" I asked him.

"Well, I was thinking that we could go and throw ourselves before Strang, and perhaps effect a reconciliation between him and Ash."

"What good would I be at that? Anyway, I seem to recall that in the equivalent scene in *King Lear,* the ruse didn't work; Lear wouldn't see Cordelia, wouldn't speak to her, until it was all too late."

"But if we somehow manage to pick up a Truthsayer on the way. . . ."

I saw. But how could we find Theo when the number of haystacks was infinite? And yet I couldn't just sit around being useless. That would merely be to repeat the isorhythms of my life.

"Come on, Philip Etchison," said Corvus, "There's a poet inside you even if you don't know it yet. Everyone *thinks* you're a poet, man, you might as well become one sooner or later; if there's anything that could get you past your mid-life crisis, it's knowing yourself for the first time."

"Yes," I said, trying to sound fervent. "Yes."

Holding onto my elbow, Corvus folded one wing across his face and whispered a word. We blinked out and stepped into an alcove in the main hallway of the temple. There was a bronze door bas-reliefed into a frieze of mythological scenes; Corvus spread his wings wide, uttered another command, and we walked through the bronze, which felt like mist on my face, moist and metallic. I gasped. We had suddenly entered the kiva, the sacred Navajo place atop the mesa in Arizona—the place from which we had entered the transdimensional portal which had transported us to the hidden cosmos of beauty and bereavement—for there, on the ground, was the sand painting that showed our family—above our heads was the tarp that had made this place into a makeshift enclosure.

The strangest thing of all was that the kiva was full of people, of varying degrees of transparency, wearing the clothing of many eras and nations. I don't know how they all fit inside this place; perhaps it was because they were infinitesimally thin; the tent held a cast of thousands. There were even people I thought I recognized: Shakespeare, Michelangelo, that sort of thing; there was even a man with flowing white robes and nail holes in his hands, though I knew he could not be the historical Jesus because of his blond hair and blue eyes.

Seeing this man, in fact, disconcerted me a great deal, since I am above all a secular person. Especially when he turned to me, transfixed me with his sea-blue eyes, mumbled to me, words that stirred my heart and brought tears rushing to my eyes; words that I instantly forgot; for I cannot set them down here; I remember only their cadent echoing. I was somewhat relieved to see the Buddha there alongside him, hovering in mid-air in the lotus position, which was a feat I had seen attempted, but never achieved, by many would-be gurus of the New Age persuasion. When the Enlightened One also regaled me in high astounding terms, which I then also forgot, I realized that I had discovered the common ground between metaphysics and Chinese food; for in a moment I was hungry again, and the truth I hungered for was ever beyond my grasp.

Then came the strangest sight of all: I saw myself, motionless, pierced through the heart by an arrow, hanging in the air above the midpoint of the kiva. The other shadow-people flitted past me; sometimes I saw myself superimposed over images of Renaissance queens and nineteenth-century sophists; I could tell, though the eyes of the shadow-me were open, that I was quite, quite dead. There was an Aztec priest behind me, wearing a turquoise mask shaped like a human skull, in fantastical robe of quetzal feathers, brandishing an obsidian knife.

I said to Corvus-becoming-Milt-Stone, "We had to die to come here, didn't we? And we're *still* dead, because there really is no return from the other side . . ."

"It's true that we cannot step in the same River twice."

"Then why did you bring me here?" I said. "We've already crossed over into the dreamtime, haven't we?"

"But Theo has gone beyond where we've gone," Milt said. "He's in a dream within a dream. Haven't you ever had a dream in which you woke up, but you were actually still dreaming?"

"No," I said, "but I've seen it in horror movies. It's almost a fixture in those *Nightmare on Elm Street* pictures my kids always insist on renting."

"Well, we're going to have to go the other way, you see; we're going to practice lucid dreaming within lucid dreaming."

"More peyote?" I said.

"Well, yes, massive quantities," he said. "So much that it must be administered the Mayan way, direct absorption into that part of the body that has the densest concentration of capillaries . . ."

Suddenly—as Corvus—he flapped his wings and uttered a piercing squawk. The phantoms of past truthseekers dispersed in a flurry of smoke and feathers. We were alone in the kiva now save the shades of Milt, myself, my wife, and Serena Somers, who, suspended in the mist, drifted about the center of the circle like ghostly Saint Sebastians. I remembered having read something about. the ancient Mayan preoccupation with hallucinogenic enemas, and I frankly began to have cold feet about the whole thing. I had died before, after all, and all at once I remembered it perfectly—the cold fire penetrating, the eerie music, the whirlwind of childhood images, and the bitter taste on my lips. I didn't want to go through it again and this did not seem like a dignified entrée into the hereafter.

Corvus shed his wings. The wings wavered, shifted shape, and presently he held in his hands two lengthy objects— halfway in size between syringes and bicycle pumps—and he handed me one. "You have to shed your clothing," he said. "Quickly now. It's easier than you think. It has ritual meaning too—naked you came into this world, and naked you leave it—you see what I mean."

He began to sing, while at the same time undoing his costume with astonishing dexterity. It seemed, indeed, that it was not only his clothing but his very skin that he was unzipping. It fell to the sandpainting in a single piece, like a deflating balloon. Inside the skin of Corvus the avian navigator was Milt Stone the *nadlé*, the sacred man-woman shaman of the Navajo; and as he stood before me I could not tell where the woman ended and the man began. Before this I had only seen Milt Stone, genetically a man, dressed in a woman's clothes and aping to perfection the gestures, bearing, the very essence of a woman; the creature I saw now was not, biologically, of either gender at all. I took it then that I was seeing the Milt Stone within, the thing his soul had become at the time when a vision had told him he must follow the way of the *nadlé*. When he spoke to me (it was no doubt an inner prejudice of mine that continued to think of him as *he*) the voice was, like that of a countertenor in an English cathedral, curiously void of sexual identifying marks. "You like my inner self?" he said. "Yours isn't bad either. I rather like the purplish aura that emanates from you." I couldn't tell whether he was kidding me or not. I had removed my clothes and folded them, through force of habit, in a neat pile to one side of the sacred circle. I saw myself for the middle-aged, nondescript man I had become. This was strange because all my life, even at the times I was most depressed, most self-loathing, there had always been something of the gilded knight in my image of myself. Tarnished, perhaps, but never an everyman.

A cauldron appeared in the middle of the circle. Around it, the figures of my family, drawn in the sand, danced like cartoon images. Above our heads, my family's corpses hovered. In the cauldron a potion seethed; Milt Stone the man-woman filled his injecting device with the liquid and handed it to me. I stared at it dully while the corpses wheeled and the paintings capered.

"You're wavering," said Milt.

"Well, can you blame me?"

"I know; this is just too weird, isn't it? But you have to look at the mythic matrix, the historical perspective. The ancient Maya used to—"

"I know, I know." I had attended a lecture by my colleague Dr. Schön, an archaeologist, and I knew all about the mystery contraptions found in the burial sites of Mayan aristocrats, only recently revealed to be the wherewithal for the anal administration of psychedelics. It just seemed so damned undignified to me.

We exchanged devices. The thing was hot to the touch and again I was afraid, but I knew that I would overcome my fear one way or another, because the many paths of possibility in my life had narrowed down to two: to stay forever in this undead dream state, or, by this death-in-death, this dream within a dream, return to wakefulness.

Then, out of the empty air, there came the sound of drums. Each beat seemed to pound my very bones. Also there came a deep and raucous trumpeting, though I saw no trumpets; but I felt a searing wind spring up and the jaws of the hanging corpses gaping wide; it seemed that the trumpeting was the wind itself, resonating through the body cavities of my family. Then the arrows twisted free of the flesh, caught fire, and fell to the perimeter of the sand painting, which also caught fire, encircling us with flame. The wind howled louder now, and the wounds of my loved ones whistled, and I could hear, behind the shrilling, the harmonies of a celestial choir.

"Hurry up!" Milt shouted.

He bent over and applied the peyote; I did the same. It was ice cold as it shot into me. A numbness spread up my torso and down my legs. The corpses were whirling now, and the singing of the wind crescendoed into a bizarre amalgam of Beethoven's Ninth Symphony and "Ninety-nine Bottles of Beer on the Wall." I thought about my sons. I thought about my fractured family—about bickering in Spotsylvania County, weeping in Alexandria, recrimination in Arizona. What right did I have to demand that my wife and children be returned to me after I'd walled myself in behind my own narcissism? No one should have a self-styled poet for a husband and father. Oh, Josh, I thought, oh, Theo . . . I tried to see the same vision I had seen when last I tried to cross the River . . . the golden boy with one arm upraised, stepping into the glittering sea . . . no image came to me.

I felt myself falling. "Catch me, catch me," I whispered, but Milt made no move, and I continued to fall long past the point where I would have hit the sand, I fell and fell and fell until I seemed to be inside the painting itself . . .

"Catch!" It was Milt's voice, echoing like a cartoon villain's. I felt something in my hand. It looked like rope but it was so light that I could barely sense it. Milt was tying the other end of the rope around my corpse, which seemed to have come to life, to be lumbering in mid-air like a Frankenstein's monster. "We have to anchor you to yourself," he screamed, "or else you'll be lost in the labyrinth of nightmares forever!"

I caught the rope. I fastened it loosely about my waist. I couldn't feel it at all; it was a magical rope, I supposed. It was like the ball of yarn that Theseus used to thread the labyrinth. But perhaps I myself was the Minotaur.

I fell and fell and then I—

Died.

I knew I was dead. I had died before. Death is the way a wineglass feels when it's been drained to the dregs. It is nothing. I felt the nothing again when the last of the feeling-stealing fluid penetrated the last nerve-endings of my body. I could see nothing, hear nothing; I could not even see that I saw nothing. But death was no longer the unknown. It was like visiting a familiar place. I welcomed the end of sensation. I floated and did not know that I floated. I did not even know that I was I. I knew there was an I, that I could reach out somehow and grab it and be in touch once more with the continuum of my selfhood, but I felt no desire for it. I felt no loss. I felt no passion.

I do not know how long it was I remained in this condition, because there was no time, only the potentiality of time. And there was Love; that, at least, was how I perceived the infinitude into which I had fallen; and that Love, it seemed, possessed a kind of consciousness.

I said (without words): "What is this place?"

But I already knew what the answer would be: it was the primal nothing; it was the cosmos in the moment before the Big Bang; it was the uncreated universe; and the consciousness I sensed was none other than that Absolute Being whose existence I, as a good agnostic and an intellectual, had always questioned.

I was hanging on to the I by a thread, by less than a thread now. In a moment I find myself extinguished, melding into the ocean of infinite Love. I cried out, "Why did you make the universe at all? If this is the way things were before . . . this utter tranquillity . . . this all-embracing oneness . . . why shatter the stillness with a cosmos? Why life and death—and I don't just mean human beings, but worlds and suns and galaxies? I don't understand," I said, "I really don't."

I believe that God was on the verge of answering me. I really do. But the next voice that I heard was the voice of Milt Stone.

"Come out of there, Phil! Another second and it'll be too late!"

"How? What are you talking about?" Waves of Love washed over me. I was sinking . . . sinking . . . sinking . . . I knew that all I had to do was allow myself to slide all the way down into oblivion and the answer to all these questions would come to me, clear and incontrovertible.

"You're sliding to Nirvana, Phil . . . it's up to you . . . you can go out, like a candle . . . or you can climb back up and save your sons."

And in the sea of Love I heard a murmuring: *You have no sons; they are illusion; all is illusion. Let go your conscious self; let go, let go.*

And I knew there was a truth in what I heard; for in my journeying down the River between worlds, I had learned that all men are islands; that the hard fabric of reality is only the confluence of our private illusions; that those we meet, those we love most dearly, are in the profoundest sense strangers to us, fellow travelers on alien roads; that love and death, father and mother of the artist's inspiration, they too are illusions.

"I don't want to come back," I said.

Milt said (and his voice was fast fading), "You have to come back. It's not your time yet. You are still tied to the world of illusion."

"No, I'm not," I said.

Enter, enter, enter, sang the voices, *enter the oneness of the all.*

But as they sang I realized that the rope was still fastened around me. I struggled against it. I wanted to cut myself loose. I wanted to enter the oneness, but even as I felt myself being submerged beneath waves of joy I also felt a nagging discontent with the New Age labeling that seemed to have been affixed to these transcendental truths. I writhed, but the rope held firm. I had to go back. I felt in the darkness for the cord, gripped it with spectral appendages that were fast devolving into hands, gave the rope a sharp tug, felt myself being pulled up. I kicked and screamed.

I raged against the withdrawal of Love's embrace, but I knew even as I was lifted out of Nirvana that the regret I felt proved I was not yet ready for extinguishment.

As I slid back up I felt a gutwrenching pain . . . a sense of agonizing loss . . . the feeling akin to when I'm desperate for the solace of alcohol and I'm desperately trying to quit . . . something I've felt a lot these days . . . but this is even worse . . . I feel that I've been wrung, twisted, flattened by a steamroller, torn apart . . . but then, when I can't stand it anymore . . . I see a vision of my two sons . . . for the first time since entering the sacred circle.

They're little . . . I think they're about ten and six . . . It's the grandparents' place . . . They're running in the woods beside the stream . . . I think they're fighting. They're screaming. I hear Theo screaming I hate you I hate you *the way kids do when they don't mean it, because the opposite thing to say is so big and powerful and magic that they can't force it to their lips. I'm right beside Theo when I hear, coming from the house, another voice, and the same words . . .* I hate you *. . . and the voice is my own.*

"No, please," I scream, "I didn't say that!"

But I knew it was true.

I had no time to react because I found myself plummeting, bursting through soft sheet metal, landing abruptly in the passenger seat of a Cadillac that was being driven by Milt Stone, restored to maleness and police uniform, and driving at top speed through desert terrain. I looked up. The roof was knitting itself back together again. I shook the steel dust from my hair.

"Welcome back," Milt said. "You seem a little shook up."

"You pulled me out of . . . out of . . ."

"I know." I saw that the rope was still around my waist; it went up right through the roof of the Cadillac. "You're anchored for a while," he said. "You pulled yourself out, really; in the battle between desire and otherworldliness, your love for your sons won out."

It was clear that the victory of my personal love against the great all-encompassing greater love was an ambiguous thing. I had to accept that. I was happy to be encumbered by selfishness. I was a human being, not a boddhisattva.

I glanced at the steering wheel and saw the gearshift, which read PRNDLL, suggesting that we had returned to the real world. But a single glance at what lay ahead convinced me otherwise.

chapter seventeen

Into the Labyrinth of Nightmares

Phil Etchison

What loomed ahead—already one could glimpse bits and pieces of it behind the forest of saguaro and twisted rock that stretched out on either side of the desert highway—was the skyline of a city. The buildings were tall and whimsical and seemed to be thousands of stories high, but that was not the strangest thing about them: it was, rather, that they seemed not to have been built but to have been drawn; they were like a vast background painting for an animated sci-fi feature. Indeed, there were flying bridges that linked the upper stories of the skyscrapers; there were zeppelinlike vehicles threading their way between them; there were fleets of aircars, swarming the structures like fireflies; and there were garishly-colored searchlights that crisscrossed the sunset. Two sunsets actually, the little sun athwart the bloated one; I wondered whether this meant we had returned to Tucson once again. Incongruously, the word *Hollywood* was etched into a nearby sandstone cliff; a mountain across the way read *Disneyland*.

"Where the hell are we?" I asked Milt, who drove on, impassive; I wondered whether he saw the same sights as I did, or whether the world he traveled in was some primal, Native American landscape of cliff-dwellings and sand dunes.

"You tell me," Milt said. "It's your son's world we're going into; you must know more about it than I do."

I did not want to confess that I had come to the conclusion than I hardly knew my son. And my close encounter with the Godhead had rendered me even less confident of the permanence of the bond of love between us. After all, had I not entirely forgotten Theo's very existence for large chunks of my existence? I was afraid of what my son might say to me. I had had a fleeting glimpse of a crucial scene from his early childhood for the first time, seen it from his point of view, seen myself as he saw me; I had felt his disillusionment. I had to save my son, but I also had to redeem myself.

Just as Milt Stone was now dressed in the garb of a police officer, I too wore the "official" garments of my profession: a kind of tunic, with a gilded border in the Greek fashion; the obligatory harp rested between my knees, and now and then let out a nervous twang.

We journeyed on; the city seemed to grow no bigger; we weren't getting any closer. I said to Milt, "Why can't you drive faster?"

He said, "I'm going as fast as I can, man; something's blocking me."

"But the highway is clear."

"Only because you refuse to see the obstruction."

"What obstruction?"

"Things happen in stages around here, Phil. You eat your soup, you get to go on to the main course."

"No more riddles, Milt. I needn't remind you of this, but I don't come from a riddling culture; I'm not used to having questions answered with other questions."

"You're right," Milt said, but didn't answer my question. We continued to move down the highway at breakneck pace. The rocky shapes on either side of the road grew ever more baroque, until at length they seemed to be monstrous sandstone statues like the monumental Ramses IIs at the temple of Abu Simbel . . . until it seemed they were actually moving their hands, nodding their heads, uttering great cavernous groans. One seemed to proffer a papal benediction; another, like a stern schoolmarm, wagged a bony finger, showering us with dirt and pebbles.

Milt remained silent; perhaps he was allowing me time to figure out the enigma for myself. There was, I supposed, some kind of test I would have to pass before gaining admittance to the next segment of the ritual. Perhaps I would have to answer three questions. I hoped they were as simple as the riddle of the Sphinx. But I feared the test would be something far more serious; that I would be forced to face some dark part of myself. That was what the obstruction was, wasn't it?

No sooner did I think this thought than a ghostly form began to materialize in the middle of the road. It was, indeed, myself—not the paunchy, middle-aged self-image I had seen back in the kiva, but a younger self, wearing black, complete with Darth Vaderesque helmet and light saber—the kind of image of his father that a six-year-old boy might have, if he was full of rage and unable to express himself.

I looked at me; the great dark me glowered, growled, rattled his saber, which filled the air with neon fireworks. The rocky figures seemed to cower behind one another.

"Time for battle," Milt said. He pulled off onto the shoulder.

"What am I supposed to do, kill myself?" I said. I didn't see how the me-creature could be defeated; wasn't it a hundred times my size, and armed besides?

"You'll figure out something," he said, and he popped the locks; the passenger door swung automatically open, and he shoved me out—not forcibly, but firmly. With considerable trepidation I stepped out of the car and walked out into the middle of the highway.

The me-monster roared and shambled about, his every footfall cracking the asphalt and exposing the yellow brick beneath; in the setting sun's light he was dark and formidable; how could I defeat him without defeating myself? When I listened more carefully to his bellowings I realized they were slowed-down fragments of my own poetry.

Perhaps I should try the quixotic approach, I thought. And at once I found myself riding a fractious steed and galloping towards the monster with a flaccid lance in my arm. I looked and felt ridiculous. The monster wore the windmill's blades like the points of a tiara, and they whirled about his head, and he rumbled with laughter and stamped his feet and swung his arms about. The light saber cut a swath through some nearby cliffs, and rubble cascaded onto the road. I hurtled full tilt at the man-windmill, jabbed the lance at the empty air, fell forward on my face and hit the pavement.

The winged Corvus, appearing suddenly by my side as my second, wordlessly handed me a sword and vanished in a puff of smoke. I only understood the use of swords from epic movies and epic poems, so, trying to wave it, I was pulled to the ground by the weight of it. I tried a two-handed approach but only managed to approach a few feet closer before stumbling again. The most infuriating thing was that this me-monster hardly seemed to notice my existence; it continued to shamble and stomp and bellow my doggerel-like juvenilia to the world. I tasted blood. I felt bruised and misused all over.

I charged once more. "I know you're there!" I shouted. "I'll kill you! I'll kill you!" This time I actually managed to slam the sword hard into the top of a steelclad boot. There was no clang; the blade sliced cleanly through nothingness; the giant was an illusion. "Maybe you don't exist," I said. "Get out of my sight. I adjure you, begone!" I tried raising my arms in an exorcistlike pose, but it did no good. The giant grew until it filled my entire field of vision, and my ears vibrated from the flat cadences of his poetry.

"Look where you're going!" I screamed at it. "I mean, aren't you supposed to be my Id or something? The least you could do is—"

I thought of Prospero and Caliban:

> *This thing of darkness I*
> *Acknowledge mine.*

Maybe that was the problem; it was I who had failed to acknowledge the monster, not he who wasn't paying me any attention. But I *was* acknowledging it, wasn't I? I had a split lip from the pavement to prove it. I had acknowledged its existence: but had I acknowledged it *mine?*

That submoronic, fustian-burbling giant?

Was that thing really me?

I dropped my sword. It was clear I had to embrace the darkness, not banish it. I stripped away my pretentious robes of poesy. The giant had grown so huge that he enveloped me utterly. I entered the me-monster's mouth; I slid down the me-monster's gullet and into the utter blackness of his belly; and I also slid into the past, into forgotten memories.

The fifties. "Leave it to Beaver" country.

I'm alone in the house and waiting for the world to end.

The sixties. Riot time.

I'm alone in my dorm room and waiting for the world to end.

The seventies. I've received my one hundredth rejection letter from *Poetry* magazine. I'm alone in a garret in Piggy County, Maryland, eating a lot of fried foods and agonizing about the emptiness of my existence; and I see Mary from my window, standing at a street corner, waiting maybe for a bus; she clutches a pile of books to her bosom very much as a Madonna might clasp the redeemer of the world, and it's a hot steamy summer, waiting for the clouds to burst. It is for an entirely selfish reason that I lean against the windowsill praying for rain. And when rain comes it is almost enough to restore my faith in divine providence. It pours. It drenches. The power goes out across the street; the traffic signal at the corner goes dark; two cars hydroplane into each other. I don't even grab a coat; I just run out into the street, run toward this bedraggled Madonna whom I have already named Mary in my mind: and I cry out, "Mary, Mary, Mary . . ."

"How do you know my name?"

"The bus won't be here for another twenty minutes . . . do you need a place to wait it out?" Oh God, you know how it is when it rains, it pushes people together, people thinking there's another person I can maybe hide behind or something, fend off the rain . . . and in only a few moments it seems almost as though our lips are about to collide half by accident half by design . . . and . . . and . . .

Mary says, "Who the hell are you, some kind of serial killer?" Oh, she doesn't say *serial killer*; I don't know what she says; the phrase isn't fashionable yet; I've been editing my memories.

. . . and I say "No, of course not . . . I'm a poet."

She looks at me. Through the sheets and sheets of rain I see in her eyes that she believes me. She is the first person ever to do so.

Do we kiss?

I can't remember.

Abruptly it's the eighties and I'm about to slug her in the face. I suddenly come to because I hear the shriek of my child: "*Don't you hit her!*" and I'm in a jumble with Mary on the bed and we're in a brutal embrace, brutal because I can't tell if it's a prelude to sex or violence.

What have I been doing? Going on and on about my inner torment, wounding myself while pretending to heal myself? I am furious. I know I could have killed. Myself or someone else. I don't know. I don't know. Is this the darkness in me?

I turn to see Theo in the doorway. He's frail, muddy, wide-eyed. I smile at him; so does Mary; it's the natural reaction, to hide our warring from our children, to want to protect them. "Theo," I say, "I didn't see you there."

Theo doesn't buy my pretense.

I don't realize yet that it is because he is a Truthsayer; I just believe it to be the clear vision of childhood. (All children, I will come to understand, begin with a spark of Truthsaying in them.) Theo looks me in the eye and doesn't speak; but I understand his silence to be an accusation.

If you're going to tell me I've ruined your life again, if you're going to tell me I stole away your future that rainy day we met—

Can it be true that in these petty domestic squabbles we reenact the life and death of universes . . . that we play out with infinitesimal precision the mythic interractions of gods and heroes?

"Hello, honey," Mary says.

I remember the rain lashing us driving our lips together and—

Theo runs toward his mother, throws himself into her lap. She hugs him to her the way she hugged those library books to her breast. I saw the Madonna in the woman on that stormy day and now I'm seeing the same image again, and I ache because my wife's embrace is no longer for me. Jesus, I'm jealous of my own child! and then he says, ingenuously, yet bringing into the open my most angst-filled thoughts, "Mommy, Mommy, maybe you should have married me instead of Daddy."

That's when I really lose it. "My life's going to pieces and here I am witnessing some cliché-ridden Oedipal drama in my own household—what a disaster." And I stomp away, away from the window, away from my son and my wife. I can hear the me-monster's thunderous footfall in my own. It *is* me after all, this shambling abomination.

I start down the stairs. I don't want to look into the eyes of my child. My other son will be more accommodating, I know. I'll call him and we'll play a game of baseball, maybe even break a couple of windows.

For some reason the stairs seem to be going on a long time. I'm descending . . . descending . . . sweating, too, because it's a muggy Virginia summer . . . or worse . . . the heat is getting worse . . . and the stairs are no longer the familiar stairs but an endless spiraling stairwell, dank and mildewed. I don't know when this transformation happened, but I am descending into the bowels of . . . I don't know, the underworld, perhaps . . . I will know if I have to cross a river and if there is a cowled old man to row it and a three-headed dog yapping at his heels and . . .

I see the River. The stairway leads precipitously downward like the narrow steps that hugged the cliffside in the town with the laetrile clinic. I see the ferryman. There is no sky, only a lowering gray canopy of mist. Sooner than I want to be, I'm getting on the boat. There is no one on board except the hooded figure and the dog. The ferryman reaches out a skeletal hand, expecting, doubtless, the traditional one-obol payment for the passage to the land of death; all I have on me is an American Express card, and it does not surprise me that the underworld is now computerized; a credit slip drops from the ferryman's sleeve, I sign it, we move noiselessly across the brackish water; in the far distance I see the same fantastical city that I have seen up there, past the highway, where presumably Milt Stone is still pulled over, waiting for me to overcome myself.

"How long till we get there?" I ask. And I'm shaking. I've relived a shameful scene from my past, and I don't see any means of expiation.

The ghastly ferryman bursts out laughing. It's the laughter of a child. His hood falls away and I see that it's Theo. "Oh, Dad," he says, "are you that anxious to be dead?"

"No," I admit.

"Let's take her for a spin, then," he says. The ferry seems to become motorized all of a sudden, and it takes off at top speed. The waters are dark except, here and there, for patches of sulphurous flame. I'm almost suffocating in the pungent air. Theo keeps giggling, and it unnerves me. "Oedipal drama indeed, Dad; you're just so fucking melodramatic sometimes."

"Are you still mad at me about that?"

"Well, you would have hit her, you know. Probably me, too. But that hardly makes our household into a seething cauldron of domestic violence. Maybe we do live in Virginia, but that doesn't automatically turn our family into a Southern novel." He laughs again. In spite of myself, I laugh a little too. "There now," he says. "It could be a lot worse, couldn't it?"

"Am I forgiven?" I ask him.

He doesn't answer.

"Come on, you *have* to forgive me!"

The boat is suddenly becalmed. Theo turns to me; he's no longer robed in black; he's just a child again; a XXL T-shirt drapes his knees. "Stop it, Daddy, stop it," he says. "Life really *doesn't* imitate art. Well, maybe, like, dude, only in other works of art."

It seems to me that we are all haunted people; but the ghosts that haunt us are often of our own creation. I know how this parallel universe business works; somewhere there's a world where I, in a frenzy of self-absorption and self-loathing, turned on my wife and children, beat them, even killed them. And even though these things did not happen for me, there still exists an echo of these events, and sometimes I bear the full brunt of their shame and guilt. Perhaps we are not islands after all.

"Congratulations, Dad," Theo says, "you're beginning to understand."

"Did I pass the test?"

"That's the trouble with you, you see. You keep thinking everything's a test." And with that Theo begins to laugh once again, only his laughter now becomes deeper and more raucous and more menacing, and the cloak of darkness gathers around him and his face is a grinning skull but I embrace him, I feel the child beneath the dry and dusty bones and—

—burst out of the me-monster's cavity like the creature from *Alien*, and found myself once again smashing through the roof of the Cadillac and attached to my dead self by the umbilical cord of my soul.

"I'm going to save you, Theo," I whispered, but this time I did not feign fervor; I knew that my child needed me; I heard his cry clear across the gulf between the universes.

We shot through the gates of the city. Inside, fire streamed from broken windows and there were multi-car-pileups on every corner. There were banners in Japanese hanging from all the buildings. People were pouring out of every sky-scraper. These were expressionless, two-dimensional people with large blinking eyes and brightly colored hair, and they wore space-age garments. The tongues of flame moved jerkily . . . perhaps twenty-eight frames to the second . . . as though we were on video. When a white rabbit in a waistcoat rushed by, peering at his watch, I realized that we had entered some kind of cartoon world, and that there was a decidedly Japanese cast to the animation here.

"The streets are impassable," Milt said. "You'll have to go on on foot."

"Aren't you coming with me?"

"No . . . I have to search for the king."

"King Strang?"

"Yes. But I'll pick you up when you're ready."

Unarmed save with the knowledge that my son was trapped within the city, I started for the city center, upstream against the crowds that surged through every street. It was easy to elbow the animated people out of the way; seen edgewise they were paper-thin; I wondered if they did, in fact, fill out into some other dimension I could not perceive, and whether they saw *me* as a cartoon figure, flat and absurd. What were they fleeing from? Was it an army of occupation? Soon I could see the thing that terrorized them, a tremendous shadow that soared and swooped above the skyline breathing fire . . . it was a dragon not unlike the witch-reptile from the final scenes of Walt Disney's *Sleeping Beauty*. And battling the dragon was a batlike creature, black and bloody-fanged, whose beating wings knocked turrets from their rooftops, whose screeching raked my eardrums. It was a *Godzilla*-style monster fight; Tokyo was being ravaged; it was a cartoon; it was a video game; and it was all real, real as a child's wildest imaginings.

It was then that I saw my son. I had reached a square at the center of the city. At the center of the square was a bronze monument, not unlike the Iwo Jima Memorial; Theo was the topmost figure in the tableau, his arm upraised, pointing toward the setting suns, just the way I had seen him at the beginning of the first journey, just before the first time I died; at his feet lay Joshua, eyes closed in death; above him was the weeping Jesus Ortega as *putto*, wings drooping, face buried in his hands; Serena Somers, too, was part of the group, standing a little apart, gazing at the horizon.

The square was virtually empty; the only citizen remaining was a man in a wheelchair with patches over his eyes, with a guide dog who whined and led the man around and around in circles. Over our heads, the bat and dragon wheeled. Sometimes the bat swerved, swooped, bit the dragon, released a shower of sulphurous blood which burned as soon as it touched stone or pavement.

"Theo!" I cried, for I knew that in this world statues were sometimes living, and those who seemed living were frequently dead. I ran up to the monument, took the broad steps two at a time, found myself within the tableau. On the dais, time moved at many different paces; for here, my son moved, breathed, and was fully human, although the other figures were still jerky, like an old silent movie.

"I've come to save you, Theo," I said. "Come on now, we can get down from here, and Milt is going to come and pick us up soon."

Theo said, "Dad, don't you know what any of this is about? Look at those monsters up there . . . they're fighting over who gets to eat up the carcass of the universe . . . but there's still life in it. As long as I'm here. I'm the last Truthsayer."

"Theo, you're going crazy." I went up to my son and tried to put my arms around him, but he stepped back all the way to the edge of the dais, teetered, almost fell to the flagstones below. "You can't let the fate of the universe depend on one

person. That only happens in fairytales. You told me only
now that life really *doesn't* imitate art."

"I didn't tell you that; it was probably just something
in a vision you saw, some pseudo-me; I've been here the
whole time."

His eyes were like marbles: bright and feelingless.

"Get thee behind me," he said softly.

"But I'm your own father."

"But you don't have the gift. Look at them. They're all
depending on me. I'm the only one who can save them. And
Joshua, too; I'm the only one who can bring him back from
the dead."

"Theo—" A sudden fury consumed me. I grabbed hold of
him, pulled him back from the edge. I shook him. "You're
my kid and you'll do as I say," I shouted, "even if you're
the fucking *kvisatz haderach*!"

Then I did what, in my whole time as a parent in the
"real" world, throughout all the hurts and misunderstand-
ings of our dysfunctional family, I had never done before.
I slapped Theo's face. Hard. Several times. I'm not proud
of this. But I didn't even feel that he was human. I didn't
even feel he was my son. I hated him. The Oedipal thing
was there too; I envied him. I was one of the blind and
he was the one-eyed man. He had a vision; he had a
purpose. I hated him. I wanted to kill him. I should have
strangled him in the womb. I had to pay him back for
everything he'd made me go through—the uncertainty, the
self-recrimination, even death itself—twice.

Only when he started to cry did I realize that my son
was still there, inside the protective shell of megalomania
he had created around himself.

"I'm sorry, Daddy," he said. He put his arms around me
and began to bawl his guts out. He didn't reproach me for
hitting me. It did not seem strange that he should seek
solace from me, the person who had caused him pain. That
was the way our family was. Our lives were played out on
a high wire without a net. "Joshua's dead and Mom's dying.
You didn't know she was dying, did you, that day . . ."

"No. It was nine years ago, Theo. Before the diagnosis."

"But *I* knew, you see! I felt the evil gnawing at her bones. And there was no one I could tell, no one who'd believe me, because I'm just a kid. And I have too much imagination . . . too much, too much."

He broke down again. Above us and around us it seemed that the city, the warring beasts, the smoke, the flames, were frozen; it was a paradox; causality and time were Möbiustripping around us.

"I didn't mean to hurt you," I said, but it sounded lame, a half-remembered quote from a John Lennon song, an inadequate analog of the truth. "I meant to say, yes, I did mean it, and I still love you." And it broke my heart, seeing my child become so childlike.

"Get us out of here, Dad," said Theo softly.

chapter eighteen

Ravaging Tokyo

Theo Etchison

So here I am in the middle of the cartoon city face-to-face with the father I've never known. It's strange, I mean, this dude just socked me in the face and he's begging me to forgive him at the same time and suddenly I don't feel omnipotent anymore. Jesus I've forgotten why I came here in the first place . . . I came to heal my family, not to drive them further apart. What's going on? The battle has raged through space worlds and myth worlds and worlds of ancient and modern history only to end up in this place that looks like a planet-sized episode of "RoboTech." And both of us are reliving a scene from years ago, a time I usually think of as the good times, before my mother got sick, only this was one of the worst moments of my life.

The brother and sister are still up there in the sky, slugging it out. They're more into the sheer destruction of it than actually winning anything. Their hatred is fueled by a kind of joy. Even though they're fighting over me, maybe they've forgotten that I'm here. "Do you think we can just slip away?" I ask Dad.

"I don't know, son. What are we going to do about Josh?"

"That's the riddle I haven't solved yet."

Serena is standing to one side of our little tableau . . . She's not all here yet . . . she's kind of translucent, like she's frozen in the act of beaming down from somewhere.

Josh is still lying at our feet. He is still dead, very dead. Maggots are wriggling in his empty eye-holes. I took him with me when they started to fight over me, but of course he's also back in the glass coffin in Katastrofa's castle; his presence here is like some kind of symbol I guess.

Dad says, "Maybe if we start to leave something will start to happen."

"Okay."

I hold tight on to his hand. He takes a few tentative steps down from the dais, and that's when the pandemonium all around us speeds up to normal. And that's when Serena becomes solid and she steps out of some kind of shimmering vortex and she has Ash right behind her.

Ash looks up at the sky. "This is the place all right," he says. "Look at them go at it."

Rubble is flying. Storm clouds are roiling around Thorn and Katastrofa as they intertwine in their deadly dance. In the city you can hear sirens; toward the sunset it's an ocean of fire.

"Are you going to try to stop them, Ash?" Serena says.

"How can I?" says Ash. "I'm only a disinherited princeling with one token castle to rule over . . . while they have all the armies of the night."

"I don't see any armies," Serena says.

"They're there all right," I tell her. "We're seeing the edited version of the carnage . . . the icon-driven simulation." The truth is that the bat and the dragon are just projections; in reality, thousands of worlds and trillions of lives are at stake; the scope of the war is something no mind could possibly comprehend. Except the mind of a Truthsayer. I do no editing. My mind is a maelstrom of raw data. I can sense every one of those deaths, every one of those planets burning, because each particle of life in the universe is linked to the River, and to me. I can feel, see, touch, taste all their torments, but I can understand nothing at all.

Serena sees Joshua at last. She screams.

"Cover your eyes," I tell her. "That's really not the way he is, I swear to God."

"He's—he's—"

"I'm working on it."

Serena kneels down beside the corpse. It's more bloated now, more blue, deader than ever. Flaming rocks are pelting us from the sky. A dragon's tooth smashes into the square and up spring a dozen skeleton warriors, lumbering toward us in sinuous stop-motion.

"Can we get out of here now, Dad?" I say.

Dad grabs my hand and we start to run. We race across the empty square. I trip a few times. I graze my knee, stagger up, keep running. We're out of the main square now and into a side street. There's a McDonalds, a sushi bar, and a Sumitomo Bank, all painted in in quick, impressionistic brushstrokes—it's just a background painting because the people inside them don't move. In the street itself there are dead people—they have burn marks all over their bodies, some of them are covered in blood. These are two-dimensional people, acetate sheet people curling at the edges as the hot wind blows them up and down the street. Maybe each one of these cartoon dudes represents like, a whole civilization uprooted, annihilated; I don't know. Fireworks explode just over our heads, and a constant highpitched keening fills the air. I'm still holding tight onto Dad's hand. It feels good to have him dragging me away, to have him leading me, even though I made this world and I am the one who sees the way out of the city . . . because this time I see that the way out is by not seeing the way out . . . the way out is by letting my father be my father.

We keep on running; still the warring siblings haven't noticed us; it's just me and Dad; I don't know what the

others are all doing, I just have to trust that we're all going
to meet up in the end, somehow, somewhere.

We run. We round another corner; we're in an alley
now. A mega-Rube Goldberg device is baking bread,
ironing shirts, washing a car, and shredding carrots
next to a storefront window. Now and then it pauses
to announce the end of the world. We keep on running, past regiments of grimfaced robots, their steel feet
clanging as they goose-step along the sidewalk and turn
sharply toward the town square . . . as they turn they
become invisible because they're celluloid too. I keep
urging Dad to hurry. Penis-shaped monsters erupt out of
apartment building windows. Women in flames roll across
a cobbled street. We run. We don't look, we don't pause.
I think we're going around in circles because at one stage
we're running back into the square and we see that Ash
and Serena are still occupying the monumental plinth in
the center, and now they're surrounded by several circles
of manycolored fire.

And now the square's filling up with cartoon people and
they're all chanting, "Freedom! Freedom!" and it's like this
bizarre rendition of the Soweto riots or something because
the robot soldiers are marching in and they're firing these
blasts of blue laser light from their eyes and the people are
crumpling, curling up, turning black, exploding.

The mega-Katastrofa has her claws on city hall now,
she's uprooting the clock tower. The bat's flying in circles
around the Serena monument.

"We're going around in circles," Dad says.

"I know."

"Why didn't you stop me?"

"I'm trusting you, Dad. Like I'm supposed to."

"But I don't know the way out of here! And this city
comes out of your mind somehow. It's the war for the
universe filtered through a ninth-grade sensibility."

"Right now my Truthsayer's instinct says to follow you."

He grips my hand harder and we run again. This time we
run through broad avenues. "We have to find water," my

father says. "If we find water, you can find the River and
we can get away."

We keep on running. I see a river crossed by covered
bridges. Behind us, rowhouses are on fire.

"Taxi!" my father shouts, letting go my hand and waving.
"Taxi!"

"Sure, Dad," I say, but sure enough a bright blue cab
pulls up to the curb. The flashing neon logo on the side
reads:

KINGFISHER CAB

FOR THE ULTIMATE JOURNEY
into the dark forest of the soul
admission free to qualified customers

Improbably, the taxi is a Jaguar. But the jaguar on the
hood is real, a big old cat that's curled up asleep around
where the hood ornament should be. The door swings open
and it's King Strang sitting in the driver's seat. His scarred
face is twisted into a leer. "My son," says the king, "it
seems you've been on a fool's errand." Full circle again. I
was running away from Strang and now I've run right into
his waiting taxi. Fucking Jesus I'm afraid.

"Get in, Theo," Dad says.

"But you don't understand," I say to my father. "We're
getting in deeper now. He's an evil king. He steals men's
souls and hides them in his scepter. He's made a pact with
the forces of darkness at the source of the River. You know
this dude's bad news."

"Where to?" says Strang.

I look at Dad and he looks at me as the fire races closer
to us, is just about to eat us up.

"I don't know," says Dad. "Perdition's edge. Ultima
Thule. Where no man has ever gone before." Trying on
different myths for size. Maybe he thinks he's Cinderella.

Strang bursts out laughing. Dad pushes me into the back
seat and climbs in after me. The door shuts with one of
those *thwhup-up-up* space-age electronic sound effects. It's

like an oldfashioned cab in back, with a glass divider—a sign
says *bulletproof*—and a little drawer for the money. There's
an incomprehensible table of rates: here's a sampling—

PURE OF HEART $1
FOUND WANTING 35¢
EACH ADDITIONAL PECCADILLO 60¢
PURGATORY rates same as BROOKLYN
$4 PER SCRUPLE FOR WEIGHED IN BALANCE

and a lot of it isn't even in English.

"So *you* are the ferryman," my father says. "When I was
going through the labyrinth of nightmares, I thought that it
was Theo."

"Fool, make me laugh," King Strang says to me.

I'm wearing the jester's suit again, and once again I'm
holding the stick with the cap and bells, and tinkling it, and
telling stupid old "knock knock" jokes to try to get the old
king into a better mood.

We careen past the corner of First and Oracle and I realize that in a way we've never left Tucson . . . or Mexico for
that matter. Maybe we've never even left Virginia. When
you dive deep enough into the waters of the soul, every
place is the same place, and yet no place is ever any place
you've seen before.

There's the hotel where we stayed that night! It's on fire.
I think I see myself silhouetted in the window, leaning
against the air conditioner while my Dad watches CNN.
He's getting up to change the channel.

"Knock, knock," I say to the mad king.

"Who's there?" he says.

Serena Somers

We'd been following their trail . . . Corvus's and Mr. E.'s
that is . . . through the labyrinth. Ash figured that, with Mr.
E.'s instinctual "father sense," we'd reach Theo a lot faster
than by any logical course of action. And that's like how

we ended up stepping out into the heart of an imaginary city . . . in the middle of a full-blast monster mash . . . with cartoon characters dying on every side. Talk about weird. Kneeling there with Josh's putrefying head cradled in my arms, I didn't think we'd ever get back to any kind of recognizable reality. Frankly I'd have settled for Congressman Karpovsky's hotel suite at that point.

So up there, battling it out with her brother, Katastrofa didn't show any interest in Joshua at all. She didn't come screeching down to wrest him from my arms. That's how I understood that he must really be dead after all; he was no use to her.

"Ash," I said, "I want to go home. There's nothing left for me here; my life's fucked up past redeeming."

"Never past redeeming," Ash said. He smiled at me the way he often did when he visited my bedroom late at night when I was a girl, my secret, my imaginary friend.

I didn't believe him anymore. He stood there, shining, beautiful, just the way he'd always been; but I was a different person now. I knew that there were things in the world that, once they happened, never got better again. Love is one of those things, and so is death.

"Come back," Ash said to me, but I had already begun walking away from him amid the chaos.

I knew he was going to tempt me with his gentleness; I knew that in his own way, as far as his kind were capable of it, he truly cared for me. He had never been in this business just to gather power, not like his siblings. But in the final analysis he too was a chess player, and I would never be more than a pawn; we just weren't the same kind. Oh, maybe he did feel Josh's death a little, but it was like maybe a pin pricking his thumb or something; he had grand schemes to think about, and no time to worry about creatures like little old me. Fuck 'em all, I thought.

I'd come a long way since being a high school kid in Virginia.

I was like totally crying when I started to leave the city square, but by the time I reached the corner my eyes were

dry and I felt pretty damn detached from the whole thing.
I knew I was probably stuck in this madcap world forever
unless I could find Theo to take me back to "real" reality.

Or could I find my own way out?

Phil Etchison

Once more I found myself reduced to a spectator. And
the scene I was watching was as mythic as they come: it
was Sir Percival and the Fisher King . . . it was the Fool and
King Lear . . . the pure redeemer and the wounded land.

I'm not sure how it happened, but after a while it seemed
to me that it was now I who was driving the taxicab, while
my son and the mad king sat on the back seat; my son told
jokes; the king sat there, magnificent in his bewilderment.
What could I say? I drove, down boulevards lit by the
burning of crucified criminals; I bridged the River half a
dozen times, each time on a bridge more architecturally
phantasmagorical than the last.

Tokyo (or Tucson) was being ravaged all around us.
Demons leaped up from potholes to terrorize young women.
In the air, an eerie symphonic soundtrack played, the ultimate Bernard Hermann score, chilling and dissonant. I had
no idea where we were going and I drove as the mood took
me—and the mood was invariably stark terror—the need to
escape from some ravening monster, some wall of flame,
some exploding ziggurat. A Chinese restaurant identical to
the one where we had begun our adventure swam into view
and shimmered out of existence.

Blindly I drove on. Tokyo-Tucson burned around us.
I threaded through rubble-strewn alleys. Sometimes the
jaguar on the hood would leap onto the windshield and
glare at me. I had a desperate feeling of being chased, but
I didn't know by whom.

I didn't even know what Theo and Strang were discussing
back there. I was only an ordinary man, after all, not privy
to the secrets of the universe. I was not even a very good
man. Hadn't I just slugged my kid repeatedly for no damn

reason except that he made me feel insignificant? What kind of a father was I, anyway?

Who was chasing me? Why was the shadow of a giant bat cast over the luminous fog in front of me? I gunned the gas, crashed through some kind of glass and metal barricade, turned around, and still there was this shadow. The jaguar was snarling now, clawing at something in the sky.

"Thorn?" I whispered.

I looked up at the rearview mirror. Strang and Theo were deep in conversation. I could hear the beating of leathery wings . . .

"Knock, knock," my son says.

Serena Somers

Maybe there was a way of getting out of here under my own steam after all. If there's one thing I'd learned from everything that had happened to me, it was like it says in *Star Wars:* everything's connected to everything else. Or was it Zen Buddhism? I remember once, when I brought Mr. E., the semi-famous poet, into school for careers day, that he told the kids that Zen and *Star Wars* espoused pretty much the same philosophy.

So there was a war going on, wasn't there? A war for possession of the entire universe or whatever. But I knew there was like another war, too, a war inside all our minds. It seemed to me that if maybe I could win my own private war, I'd be able to claw my way free of Theo's universe.

And what *was* my own private war? Hadn't I conquered my own fear of my self-image the day I sacrificed my virginity to save Joshua's life? Hadn't I just accepted my own humanity by turning my back, at last, on Ash, my supernatural companion? Hadn't I come to terms with my ambivalence about my sexual nature the day I met and merged with the alternate version of myself in the lobby of a Tucson hotel?

Before I knew it, I found myself walking into that very lobby. It didn't surprise me one bit that the hotel would be here. It seemed almost inevitable. The glass doors swung shut behind me and there was all this fire outside; I knew that if I tried to leave I'd be burned alive. There was nobody in the lobby but there were a lot of half-full wine-glasses in the reception area and where there was this piano bar, there was a glass stuffed full of dollar bills, as if the piano man hadn't even had time to get his tips before he had to leave.

There were Karpovsky banners everywhere, and wadded-up Karpovsky fliers littering the floor, and all kinds of other Karpovsky débris. It was very warm in the lobby; after all, the city was burning all around us; I was surprised they still had electricity.

I walked around the lobby several times. I was waiting for some kind of sign I guess. That's what usually happened in the past, I'd get a visitation from Ash or something and I'd know that the next stage of my life was about to happen. I didn't get a sign as such. I hung around the reception desk for a while, waiting for a phone call from on high; there was nothing. I poured myself some coffee out of the machine. It was cold but it kind of cleared my mind a bit, like Drano.

I started to wonder if maybe I shouldn't have walked away from Ash that way. Would I have really done that if I had all my shit together?

No one was going to tell me where to go from here. I was going to have to take the next step myself. And now I realized what it was going to be and why I'd ended up walking into this place, the last place I ever wanted to see again.

I knew what was going to happen.

The merging of personalities wasn't complete yet. There was another Serena Somers somewhere in this hotel. Maybe more than one. I was going to have to hunt them down one by one. I had the feeling that some of them weren't going to be that willing.

I looked up at the clock. It was totally weird but I could have sworn that the date and time were the same as when I met the first other Serena Somers. Maybe time had been

standing still since that moment. Or maybe Theo'd made
a bend in the River and brought me back to the same
coordinates.

I switched on the speaker on the receptionist's console
and I dialed Karpovsky's suite.

Serena answered the phone.

chapter nineteen

_____

The Third Serena Somers

Serena Somers

Serena said to me, "I've been waiting, Serena. Come on up. Knock on the door—three short, one long, you know, like Beethoven's Fifth. I'll let you in."

I put the phone down. My heart was pounding. This Serena had an edge to her voice, and she seemed used to ordering people around. Maybe she didn't want to be absorbed into the rest of me. But I had to make it happen somehow.

I took the elevator up. There was no noise in the corridor except for the distant hiss of the burning city, and now and then the crack of a collapsing building. At the end of the hallway, next to the doorway to Karpovsky's suite, there was a panoramic window. It was night and the fires burned brilliantly for miles, all the way to the edge of the mountains. In the sky, you could see the bat and dragon outlined in fire, like animated fireworks. Below, in the avenues, antlike people swarmed away from the city center pursued by rivers of flame. Yeah. Rockets' red glare, bombs bursting in air, the whole works. It was even more spectacular than the CNN footage of

Baghdad under fire. Mostly because it was the view from the inside out.

I knocked on the congressman's door.

It flew open and there stood, not the third Serena Somers, but Katastrofa Darkling.

It had to be her. She was wearing this tight-fitting snake-skin one-piece garment and glittery eye shadow and she had claws instead of fingernails and her eyes were the eyes of a dragon, metallic and predatory. And at the same time she kind of looked like me, too, especially around the lips.

She held the door open and said, "Come in, won't you, Serena dear."

I said, "This has got to be some kind of joke."

"Joke?" she said, and she made the word sound like a hiss even though it contained no esses. "Serena, dear, you disappoint me. Don't you recognize yourself?"

"You're Katastrofa Darkling," I said. "You're my worst enemy. You stole the person I love. You made him die. I'll always hate you."

"It's true," she said, "I am all that. But I'm also you. And now, as you can see, it's time for me to take you back into myself."

She spread out her arms as though to embrace me. I felt a blast of heat . . . a heat that raced through my veins and lanced my heart . . . I could feel that she was the source of the fire that was bringing the city crashing all around us. Jesus, you're stupid, I told myself. You thought she was going to be reluctant to merge with you . . . but it's the other way round . . . she's waiting to pounce and it's you who are scared of being sucked into the jaws of the dragon.

A last-ditch effort: "If you're Katastrofa, how come you're still out there, battling your brother? You can't be in two places at the same time."

"Why not?" She smiled. Her teeth glittered with reflected fire. "You know that *you've* been in more than one place at the same time. If one person can occupy two spaces, why can't one space house two persons, and each one lay an equally valid claim to be the true occupant?"

"You're lying," I said. "You've taken possession of the other Serena Somers. She's a prisoner inside you. It's some kind of trick. I know myself pretty well and I know there could never be a Katastrofa Darkling inside *my* mind."

"See for yourself, sis," she said. "How dare you presume to think that the rah-rah virginal purity aspect of our personality has got to come out on top? We sluts have a right to be heard, too. . . ."

"What are you talking about?" I elbowed her aside and entered Congressman Karpovsky's suite, except that when I got inside it was a totally different place. The congressman's office maybe? But I couldn't remember if I'd ever actually set foot there before. It was D.C. though. You could see that through the window behind the big desk cluttered with papers and yeah, the big crystal whale and the bronze eagle, that image was perfectly clear. . . . What was I doing here? I sifted through the memories of my two selves . . . Serena One, who'd kept herself pure and fat, who'd dreamed of Joshua Etchison, saved herself for him, fled the congressman's advances like the plague . . . Serena Two, who had succumbed to a degree, but had managed somehow or another to misdirect the congressman away from the final penetration . . . whose line in the sand was a lot closer to the enemy than mine had been . . . was there a third Serena who had gone all the way, Serena the Slut? In high school I'd been called a slut of course; it was common knowledge that the entire male population of the school . . . of G.W. Junior High for that matter . . . had done me. Except that it wasn't true. It was a myth, kept alive by my own reticence and by locker room macho tall stories.

But was there another Serena who had lived through all of those tall stories?

I went into the congressman's office and I saw myself sitting in a high-backed chair across from Karpovsky. Only the top of the congressman's hair was visible because he had swiveled away from Serena Three and was gazing

out over the city. A New Age CD played softly in the
background. It was a concession to the image the handlers
had built of Karpovsky, as someone caring, sensitive, profoundly understanding of the yuppie sensibility. The crystal
dolphin was another such emblem. I bet that even the prof-
essorial clutter on the desk was carefully arranged between
interviews by a continuity person.

I started to say something to the other Serena but it
was like there was a glass wall between me and the rest
of the room. I banged on it, I shouted, I kicked. Serena
sat there. I could even hear her breathing, but she was
totally unaware of my presence. The Serena that I saw was
unmistakably me, but everything about her was tinged with
Katastrofa . . . I could see it especially in the fingernails
and in the lips . . . and that skintight, scaly dress . . . and
the eyes, of course . . . the eyes of a hungry reptile.

I heard Karpovsky speak the words that were common
to the memories of both Serenas One and Two: except
they were addressed to different mes, one to a me in a
conservative two-piece outfit from Lord and Taylor, sweating because my bulk flowed uneasily into the folds of the
blouse; the other me in a halter top that barely concealed
what little there was to see of my breasts: "Why do you
want to work for me, Serena?" He was leafing through my
application.

I heard Serena Three say, "I believe in your message.
And anyway, Congressman, you're kind of cute."

Serena One had like blurted that out, regretted it, sat
tongue-tied for the next ten minutes while the congressman
practiced his national health speech; Serena Two regretted
it too, but figured she was in too deep now to climb out
of the water. But the way this snake-Serena said it, it was
totally flirting with the congressman, I mean *brazenly*, the
way the slut-Serena of my junior high's mythology would
have uttered it. I was appalled but I couldn't look away as
the scene was played out.

"I'm glad you believe in my message, Serena. Love one
another. That's the most important thing of all, and anyway,

as you know, it's from the Bible. Those fascist fundamentalists should know that liberals can quote the Bible just as well as they can, isn't that so, Serena?"

"Yes, Congressman."

"Would you care for a joint?"

Serena Three giggled. "I hate getting stoned before lunch, Congressman, but if you insist—"

That's not what I said! I thought, but another part of me said, I wish I *had* said that. I watched in disbelief. I still hadn't seen Karpovsky's face but now he turned just a little way and I could see a gloved hand idly rolling the joint as the phone rang and the receptionist buzzed the congressman about some meeting that he was supposed to go to with the Rev. Jackson.

"Put it off for an hour, will you? I'm TQ at the moment."

I wondered what TQ meant. "Taking a quickie," perhaps? It didn't sound good. The congressman was all confident, knowing that I was a done deal, a tidbit sitting there waiting to be scarfed. I hated him. Because he started off on his spiel now, the spiel both mes remembered: "You see, Serena, I'm a *big* man. Who's gonna change the way the world thinks. I have inside me this huge and overwhelming compassion for the sufferers of this godawful planet of ours. But I got tragic flaw, too, you understand that? Just like your Oedipus, your Hamlet, your big heroic figures . . . I'm a lonely man. A man who never had a childhood. Did you know that my father used to beat me? He was an alcoholic. I've never told that to anyone before. And here we are, you and me, and you're so fresh and young, like an unplucked flower, and . . ." It made me sick because it wasn't the first time he'd told anyone that before. It was what he told all the girls. By proxy for that matter because it was in his autobiography, *Poor White Trash*, which many people who knew him in his childhood say was bullshit—he grew up in suburbia, not a coal-mining town. So they say. I'd heard it many ways, enough to make me disbelieve most of what he said anymore. I don't blame him for lying— maybe a politician *has* to be a pathological liar, how else

could he fool everyone, unless he fooled himself first?—
but well it made me sick because I knew that Serena Two
had swallowed it hook line and sinker and Serena One had
actually started to cry.

But Three, she just sat there all cool, adjusting her pout
level to go along with his intensity.

"You're young and I'm old and weary and withered,"
said Congressman Karpovsky, "a great man with a tragic
flaw, an uncontrollable libido. . . ."

"Cut the self-serving bullshit, Congressman," said Three.
"I know you want to have sex with me." She shivered her
dress onto the floor. She shook her hair and all at once it
was wild, like the Bride of Frankenstein. When I saw her
naked body I was amazed that I had the potential to look
like that . . . as curved and bouncy as the ocean.

The congressman's leather chair swiveled around and
he was a cartoon congressman. He was all flat and his
face was painted in swift impressionistic strokes and his
eyes were completely blank. How could someone like that
be frightening? I banged my fists against that forcefield
again. I thought I could feel it give a little. Serena Three
was oozing her way over to the desk now. She skimmed
her fingers along the crystal dolphin, teasing, the way men
think a girl likes to caress a penis. And the thing is that my
own fingers prickled with the smoothness and the cold . . .
and I knew for sure that that was another me in there . . .
I could feel her thoughts racing through my own head and
her thoughts went something like this:

Fuck fuck fuck fuck fuck (and an image of an old man
getting up from a sofa and wandering down the hall) *fuck
fuck* (in the wheezing voice of an old man maybe someone
with asthma and) *fuck*.

Jesus I thought, what is she thinking about, who's the
old man? Serena Three sidled over to the desk. She was
talking the whole time in a kind of immature parody of a
sexy voice, saying stuff like, "Gosh Congressman you are
so attractive so mature so beautiful I want to envelop you
in my arms I want to want to want to" oh, it made me

sick and angry, I screamed at the top of my lungs, "Get away from him, he's just a user, you must think you're totally worth shit to throw yourself at a man like that," and I felt like this dirty feeling, this despair, seize hold of me as I watched this Serena-serpent kind of shimmying and jouncing in front of the congressman's desk. Now she was sort of riding the crystal dolphin, rocking herself back and forth against it as though it were a dildo. Now she was climbing up on the desk itself and kneeling in front of the cartoon congressman and undulating her hips in his face and pulling at his tie and still those celluloid eyes were blank, pupilless. Behind the congressman's head, in the window, Washington by daylight was dissolving, and a different backdrop was showing through . . . the burning city terrorized by animated monsters . . . and Serena Three was smiling now, tugging at the congressman's tie . . . the tie fluttered across the room, making a cellophane-crinkling kind of noise, an echo of the roar and hiss of the flames outside. I had to smash through to her. "Help me, Theo," I cried out, thinking to myself, this is Theo's world, maybe he can hear me. My clenched fists were getting bloody.

They were embracing, the two-dimensional Karpovsky nude now, folding himself around the 3-D Me Three like a big pink sheet of gift wrap. I couldn't take it. "Theo!" I shouted again, and then I felt a surge of power flow through me, like they say you get when you're high on angel dust, and I crashed through the barrier and there I was, trying to pry the two of them apart.

Serena Three pulled away furiously. Time stood still except for the two of us. Karpovsky was intertwined around the empty air. Outside, the flames were all frozen in place. I grabbed Serena by the arms and she spat in my face. "What the fuck is going on?" she said. "And who the fuck do you think you are? Is this good angel bad angel time or what?"

"Mellow out, sis," I said, "we have to talk."

"You're not my sister," she said.

"Am too."

"Get lost."

"Serena, Serena . . ." I dodged another wad of spit. Even in her anger she exuded sexuality. Even though I was trying to chew her out, I realized that I envied her too, envied how easy it was for her to shrug out of her clothes and get it on with a total stranger. "Listen to me," I said. "You're part of me. We've gotten split off from each other, but we have to listen to each other, to help each other out. Otherwise there's going to be trouble."

"You'd better get out of my mind," said Serena Three, "or there's gonna be trouble. I know what you are. You're the mind-eater. You're going to swallow me up just like you did that other bitch, the pricktease, the one that wouldn't let Karpovsky stick it up her even though she let him do *everything* else . . . that fucking hypocrite."

I held onto her tight. "Maybe you're not going to like this," I said, "but it has to be done." I guess I'd known ever since Katastrofa flung open the door to let me into the hotel suite. I had to accept that there was a Katastrofa creature inside me . . . that there were dark parts of me that I not only had to accept but I had to come to love, willingly and without recoiling from them. That was why I had been brought back to this juncture in my life; it was a major splitting-off point, a place where many mes had branched off; a node, you could call it, in the private River that was my life.

"Don't do this to me!" Serena Three said. "You were never there when I suffered all those awful things. I was hurt and you were healing yourself with Snickers bars and lard. I hate you. You don't even know about the old man who fucked us when we were little."

"Nobody fucked us," I said, "I was a virgin until . . . until Josh . . ."

But she'd said something that chilled me shitless. I *did* remember an old man. Or was it a dream? I could remember the smell of him . . . *cloves, sour wine, and a sick-sweet smell that I couldn't have known was semen and . . .* who was he? It couldn't have been a just a dream, could it? I was wavering and it was an effort to hold Serena Three, to keep her from squirming out of my grip. I did it though. This was important.

"Leave me alone," said Me Three. "Leave me alone, Serena. Because I'm scared."

It had never occurred to me to look beyond the immediate reasons for the eating disorders of my teenage years. Now, maybe, there was something. Something I'd never remembered before, let alone faced; because elsewhere, in a different universe, another me had taken the pain for me.

"Oh, Serena," I said softly, "I'm sorry."

—and felt a momentary glitch or blackout as she and I began to move into one another. And saw the congressman begin to move, flesh out, expand into the third dimension. And saw, behind him, in the window, the flames fan out and leap up to the sky. As Serena Three's mind melded with mine I was flooded with anger and bitterness. I remembered encounters with nameless boys in filthy school toilets filled with marijuana smoke . . . I remembered the withered fingers of the nameless old man . . . a friend of my parents, maybe . . . I think I called him uncle, uncle . . . those papery fingers trying to spread the lips of my vulva, rasping . . . the smell of old wine and cloves and . . . they were so vivid that I knew that even if I hadn't experienced them myself, the mind that had, the mind that had been tormented and warped by these things, was as much my mind as the mind I'd carried inside my skull since childhood.

The anger that finally broke loose was like when you're floating down a River and suddenly you reach the cataract and the water's exploding all around you and there's nothing you can do now but hold on and fall and fall and hope you won't be dashed to smithereens by the rocks, and that's how I felt when I rushed at Congressman Karpovsky, who was inflating like a rubber balloon now, filling up with hot air . . . I grabbed that crystal dolphin and I just started clubbing him with it and . . . I screamed at him, just screamed and screamed without making any sense . . . and finally the congressman just popped and the air came all rushing out with a tremendous farting thunder sound and he was whizzing around the room and shrinking and shrinking and I ran to the window, smashed the window with the dildo dolphin, watched the congressman go zooming off into the flames, and . . .

I looked up into the sky. I smelled the smoke of the burning city. The fume-filled wind billowed around Karpovsky's office. Papers were flying. Katastrofa—the big Katastrofa who'd owned a piece of Serena Three's soul—the dragon writhing up there in mortal combat with Thorn—Katastrofa was wounded! A torrent of fire-edged blood was spewing from a gash in her side, sizzling as it baptized the ground.

I screamed up at the howling dragon: "You can't steal my boyfriend from me, Katastrofa, and you can't steal me from myself! The more you fight me, the more myself I'm going to become!"

Oh, Jesus, I exulted, I was proud, I was bursting with joy even though I still had no idea how I was going to escape this world. I knew that I had the power within my shattered selves, the power to tap into Theo's vision, the power to wound the dragon, woman power.

chapter twenty

Soul Vampires

Theo Etchison

I'm not sure how it happens. One minute Dad's pushing me into the taxi, the next the taxi driver's sitting in back with me and Dad is driving, pretty damn aimlessly as far as I can see, cutting through parking lots, going the wrong way on one-way streets . . . I mean, not that it matters when the whole town is crumbling all around you.

And here I am, the joker once again, telling the mad king bad jokes which barely cause him to raise an eyebrow as he sits there, clutching his scepter with its soul-catching jewel, brooding so hard you can almost see the black cloud hovering over his head. I've exhausted my supply of knock knock and dead baby jokes, and now I'm doing Dan Quayle jokes . . . anyone remember him? . . . which are met with bewilderment.

We dodge a few fireballs and King Strang says, "I hope that man knows what he is doing."

"He's a poet," I tell him.

"Ah, a kind of Truthsayer then."

"One who has lost his way," I say, which is the truth, and I'm hoping that the bulletproof glass and the noise of the explosions around us will prevent Dad from hearing it. And it's true that he doesn't look around. He's too busy chasing something that looks like his own shadow . . . but sometimes it's the outline of a bat. I realize that he's about due for some private confrontation with Thorn . . . maybe it's about, like, who has the right to possess me. When are they going to learn that I can't be owned? I can only give myself. It's a truth no one ever wants to hear.

I turn to King Strang. He's a man in pain, I know that, I can feel it. He's also, at times, a very evil man; I feel that too. Maybe he regrets it, but I don't think he really regrets it enough. What I feel from him I feed back to him in the form of bad jokes. When it looks like he might laugh, he cuffs me with the back of his hand. I shake the bells. I don't know why I'm doing this except I think it's something to do with keeping him going a little bit longer, treading water, maintaining the universe in a holding pattern until we can perform the healing.

The next thing that happens is that we're hurtling down a blind alley. I can tell there's no exit because you can't see the burning city down the way, only darkness. All of a sudden, I see why my father is headed there. A circle of light has formed on the far wall and in it, silhouetted, is a bat—just like the bat-signal in those *Batman* comics.

My father's all cussing at the image, something about "stealing my son, my son . . . ."

"You can't take him on, Dad," I say. "He's too powerful. That's only a shadow of a shadow of Thorn that you're seeing, not even a scruple of what he can do . . . oh, Daddy," I said, "don't go after him, you're gonna crash us into that wall; it's a trick. . . ."

King Strang put his hand on my shoulder. "Continue with your jokes, fool," he said. "He knows what he is doing."

Then Strang clutches at his heart as though he's received a sudden wound. I sense it too. I think I know what it is. I think that Katastrofa has been struck. It has something to do with Serena.

The bat-thing rears up and even though it's a shadow I can see the blood dripping from its jaws and then my Dad guns the gas and we go crashing into the wall, which evaporates into a blood-tinged mist, and then Dad is suddenly gone and the car is careening out of control in the middle of a hundred-way intersection. . . .

"Do not fear!" says Strang. "Attend to your duties, fool."

Phil Etchison

And all at once I found myself again wandering through the corridors of my past. In the bedroom again with my six-year-old son, about to strike my wife, avoiding his reproachful eyes.

"We've been through this," I told him, breaking out of my memory and addressing the child within the child. (Was this an endless loop, a perpetual *Twilight Zone*ification of my inner reality?) "I've fought the me-monster and I've started a rapprochement with you on this, Theo; don't make me relive it yet again."

Theo only looked at me: solemn, his wide eyes glared through strands of muddied hair.

"Give me a break, son," I said.

At that moment, Mary, too, detached herself from her corporeal form and said to our son, "You do have to forgive, you know. Forgiving your parents is the beginning of maturity."

Theo didn't speak.

The entire room began to shimmer; the walls became drops of blood; we were in a cavern, and my wife, a statue, stood amongst a thousand candles, her hand raised in benediction behind the altar rail. From outside came the sounds of the Day of the Dead: salsa music, cheering crowds, laughter, the tolling of bells, a *dies irae*. Mary was no longer able to speak, but her authority had grown considerably. Women in black robes were kneeling, crossing themselves, beating their breasts, weeping into paper cups, creeping forward to bathe the statue's feet with their tears. Children scurried this way and that, chattering, eating, hustling the tourists. But it was all window dressing; what mattered in the scene was me, my wife, my son.

"Was I the one who made you turn to stone?" I asked the limestone Madonna.

Theo said, "Oh, Dad, all men and women are made of stone, until they're touched by the breath of life."

His lips had not moved.

He continued: "Dad, Dad, we always have to be vigilant; the breath of life passes by more swiftly than a downstream current; but the quality of stone is always in us."

"You don't sound like Theo," I said, "more like a cardboard cutout of some nineteenth-century philosopher."

Theo laughed. Without moving his lips.

"I'm really having this conversation with myself, aren't I?" I said at last.

He just went on laughing.

It must be true. Each of the figures in this vision was a figment . . . a fragment of my own shattered consciousness . . . my versions of what these characters might say and do . . . I was doing, I suppose, what psychotherapists make you do . . . take the characters from a dream and put words in their mouths. But perhaps I was merely rationalizing . . . a dangerous thing to be doing at this stage in the universal madness.

I became giddy, as though I'd had a hefty noseful of nitrous oxide. As the image of my wife looked on, I embraced my cold son, hugged him hard to my chest: I said, "Maybe you are only me, but I still love you," and other nonsensical things; but as I bent down to kiss my son on the cheek, he shattered.

Like porcelain.

And another figure came swirling out of the pieces of Theo: he was tall and he was batwinged and he had slate-colored eyes, and I heard the distant conch-call of Cornelius Huang, and I knew that Thorn was here, and that by no means could Thorn be considered a part of myself.

"Get thee behind me," I shouted at him, making the sign of the cross for good measure, though I'm not a religious person. Perhaps the symbolism alone would be enough to defeat him.

Thorn laughed: it was Theo's laugh.

I said, "Get out of my vision; you don't belong here."

"Such hubris," Thorn said. "How would you know anyway?"

"I'm inside my own mind, and I'm only talking to pieces of myself; that's how I know. Within this little circle of my brain, I'm God."

"Oh, Phil," said Thorn, "you are so wrong. I am, indeed, a part of you, the part you most detest."

"Don't be ridiculous. You are the one who stole Theo from me. You're the enemy, the darkness. You're a fucking vampire, for God's sake. I don't even know how you can stand to be here, with all the holy water and crosses around."

I was trying to be flippant, trying to dispel the disturbing notion that perhaps he might be right. But I was becoming afraid. When the vampire did not answer me, I babbled on, filling the silence between us with bluster and self-delusion: "I've already battled the darkness within myself," I said, "I fought the monster within myself in order to get to this city in the first place. I've overcome the darkness, I've harrowed hell, and I'm too weary for another battle."

A hymn to the Virgin welled up somewhere in the depths of the cavern.

"You can never be victorious over yourself," said Thorn, whose features were warping as I watched, resembling more and more my own. "The fact of the matter is, you fought a monster . . . you as your child perceived you once, when he was too small to understand that you are flesh and blood and full of human frailties. I represent a far more insidious version of yourself . . . the self you've never faced . . . your vampire nature."

"That's ridiculous," I said, "I hate the sight of blood."

Cornelius Huang stood next to the statue of my wife now, and he lifted the conch to his lips seven more times, pausing between each blast for an apocalyptic flourish of his instrument.

"It's not blood you suck," he said, "it's human souls."

"Sure," I said, feigning sarcasm; but I felt the prick of terror run up my arms and scalp. "I'm a soul vampire."

"Think about it," Thorn said. "You fancy yourself a poet, don't you? And what do you do, as a poet? Don't you fling yourself on suffering and pain in a veritable feeding frenzy? Don't you distill the grief of others into words, and sell those words for a dollar apiece to *Poetry* magazine? Haven't you traded the souls of your closest family members for the poetry chair of a mediocre university? Isn't it true that you've exploited your wife's illness all the way to being shortlisted for the American Book Award? And your son Josh's death . . . what do you really feel about that, you with your visions of flaming angels falling into the sea . . . do you not see another slim volume of pained metaphors and unlikely classical allusions, another credit towards tenure? You use people, Phil; I only devour their blood out of biological necessity; it is you who are truly the vampire. How can you say you don't partake of my essence?"

There was no answer to these accusations. But what was I to do? Embrace the vampire as I had embraced the me-monster? Suddenly I found myself standing at the edge of a bottomless pit. I was a kind of Wile E. Coyote, and the Road Runner was beeping at me from the other side of the chasm, and I was seized by a force far greater than myself, a force that demanded that I try to leap the gap though hell itself should bubble underneath . . . and the vampire who stood beside me said, "Accept yourself. Accept that you are nothing more than a stealer of souls."

"No!" I cried. "I can't accept it." And yet how easy it would be to take that single step, to fall and fall forever, to kick aside the safety net of self-esteem and perish in the quagmire of self-loathing. I wanted to. Poets were just leeches, after all, weren't they? I'd joked about that often

enough. And thought it true more often than not, though I
had never dared to think it too long for fear of losing forever
the illusion that my life had a purpose.

"But isn't *everything* an illusion?" the vampire said, reading my thoughts.

I gazed out at the chasm. I despaired.

"What kind of poet are you anyway?" the vampire
screamed. "Have you ever dared stand alone at the brink
of the void, have you dared face the emptiness that is
yourself, the utter meaninglessness of the human condition?
Of course not. How could you, sitting in your comfortable
suburban home with its picket fence and well-kept lawn . . .
hypocrite!"

I continued to stare at that which yawned before me.

"Jump!" cried the vampire.

I could hear the word reecho and reverberate in my
mind . . . *jump jump jump jump jump* as though there were
a crowd down below jeering egging me on daring me to
take the infinite leap accept myself for the nothing that I
was accept the darkness accept the reality there is no truth
there is no life there is only despair despair despair. . . .

And then I thought: Haven't I stood on the edge of
Nirvana itself, and listened to the voice of the universal
spirit? And wasn't what it said to me the mirror image of
what Thorn is saying now?

I remembered the siren whispering of universal love.
Had I not resisted it? Wasn't I still fastened to my corporeal self by an invisible rope? And wasn't that rope
spun from my desire still to hold on to the things I yet
loved, my children, my wife, and even that picket-fenced
suburban home with its lush lawn, vividly green in the
aftermist of a Virginia rainstorm? The Wile E. Coyote
image popped back into my mind. I've always considered
Wile E. to be the true embodiment of the human condition, and his quest for the Road Runner to be a virtual
analog of man's quest for the divine, the unattainable,
God himself; and here I stood at the coyote ledge, and
despaired (as Wile E. must have, oftentimes, when the

latest product from the Acme company failed to operate as advertised)—and what was so damn bad about being Wile E. Coyote? And what was wrong with being racked with despair?

Love and despair were what defined me as human.

"Jump," said Thorn—I felt the parallel with Christ's temptation all the more clearly—"jump and everything will be all right. You have nothing to live for anyway. But once you jump, you'll be transfigured. The despair will have no meaning. You'll be buoyed up by flights of angels. You will have sucked in despair and conquered it, and you will again be the hunter, not the hunted."

"I'm not going to jump," I said. "I don't want to be a God. I don't want to be the Void. I am a man."

I felt the tug of the rope around myself, and I knew that the knot held firm.

Thorn screamed.

Serena Somers

And then I found myself back in the town square. Katastrofa's blood was raining down from the sky. Thorn was wounded too. His blood was a brilliant blue color and it glowed as it spattered the clouds and the flagstones. They were both wounded but they still fought. I knew it was to the death.

And well, I could feel the wound in my own soul, too, because now I knew that Strang and Thorn and Katastrofa and Ash weren't just dream people, figures out of a real-life sci-fi fairy tale, but also part of us; that the war in heaven was like, the war in our hearts as well.

I saw Mr. E. standing at the far side of the square. I started to walk toward him. He seemed different, cleansed almost, as if he'd had a totally intense therapy session. He caught sight of me and began coming in my direction as well. The square was littered with corpses, both human and celluloid. "Mr. E.," I shouted, "Mr. E., where have you been?"

Theo Etchison

Now we're busting through the wall and the jaguar taxi flies out over the city square into a rain of manycolored blood. The taxi skids to a halt beside the monument in the center of the square, which is I guess really a kind of transdimensional travel nexus or something, because the group of statues never seems to have the same people in it: this time there is only Corvus.

He's huge and white and feathery. His marble face is veined in streaks of emerald and lapis.

Slowly he softens. The flesh emerges from the stone. The jaguar—I mean the living hood ornament—growls. He leaps off the hood and bounds up the steps toward Corvus. He crouches, clawing the stone; he roars.

"Let us see what he wants," King Strang says. We leave the taxicab.

Corvus kneels before the king.

"Have pity," he says to him, "have pity."

chapter twenty-one

The Fall of the House of Darkling

Theo Etchison

There's Corvus kneeling in front of his king and liege lord; I know that Corvus, unlike the servants of Thorn and Katastrofa, still believes that King Strang is the King of Everything. And he's all saying, "Pity, pity." Pity on who? What difference can a mad king's pity make? I take Strang by the arm and lead him toward the birdman. Strang's eyes are misting over; maybe he's crying, but maybe, maybe he is going blind. . . .

"Where am I going?" he mumbles.

"This way. This way." I tug his sleeve a little. His robes are stained with blood, tears, and dirt; his scepter must weigh a ton, with all those souls trapped inside it; he staggers toward the steps, where Corvus is kneeling with his wings spread out behind him, draped all over the steps, humbly staring at the bloodstained flagstones.

"Pity, pity, O King," he says. His voice is barely a whisper; meanwhile the sky is thundering and burning; we have to strain to hear him.

King Strang struggles to stand erect. He shakes his fist at the sky and screams: "Betrayal! Betrayal!" at them; but the bat and dragon do not even bother to glance down because they're so busy ripping at each other's flesh.

"King Strang," I say, "listen to what Corvus has to say."

"Yes, what is it?" he growls. There is a lot of jaguar in his growling. Corvus trembles. I don't know why. Hasn't Strang given up his dominion over the universe to the quarreling siblings? What power can he wield over Corvus?

Corvus says, "My lord, you must forgive your son. This is not the first time I'm begging you to do it, and it won't be the last."

Strang says, "I cannot."

"My lord, look up there. Who is it who rends your world in twain? Not Ash. Ash is the one who has always loved you. Ash is the one who spoke the truth to you, the truth you know in your heart but dared not face; only speak the word, my lord, and admit him into your presence; perhaps there is still time to heal the rift and make the River flow once more through all the universes; you can do it, you and Ash and the Truthsayer, the three of you together."

King Strang is leaning on my shoulder. I can see a lot of emotions battling it out in his face. I don't think anyone has dared speak this frankly to him before. But I know Corvus is right.

"What do you think of all this, fool?" the king says to me.

I take the bells and shake them. The music seems to soothe the king a little, and, as Corvus sweeps the blood from the steps with his snow-white wings, he sits himself down on the marble, still holding on to my arm; his hand is withered and unsteady.

I shake the bells again. I tell the king the truth, which is my duty. "King," I say, "Corvus is right. Whatever possessed you to split the kingdom in three anyway? You must have known that it was going to start a war. And you shouldn't have tested your three children the way you did. It's never fair to ask your kids how much they love you, because kids always lie when it comes to love. Kids don't love their parents in a simple way. The love they have is always riddled through with pain and wishful thinking and anger. You know that. You had parents once."

I feel the king's hand grip tighter; I know that I'm stirring up his rage. But I can't stop telling him the truth. "You owe it to yourself to forgive Ash," I say, "look into his heart and you'll see so much of yourself: you'll see the stubbornness. You'll see that like you, he doesn't like to talk about things. He sees the world in feelings, not in words. That's why he couldn't bring himself to flatter you like the others did. You know that if your father had asked you the same thing, you would have answered the same way. You've done your deal with the darkness, and you're wasting away from the wounds that you gave yourself in exchange for the power to rule the cosmos, but you were once the kind of person your son is, noble, loyal, and unafraid. Admit it to yourself, Strang. When you see him, you see the things about yourself that you've thrown away. It's that that makes you angry. Not some imaginary betrayal of your love. It's yourself you hate, not Ash."

At first it's painful for me to talk this way to him. Every word I say is a stab-wound. But after a while I really get into it. I mean, I never thought of myself as like a sadist or anything, but it felt good to lay it all out for the mad king . . . good the way it feels good when you've been rolling in the mud and you're scouring all the shit off with a strong abrasive soap . . . fucking Jesus it feels good. I'm really rattling those bells, man, they're clanging and banging and it's almost louder than the noise all around us.

I look behind me and I see that my Dad and Serena are nearby, leaning against the taxicab. And Serena says: "He's not gonna go for it, Theo. The last time Corvus tried to get him to do it, he almost killed us—we barely got out alive!"

The way Strang is, it's kind of like a volcano getting ready to erupt. I feel the roar building up inside him: first he's quivering all over and I grip him harder, trying to steady him, then he's all shaking and then at last the fury comes all at once and he flings me away from him and I go flying onto the steps and I hear my own skull thudding against the marble like it's thundering inside my head and I think there's blood running down one eye oh God, the pain, and through the red-mist-blur I can see King Strang rear up, the scepter glowing, his eyes reddening . . . it's a shadow of the old powerful ruler of the cosmos . . . just a pale ghost of what he once was like . . . though I'm sure it's enough to strike down dead me and Corvus and Dad and Serena . . . but you know I'm not scared and I'm not planning to run away at all . . . because I feel his sadness underneath all that anger, and so I cry out even though I'm hurting all over, "King Strang, don't do it . . . you know I can't help telling you the truth . . . if you don't like it you can just think of me as your fool . . . your jester . . . your word-twister. . . ."

He's astonished that I'm still defying him. He hesitates for a moment.

Then he says . . . simmering down a little . . . bottling his rage again . . . he says, "I will never accept Ash back into my heart. He is dead to me . . . dead forever."

Corvus says, "Nothing is dead forever, my lord."

"Never," says King Strang, "never, never, never, never."

But at that moment the war between Thorn and Katastrofa comes to an end. On some level I guess the millions upon millions of starfleets and planetary armies just blow each other all up and the universes are littered with a jillion corpses, man and alien. But that's not what we see, I guess, because it's *my* vision of things that shapes what we perceive.

We all look up at the same time because we hear a gutwrenching shriek, so loud that it drowns out everything around us: the fires, the crashing buildings, the screams of the dying . . . and we see that Katastrofa is flailing up there among the clouds . . . A hail of dragonscales is pouring . . . it is Katastrofa who's shrieking, shrieking and transforming . . . She's a red dragon, a green dragon, a

white dragon . . . she's a crystal dragon, a sea dragon, a
fire dragon . . . she's a woman as she plummets down
toward us . . . and Thorn, the bat, is ripping at her throat
the whole time . . . we hear a high-pitched squalling,
the bat-sonar gone haywire, whining in our ears . . .
they are diving earthward together . . . they are becoming human. . . .

In the few brief moments that it takes for them to fall,
it's like we live through the lives and deaths of a million
civilizations. We're not just standing in the center of a
cartoon square with the city in flames around us. We're
also seeing planets ripped from their orbits and hurled
into one another . . . and star systems blowing up . . . and
million-starship-fleets stranded forever in the warped folds
of spacetime . . . and a lone child crying . . . and the jan-
gle of unfinished symphonies and pulverized poems . . .
and everywhere scream upon scream upon scream and . . .
and . . .

. . . and then they hit the pavement

It's not the kind of thud you hear in movies when a body
flies out of a skyscraper window . . . it's a dull, empty,
echoless kind of a sound . . . I guess we're all expecting the
big bad sound effect because it takes us several moments
to realize that Thorn and Katastrofa are lying on the monumental steps in front of us, intertwined in each other's arms,
limp, broken, dead.

And not just them but thousands of territories cut off
from the flow of the River . . . civilizations sundered from
their roots . . . the universe no longer a whole but jigsaw
fragments . . . shattered . . . decaying.

"Quick," I say to the king, "you only have one child
left . . . make peace with him . . . Come on, man, it's your
only option."

But still King Strang says, "Never, never, never."

Above the corpses of the two Darklings, on the plinth at
the top of the steps, my brother still lies, still dead. Just as
he still lies in his glass coffin in the dwelling place of dead
Katastrofa. Just as he still lies at the bottom of the Pacific

Ocean offshore by a Mexican town, back in the real world, real time. He lies there feeding the sharks and lobsters.

And this is what I'm thinking: I'm remembering Thorn: how he haunted my dreams with his slate-colored eyes, long before I knew that my dreams weren't really dreams. I'm remembering that, in spite of all his callousness, he always believed he was doing the right thing. I'm remembering how he captured me, how he boasted to me, how he killed and drank his subjects' blood, how he exulted in his power of life and death. And I'm also remembering his loneliness. Yeah. The slate-colored eyes. I go over and kneel beside the twisted bodies and the slate-colored eyes gaze up at me, as soulless in death as they were in life. He'd wanted me to share that soullessness with him. Perhaps he had even loved me. His death makes me cry. I wonder why. Perhaps because, for all his evil, there was something of my father in him, in a way; I know that it was something between him and Dad that dealt him the death-wound.

I close those slate-colored eyes; the lids are stiff. And cold. I'm crying. I mean one of my eyes is crying, because my other eye has been part-closed by scabbing blood, and has no tears.

"You see!" I say, turning to the king. I feel pitiless and bitter. "This is what comes of all your games . . . who the fuck is the fool, King Strang, you or me? You tell me that. You fucking tell me!"

King Strang begins to howl.

Around us, in the city, the fires are already beginning to subside. A wind has sprung up and there's also a drizzle. And there's light now; one of the suns is rising. I realize that there's only one sun now . . . and that the city's not as cartoonlike as it was . . . the corpses in the square around us are becoming three-dimensional . . . the lurid colors are becoming more subdued, drab even.

Corvus flies up and hovers over the king, trying to shelter him from the wind with his outspread wings.

Next I look at Katastrofa. There's very little of the dragon left in her; the glitter of peeling scales at the corners of her eyes, maybe, the metallic fingernails. Jesus she's beautiful. I remember the way she did the gingerbread house number on me, and the way she held me, and how confused I became because her closeness was driving me crazy, I mean, making my thing thrust up and making me just shiver all over with these brand new desires; I remember Joshua in the glass coffin.

"I think they would have gone on fighting until the end of time," Dad says. "But we wounded them. Serena and I, I mean. They were like gods at first. I think that when Serena and I faced these dark archetypes in ourselves, and acknowledged that the dark gods lived in our own souls . . . that meant that the opposite could also happen . . . that the dark gods had to acknowledge a humanness within themselves . . . which made them vulnerable . . . to ourselves and to each other."

"Oh, Mr. E.," Serena says, "you're overintellectualizing everything again. You want to impose some big old structure on everything, even on chaos itself."

Dad laughs. Bitterly, to stop himself from crying.

"Oh, Theo," he says softly, "come home."

"I can't, Dad."

"You have to. Forget about gluing back the pieces of the universe. It's broken and it can't be fixed. You can't reconstruct a Bible out of a million palimpsests. But maybe we can find a corner of it somewhere that'll stay stable for a little while. Long enough for us to live out our lives. Why should we care anymore?"

"You're forgetting Mom," I say. "And Josh."

And the king goes on howling. Like an animal he howls, and he tears at his garments and you can see that his wound is festering. He's gone over the edge. His mind is in a million fragments, and so is the universe. There's one more journey he's going to have to take, and I'm going to have to go with him.

How can I explain to Dad why we can't go home yet? Poor Dad. He sees the way before him only one step at a time. Maybe I should say poor me. Because I see all the steps, every direction, all the strands, all at once, and it makes me crazy. Truthsaying is a curse. I wish that I were blind.

Blindness. . . .

The king crawls round and round in circles, howling.

I realize that he is losing his sight as well as his mind. I also know he's still not going to accept Ash . . . because even in his degradation he still can't rid himself of his pride.

Once more, the future of the cosmos seems to be in *my* hands.

The city is becoming very still. A light rain has started to fall and the plumes of flame have become clouds of smoke. King Strang is slowing down . . . my father and Serena seem to be frozen in place . . . my brother's corpse is calcifying . . . all of them are turning to stone.

It has become utterly silent.

I know what has happened. I'm trapped in a single moment of time. I've made this moment, stretched it out, looped it, so that the world stands still and gives me time to make my next move. I am outside time. This moment exists so that I can see the way ahead; it captures the whole universe in a still photograph.

I'm standing in a forest of statues. They are all made of stone, like my mother is when she's here on the other shore of the River, because she, too, is outside time, existing so slowly that a civilization can spring up and be extinguished while she's taking a single breath.

The world is on hold. It's waiting to see what I'm going to do next.

Black and white. Color has drained away. Only my pied clothes are colored now, and my hands, when I look down at them, are barely pink. The drizzle in the air has frozen in mid-fall, and when I pass my hand through the raindrops there's no sensation of wetness.

Where must I go now?

My marble drops out of my sleeve.

It skitters up the steps, up the ninety-degree angle of the stone . . . like in a macrocosmic game of Marble Madness . . . totally defying gravity. I realize it's trying to get me to follow it. The marble rolls up to the middle of the plinth at the center of the monument. I take the steps two at a time and race over to where it's stopped. Just as I reach down to grab it, though, it like blinks out. It's gone.

But I and the marble are one. I try to see the marble in my mind . . . a manystranded orb spinning in a starless void . . . I see it, I reach out for it, through and past the dimensions of space and time, see my arms vanish as they sink into some other cosmos, feel the marble's smooth surface touch my invisible hand. . . .

I step out of the world, out of the lattice of illusions, into a place that's colder and darker than the human mind can imagine.

book four

the forest of the night

Quiero bajar al pozo,
quiero morir mi muerte a bocanadas,
quiero llenar mi corazón de musgo,
para ver al herido por el agua.

I want to go down to the well:
I want to die my death, mouthful by mouthful:
I want to fill my heart with moss
To watch the boy wounded by the water.

—Lorca

Tales of the Wandering Hero
by Philip Etchison

4: In the Darkest of All Forests

The time of reckoning had come; I stood
Before the gates of hell; I had come far,
Braved men and monsters, answered riddles, slain
The sphinxes that afflict men's souls, unchained
The princess from the rock, sung songs to move
The rocks to tears, to change the River's course.
Behind those gates lay the forbidden fruit
Moly, the herb of immortality,
The quince of sexual awakening.
A fearsome voice cried out to me: "The password!
Utter the password, or be doomed forever
To wander among the lifeless shades of Hades."

I knew no password, so I temporized:
Plucked from its socket my one remaining eye,
And cast it, bleeding, past the iron bars.
I saw no more. With blindness came true vision:
I saw that I could gain the golden apple
Only by vanquishing my longing for it,
And conquer death but by embracing it,
And reach the quest's end only by acknowledging
I needed the quest no longer.

                There I stood:
Racked by the final quandary, out-paradoxed;
Unable to advance without retreating

Sightless yet gifted with a godly foresight,
My loaf, my condom, and my kiss long since
Consumed in the arduous wandering. I wept,
And from my tears there flowed a mighty River
Encircling the dark forest.
Eternity long, eternity and a day
I wept. The water rose. The universe
Itself sank in my sorrow, and was drowned;
The stars fell from the sky; and I myself
Fell like a droplet into my own grief,
Infinity, infinity plus one.

In time, the flood subsided. I myself
Became Deucalion to some brave new world,
And ruled over a prosperous domain
Until an age had passed. Then, on my deathbed,
An angel led me to the gates of hell,
Beyond which lay the fruit, the herb, the pomegranate,
The pearl, the grail, the jewel, the orb, the crown.
I knew then that the kingdom I had ruled,
The cosmos flooded by my sightless eyes,
The long eternities that had transpired,
Had been as substanceless as dream, and I
Still stood before the gate, not knowing the password
That the portal's guardian still demanded from me.

I knew no password, so I temporized;
I reached up to my eye, to pluck it out.
But this time it was different. I was blind.

chapter twenty-two

The Riddle of the Sphinx

Theo Etchison

. . . and step into the forest of the night.

I'm alone. I don't know this place, but somehow it feels like I've always known it, like I've been destined to come here all my life. It's dark and I can't see, but I can hear the rustling of the treetops, and I know it's a forest because of the noises and the wet vines brushing against my face. It's hot here. It's probably tropical. Yeah. Exotic birdcalls and chittering monkeys and darkness so dense it's a kind of mush you breathe in.

I keep on walking. There must be a clearing somewhere, or at least a break in the canopy where the sunlight can get through. There has to be. I keep walking. I don't keep track of time because where I am is timeless. It's the dream world of the dream world.

I keep on walking, like I've done so many times in the forest of the night. It's so dark that like my eyes go crazy and begin playing tricks on me. I see hazy whorls of color that swirl slowly around me. Where is the River? Wasn't I following the marble when I like teleported into this place? I can't see the marble so I try to reach out with my mind . . . there's a throbbing sometimes that let's me know where the marble is, but now when I reach out my mind touches only blankness. I bend down and scrabble around in what must be mud and rotting leaves and finally I think I touch something smooth and round, and I hold it up in the palm of my hand thinking I'll see the intertwisting filaments. Instead there's just a general dull flow, as though the strands have become so jumbled they are all one mass of indistinguishable light.

That's because of all the things that have happened to jumble up the River. Strang's contract with the dark forces kind of dammed up the flow of causality, I guess, and the dam had to burst sooner or later, and the catalyst was the dividing of the kingdom, the accelerating of the war, and the crazy changes that happened because I got dragged into it all. The universe is about to blow and—like in every good superhero story—it's come down to one lone man versus the forces of evil. Sounds melodramatic, huh. It feels like shit. It's probably not even true.

Here I am, walking through the forest of the night, stuck in the labyrinth without a map. It's dark and humid and there are noisy things buzzing against my face, too big to be bugs, too small to be rats.

I keep on walking. After a while I become conscious of a faint smell of fish in the air. Well it starts off like fish but it ends up as something a lot more disturbing because it makes that dream I've been having surface once more I mean the dream about *gliding down the River and me all slick with sweat and sliding deep deep deep into the bridge of thighs no sighs thighs thighs and the forest is a thicket of hair human hair that smells like a fish like a woman slippery and wet and* I'm trembling all over as I trample the forest floor with the mud squishing between my toes because I'm not dressed as the jester anymore, I think I lost my clothes somewhere, maybe the moisture ate them away like acid.

The forest seems to thicken. So does the smell of womanflesh (I'm sure that's what it is because I've heard Josh making crude remarks about sushi and cunts) but like, it's a much stronger stench than I expected, I mean it totally clogs my nostrils and makes it almost impossible to breathe and I feel as if the whole earth has transformed itself into a monstrous woman (I don't mean the fifty-foot woman I mean one that's the size of the entire planet) and the dense dense rain forest that I'm squeezing through now is somewhere in the cosmic woman's genital area and heading straight toward the center of the world, the fiery core, the womb . . . if the earth is a woman am I the sky? I guess this doesn't make sense but I'm starting to get these memory flashes that go back earlier than I've ever remembered before. I mean like, the taste of a nipple, the spurting of fresh hot milk, totally pouring into me and me hungry, hungry, just one monstrous screaming hunger. I remember lights screeching overhead, they're screeching because I don't know the difference yet between hearing and seeing and feeling and smelling, the world around me is a churning blender. The hunger's all that's driving me and I'm screaming with my throat all raw and the lights above me screaming and touched by screaming metal then dunked into screaming water screaming screaming. And then I remember something else. Warm, enfolding, blissfully dark. It quells the hunger. It awakens another memory: the wombwarmth, the dark cavern in which I am God. I've never remembered this before but the memory is all there, a whole touchy-feely image, not a lone fragmented image like early memories usually are. It's the first time in my mother's arms. I'm sucking in the milk now and the screaming is slowly receding. I'm sinking back into the memory of being a God . . . yeah I'm sinking back into the infinite sea.

In Mrs. Dresser's social studies class we are learning about ancient cultures and she tells us the story of Oedipus Rex. There was a man who solved the riddle of the Sphinx then accidentally married his own mother and brought down a curse on the kingdom of Thebes. *Later I say to Dad, "This is bullshit, Dad; it wasn't his fault. What a stupid thing to happen to this dude, I mean, like he saves their whole city, and he even marries this woman who's old*

*enough to be his own . . . well, actually is his own mother,
probably only does it out of pity for the poor old woman
who's stuck there in the palace and can't, you know, get
any." Dad laughs and he puts on a CD of a Tom Lehrer
song, and we both laugh sitting in front of the fire, it's
February in Virginia and school's probably going to be
canceled tomorrow because it's snowing like there is no
tomorrow. And then Dad says, more seriously, "Well, it's
not just about some 'dude' who accidentally has sex with
his mother, you see. It's about everyone who ever said 'I'm
gonna kill you Daddy and then I'll marry Mommy,' and you
see that makes it about me and you . . . not just a bunch of
musty old Greeks." "That's dumb, Dad, I'd never say that,"
I say, and this is a long time before the incident down in
Spotsylvania County when I actually do end up saying it
and meaning every word of it. . . .*

End of flash. I'm trudging through undergrowth again,
With every step the air gets more intense. I'm sucking in
creepy crawlies with every breath I take. There's creatures
slithering up my arms. I hold the marble in the palm of my
hand like it's a candleholder, try to awaken the amorphous
glow that used to be all the strands of the River. Slowly the
marble begins to shed light in the jungle. A flash of neon
brilliance swoops by. One of those tropical birds, like a
toucan or a quetzal, so bright it stings my eyes, already
smarting from the acid drizzle.

After a while the forest thins out a little. I'm standing
in a circle of Joshua trees. Far far above my head there
is a circle of light. It doesn't come from the sun because
though I'm standing on the surface of the womanwood, this
place is also deep inside me, the place where all memories
converge, the place where everything I've ever been scared
of lives, the place where the thing under the bed has gone
to hide and will never die.

I'm inside out, my skin is turned around and I'm standing
in the part of me that's my soul, the part that's more than
man and woman . . . the way Detective Stone is when he
does his own kind of Truthsaying, when he becomes the

messenger from the spirit world. The faint glow brightens to a half-light. The place is a cave. It's the cave where you fight the dragon to get the treasure. It's a cave though it's still a forest. The stalactites and stalagmites are the trunks of giant trees, and the tunnel walls are thick with vines.

I see the coils of the dragon here and there. She fills every twist and turn of the tunnels inside me. It's the glitter of her scales that's giving off the pale blue light. I suppose I'm going to have to fight the dragon now. Isn't that what saving the universe is all about? No use being afraid. It has to be done. But I can't even see where the dragon begins or ends. And I have no weapon except . . . except the sword that I find myself holding in my hand. It's glowing. It has no weight at all. It must be an illusion. But I heft it from hand to hand and after a while it feels like it's always been there. But where is the dragon's heart? I cannot tell.

The cave is rumbling. The dragon's surface begins to ripple. The dragon's slithering through the tunnels. I can't even tell if she's heading toward me or away from me. All I know is that the noise is crescendoing and pieces of the ceiling are falling, although they hurt me about as much as if they were made of Styrofoam. At some point I realize that I'm wearing full armor . . . not real armor, clanky, heavy, and centipede-jointed, but a weightless suit of light that hugs my naked skin. I guess I'm about as ready as I'll ever be.

"C'mon," I scream, "Come out and fight."

I don't see any treasure. Maybe it'll show itself after I've slain the dragon. I run full tilt toward her, waving my sword and shrieking out an imitation of a bloodcurdling heroic warcry in my puny voice. The Joshua trees that are the cave close in on me. It's like that part in *Macbeth* where the trees are marching toward the castle. The dragon seems infinitely big and I know that there's no way to defeat her because she is the dragon that coils around the tree of the universe and I know that this jousting is a ritual, preordained for me since the beginning of time, when everything was still called by its true name and all people were Truthsayers. . . .

The dragon moves. She seems to uncoil with agonizing slowness yet she is too fast for me and when I think I've reached her she is gone, and me just leaping from clawprint to clawprint seeing the burn marks of her breath against the cavern walls and her in the distance, a snake of sizzling light, further down the labyrinth.

I'm really sprinting now but the dragon isn't any closer. The trees are racing past me and I see people hanging in the branches . . . my Dad, my brother, Serena, and dozens of other people that have touched my life . . . all chained to the branches of the Joshua trees and crying out in pain and calling on my name, *Theo Theo Theo save us save us* . . . and I keep running. There's a high wind in the tunnels still saturated with the womansmell and I'm running into the wind and it fills me with unnamed, untameable desires . . . it makes me bigger than myself . . . it terrifies me . . . it elates me. I don't know how long I'm tilting at the dragon but I'm not exhausted, I guess it's the adrenaline rushing through my blood, the blood that hurtles like the screaming wind . . . and I still can't catch up with the dragon.

Sometimes it takes all the running you can do just to stay in the same place . . . isn't that from one of the *Alice* books? It's a line that echoes through my head as I pursue the dragon. I realize I have to stop. And I do, and it's like colliding with a wall of memory, and images burst out everywhere, uncontrollable: Dad reading to me when I'm really little . . . Josh breaking a window . . . the stream beside my grandparents' house and . . . embracing my mother and feeling the disturbing emotions and . . . I stop and I've pierced the dragon through the heart . . . the skin is sloughing even now, curling up, withering, flying, and where the dragon's heart was is a whirling, dancing flame . . . and I'm inside the dragon now, inside the cage of bones, and the bones are melting together and weaving themselves into a wall of limestone and in the distance I can hear salsa music playing and I know that I am in the cave of the weeping Madonna and that behind the altar railing stands my mother . . . and there she is . . . my mother yet more than my mother . . . unfrozen from her statue stillness because in this secret place space and time are what we make of them . . . she's standing in front of the altar and behind her there's a celestial choir, Jesus flits back and forth about her head tossing rainbows in the air, and on the altar there's a chalice, and over the chalice, suspended, is a piece of a waterfall, the water trickling into the cup yet never filling it . . . the water turning to the color of blood as it touches the silver. . . .

My mother is standing in front of the chalice with her arms outstretched. She doesn't have the wild-eyed madness in her face, or the dull-eyed desperation of the cancer. She's how I remember she used to be before the illness came. Her hair has all grown back and it's the color of my own hair. She's smiling at me. "You've made it through to here," she says at last, "to the secret cavern of your soul."

"Is the cup what I think it is?" I ask her.

"Yes," she says. "It's the cup that can only be touched by the pure fool; it is the cup that continually replenishes itself from the source of the River; it's the cup of the water of transformation; it's the cup that heals all wounds; it's the Holy Grail."

"Then how come I can see it? Maybe I'm a fool, but I'm not so pure."

"You're pure enough to be a Truthsayer."

"You mean because I'm a virgin?"

"Partly, Theo, but it's more than just virginity; it's your Truthsaying; it's your ability to see through to the heart of things. Do you want to heal the wounds of the world? You must take the chalice and use its inexhaustible supply of the water of transformation to renew the universe. Isn't that why you came here?"

"But why were you a dragon? Why did I have to fight you? Aren't you my mother?"

She smiles again. I want so much to run up to her and put my arms around her and for us throw off these absurd high fantasy costumes and go home, but something prevents me. She's my mother but she's also mother to the world and that makes her more than woman.

She tells me—and her words are echoed in the wind through the cavern and the sighing of the sea—"Theo, Theo, you fought me because every hero must fight the dragon. In the ancient dream time, Apollo fought the earth-serpent-mother of the world for possession of the oracle of Delphi. He wanted to wrest the art of Truthsaying from the mother of the world. The Truthsayers have been battling mother earth ever since that time. It's not a war that you can win or lose. It's the war that keeps the world afloat. It's a war of love as well as death; because, Theo, you know, you love me more than anyone in the world . . . at least, for a little while longer . . . until the day comes when you leave the nest, you start to look outside the house, and you find the woman who is uniquely yours . . . do you understand what I'm saying?"

I think so. But there's a music in her words that touches me far more than their meaning ever can. "Mom . . . what am I supposed to do now? Take the chalice and heal the world, right?" I go right up to the altar railing. Only a few feet separate me from the thing that human beings have spent lifetimes seeking. Only a wooden railing stops me from embracing my mother. What does it mean? Why don't I just take her at her word, leap over the barrier, grab the grail, renew the universe? What kind of universe would the renewed universe be? Will it bring Josh back to life, and return Mom to my father's house, healed of her sickness? Somehow I don't think so. It's not the right answer to the riddle of the Sphinx.

My mother reaches across the railing. Our hands touch and I am afraid because this touching is where the dream begins, the dream of sweat and water and fish and things I cannot name though I know they come from the world of sex, the unknown territory that has begun to haunt my fantasies . . . "What are you doing, Mom?" I ask. I can't help myself. She pulls me forward toward where I know our lips will touch. "Mom, does this mean what I think it means?" I say, knowing that in the woman there is still the serpent.

"Tell me, Theo," my mother whispers, "if you were Adam, would you have wanted to stay in the Garden of Eden for ever?"

That's when I finally understand that there is a choice. In my innocence, I could seize the chalice and return the cosmos to its pristine state, as innocent as myself. I could remake the Garden of Eden. Everything would be healed; we would all be creatures of joy, dancing for all eternity in the radiance of perpetual morning. But is this a good thing? Isn't leaving the Garden a good thing too, like growing up, putting away your toys, disobeying your parents for the first time, and knowing at last that there must be death in order for life to have any meaning? I'm a Truthsayer. I see the true nature of things. I see that paradise is also hell, that to live forever without pain is also to be forever unborn.

I could give up my innocence. I could receive knowledge, and I know that the price of that knowledge is going to be my eye . . . my inner eye . . . that the power of Truthsaying would gradually be sucked away from me . . . because I would no longer see with the eyes of a child. Is that what I want?

I'm scared. Fucking Jesus I'm scared because no matter what I choose there is a terrible price to pay.

"You've stayed a child so long," Mom says, "it seems as though you've been stuck, refusing to grow; but I know you hear the call of your own death, which is also your own restlessness, your own need to live."

"If I heal the world now, Joshua will never come back, will he?"

"No."

"We won't even be people anymore, will we? We'll be like total zombies."

"But happy."

"Yeah." It's then that I realize that I don't want to be a Truthsayer anymore. And I have to pass the burden on to someone else. I start crying. I don't know, Jesus I hurt all over. I don't want to give up my special gift of seeing. But I want to become something too, even if it means suffering through adolescent angst and pimples and sexual frustrations and all the other shit I've seen Josh go through. And I realize now that I *can* pass on the burden.

I've been to the River's edge, where the unborn heroes float downstream in their little rush cradles. I've swallowed the essence of Joshua into myself. That's why, even while I was gazing down at his putrefying body, I could still feel him close by. He's inside me. I can plant him in the body of the One Mother, and I can make *him* carry on the destiny of Truthsaying. But to do that, I'm going to have to. . . .

"I know it's unthinkable," she says. The altar railing has evaporated into the swirls of incense. "It's the biggest taboo that humans have. But you and I aren't just human beings; we are also forces of nature, we are gods. There are two ways to renew the world—to return it to a state of utter entropy—or to fire it up with the tension of a lovemaking that is also a deathmaking. You must give up your innocence; you must make love to me; and you must pay the price by giving up your vision. Or else—"

But you know the strange thing is I don't feel sad about it at all. I know that the universe is kept in the air by a monumental feat of juggling. I can't let it drop. My blood is pumping and my mother has bared her breasts to me and I drink in the memory of milk and the feeling of omnipotence in being at the eye of the cosmos. I throw my arms around her and I'm seized as though by a mighty wind and I hear the jangling harmonies of angel choirs and the percussion of our syncopated heartbeats. She overwhelms me, she surrounds me; she is the forest of Joshua trees; she is the sea. Our love is a tumult of joy that shakes the very orbits of a trillion worlds. I dive into the womb of the universe, pass through the event horizon, traverse the utter darkness of the singularity, break through the threshold in a shower of exploding starstuff . . . I am reborn.

And then, when the tempest dies down, when the world is dim enough for me to look on once again, my mother and I walk slowly down the steps, hand in hand, into the city square where the others, time-frozen, have been waiting.

I'm still shaking from the sexual encounter that was more than sex. I'm more confused, not less, because my Truthsaying vision has already begun to fade. I've managed to juggle the universe, but I've had to let myself drop.

"We're back," I tell my Dad.

But he just stands there gaping at Mom. He is remembering all sorts of things that happened before I was born; and now those images are closed to me.

I know he will never understand the journey she and I have returned from, and I know things will never be the same again between him and me.

He doesn't know that my gift is slipping away from me, that soon I'll be blind to the true nature of things. I'll be just like all the others.

Jesus, it better be worth it.

chapter twenty-three

Oedipus Rex

Phil Etchison

No time passed. In less than the twinkling of an eye, the fabric of space over the plinth atop the monument in the center of the cartoon city unzipped itself and Theo and Mary stepped out, hand in hand; I caught a tiny glimpse of the fearsome world they had left behind, fleshy, palpitating and sulphurous, and then the gap between the worlds closed up behind them.

Everything began to change. The body of my other son, which had lain, putrescent, on the marble steps, was no longer there. The dark clouds overhead began to break apart, admitting a supernal radiance, as in a *Transfiguration* by Raphael.

"We're back," Theo said softly. I looked from him to my wife. Something had happened between them. I didn't think that Mary was dying anymore. Her face was positively glowing with health and joy, and it was not just that she was standing dead center of the shaft of heavenly light, her long hair stirring a little in the wind that is cooling the smoldering city, and she was wearing the same dress she was wearing the first day we met . . . the summer dress drenched with the hot Virginia rain.

"I've brought Josh back," Theo said. "But I had to pay for it."

He ran toward me, he buried himself in my embrace; oh God, he was a frail thing, spindly, awkward, and his dirty blond hair was matted with sweat, and there was so much bewilderment in his eyes, so little of the searing certainty I had come to expect of him. "Oh, Daddy, Daddy," Theo cried, "was it worth it?"

"I don't understand," I said. "Where is Josh?"

"Inside me," Mary said.

I smelled on my son the smell of a woman, a smell intimately familiar to me because it was the fragrance of one particular woman, a woman I'd cherished for twenty years, a woman I'd given up everything for, even my own sanity; and I was consumed with rage and bewilderment.

Serena Somers

So Theo had made the same sacrifice I had made . . . and for the same reason . . . because we both loved Josh. I could tell what was dawning in Mr. E.'s mind; I could tell that it made him very nervous. He and Theo stood there, hugging each other, but when Mary said that Joshua was inside her I could see him stiffening, turning away.

"Dad, don't turn from me," Theo was saying. But what was going through Mr. E.'s mind wasn't something you could logically argue about. My heart went out to both of them because like, Theo was bawling his guts out and Mr. E. couldn't find it in himself to comfort him; Theo had wounded him in the act of fulfilling what he most desired.

Phil Etchison

Mary said, "Don't be angry, Phil. I'm not dying anymore. Theo has taken our pain upon himself . . . don't you see that?"

But I wasn't feeling very rational. I had been cuckolded by my own son, hadn't I? I'd had no major role in the drama to start off with . . . wasn't it always Theo who was the Truthsayer, the redeemer of the world, the one who knew the answers? "I'm an insignificant appendage in my own family," I said. "I'm like Joseph, a village carpenter who's conveniently around to give God's bastards a name. . . ." Why was I so bitter? Was it that Mary was back, Mary, more beautiful than ever before, untouched, it seemed, by all the tribulations that had wrenched our family . . . and I'd somehow expected even more? Was it that my son had harrowed seven hells while I stood impotent, and now by his victory over the darkness had rendered me more impotent than ever?

Mary said, "You don't understand, Phil. It wasn't what you think. We danced the dance that brings forth the light. You have to look at it mythologically. Josh is inside me again. He'll be twice-born. He's going to be the most powerful Truthsayer of all. And to bring him back from the dead, to reverse the entropy of the cosmos, Theo gave up his most precious possession . . . his gift . . . and his innocence."

But there was in me an ugly thing called jealousy, and I just couldn't see all these cosmic verities, because unlike Theo, unlike my wife, I was not a god, and I was unlikely ever to become one. I had always known I was less than a poet, but now I knew also that I was less than a man. Why couldn't they see that? But they could, you see. And they pitied me for it. And their compassion made me even more bitter.

Theo Etchison

My vision is ebbing. Before, the world was fluid, because there were illusions piled on illusions, and I could see through all of them like they were so many overlays of acetate, so many cartoon animation cells . . . I could see through all the falsehoods to the bedrock of reality. But now the illusions themselves are becoming solid.

My father has stepped back. I don't know who to turn to. When I turn back to Mom, I can't meet her eyes anymore.

Standing farther off is Strang; like me, he is losing his vision; he is entering an inner world of madness. Behind him is Corvus; behind them both are the intertwined corpses of Strang's two elder children; and hovering overhead, its spires peering from the thinning clouds, is Caliosper, where Ash is waiting, alone, for word of forgiveness from his father; and I know it's not going to come.

Saving the universe fucking sucks. I've brought my family together again, but it looks like there's no room in it for me. I've been crying like a baby and my father's heart has turned to stone. He'll never understand because he's never seen, never breathed the air of these alien worlds; he's been in the theater watching the movie, but he's never *lived* it. Jesus I'm bitter. But I see that he is too. And yeah I blame him. I blame everyone.

"All right," I tell them all. "I'm going now."

My father says, "Where? What do you mean?"

Mom says, "Phil, Theo has to go away for a while."

I fling the worthless marble onto the steps. The marble cracks the stone and through it I see the surging waters of the River. Suddenly everything's shaking, I mean the whole city seems to be splitting up into a million shards, and beneath them all you can see the River. It's angry. It's been stirred up and it's about to burst the seams of reality. A geyser starts spouting where Joshua's body once lay. I start to walk away from my parents . . . I go toward the crazed old man who once was king of everything.

"Truthsayer," says King Strang, and he pets my cheek.

"No way, not anymore," I say.

"There is another journey we must take," he says, "you and me together."

And though my gift is fading, I feel the truth of what he's saying. The pavement's cracking beneath our feet and the water's lapping at my calves. Doorways are opening all around us. We could step into a million other worlds. My father and my mother are standing close together, staring at each other, poised in the tense moments before reconciliation.

There are things I must do before I lose my powers forever. There is a way to heal the universe without destroying free will . . . and I know that Strang and I must go on the journey together . . . before he becomes completely blind . . . before the truth slips away from me forever. I've glimpsed the Holy Grail, and I know its power comes from the source of the River . . . but we must go there, he and I, we must travel together through the schizophrenic labyrinth of his mind . . . to the place where Strang made his bargain with the powers of darkness . . . we ourselves must stand at the source.

Dad is striding toward me now. He's trying to use reason; he's fighting his own emotions. "Don't go, Theo," he's saying. "I know that you're acting out all these cosmic roles, preordained since the beginning of time. Sure it disturbs me, but I'll get over it. Jesus Theo, don't walk out on us. You're my son. I love you."

"I know you do, Dad," I say. There's so much I want to tell him. How much I've loved him when, Sunday mornings, he's sat us down and read to us great bleeding chunks of shiny poetry, the words all jingly and grand, echoing in my mind for days and weeks afterwards; how much I believed in him when we played the game of *Trust Me* and drove blind through clashing universes; oh I'm aching because of how much I love him, but I know that I must go. It's the whole Garden of Eden thing. I have to slip away from him. To be exiled is the beginning of maturity; to be blind is the beginning of wisdom.

I reach out to take the old king's hand. Corvus is beside us now, spreading his wings to shield us from the wind.

"Goodbye for now, Dad," I say. I kiss my father gently on the cheek.

I don't kiss my mother; we've gone beyond all that.

Serena Somers

Watching what was happening between the Etchisons was painful. But I knew I wasn't just witnessing the breakup of their family; there was something else going on . . . the beginning of something.

The city was coming apart at the seams. Water was sluicing up out of the ground. Theo and King Strang were standing one moment, Theo leading him by the elbow the way you help a blind man cross the street, and then they just stepped out of the universe and were gone. And Corvus followed them, not even saying goodbye.

Yeah, there were all these turbulent feelings in my head, but there was also this urgency because I knew we were going to drown if we didn't get out of there fast. Mr. and Mrs. E. were just standing there, looking into each other's eyes, maybe thinking about how they'd let their son slip through their fingers . . . and it was up to me to grab them both by the arm and propel them toward the nearest exit. The exits were continually changing, they were like these windows into other worlds that popped in and out of the air around us. But I followed the sound of salsa music because that was the last thing we'd been listening to in the real world . . . and there was the gateway . . . through it I could see thousands upon thousands of candles, and children in skull makeup dancing, and women weeping and beating their breasts in front of the altar railing, and . . . "Let's not stick around anymore, guys!" I said, and I pushed Mrs. E. over the threshold into the other universe, and she was holding on to my hands so I guess I came tumbling after, and Mr. E. had a hold of the other hand so he came through too, and the next minute we knew—

Phil Etchison

I had landed, flat on my backside, on the hard cold limestone floor of the cave.

"*¡Milagro . . . un milagro!*" one of the kids was shouting, pointing at us because we had, presumably, materialized in front of the altar in the grotto of the weeping Madonna.

"Mary?" I said.

I turned and saw the statue of the Virgin.

Jesus, I thought, it's happened again, she's frozen into stone again, it was all just a dream when I touched her and smelled her perfume and caressed the soft hair as it billowed in the wind and—

The limestone began to crack. The sound was like a sudden thaw of ice in the spring, up in the far north, a thundering elemental bursting. Some of the celebrants were cowering behind the rows and rows of candles and decorated death's heads. Again and again I heard them whispering, "A miracle! A miracle!" Mary emerged from the rock. She wiped the white dust from her eyes and stood behind the altar rail, a living woman in the place of stone.

Softly she said, "Phil, I've awakened from a long and terrible sleep; I've dreamed the birth and death of universes. Am I in the real world now?"

"Yes," I said, though I was far from sure of it.

"I'm going to have a baby," she said.

We embraced across the altar railing. My bitterness was slowly beginning to fade. It was good that we were finally going to have children. That was why we had come down to Baja: we wanted to spend a few romantic weeks together, doing what the doctors had said could not be done, curing my wife's infertility with an outpouring of passion.

I'd had so many daydreams about children: about strong tall sons playing catch by the stream next to the cottonwoods that ring my father's house in Spotsylvania County, about a beautiful young child who knew how to say all the things I left unsaid, who grasped the truth without the tortuous twists of logic and philosophy; who would be my best and most beautiful poem. I'd daydreamed about going on adventures into fantasy kingdoms, manufactured great epics in my mind of which the eponymous heroes were my offspring . . . woven the great classics together . . . fantasized even about myself when old and wandering, doling out pieces of my kingdom à la Lear, losing my mind . . . I could hardly believe that fantasy was about to become reality, here in a grotto known for its miracles, in a foreign land, at a festival of the dead.

"Serena," I said to the woman who had served as our surrogate daughter all these barren years, "Mary's going to have a baby!"

"Congratulations, Mr. E.!" she said. But then she added, darkly, strangely, "But don't forget the other one."

"No," said Mary, as she kissed me over the wooden railings, "don't forget the shadow twin, the one who is wandering in the outer darkness, who blinded himself to plant your son in my womb."

Words of great mystery, sublime, poetic, dark, unfathomable words; I did not understand them. But that was to be expected on the day of the dead; it was a day of magic, where the boundary between the real and the dream fuzzied itself, and the dead could come back to life.

chapter twenty-four

_____
_____

Congressman Karpovsky

Serena Somers

The world was settling down once more into some kind of semblance of stability. The Etchisons and I walked back along the beach; I had to get back to my job handing out Karpovsky buttons. The festival was in full swing. It was exciting I guess: there were fireworks and there were bands and there was a procession of skeletons carrying candles and there were booths selling horror candy, and Mary was back with us and no longer mad or dying. There was still a wrongness in our world though, because Theo was out there in the wilderness with the mad king, and because Mr. E. no longer seemed to remember the hell we had harrowed together. Mr. E.'s memories were totally elastic, like the fabric of reality itself.

I had a little unfinished business too.

That's why I kind of snuck away from the two love-birds—they were holding hands and whispering in each other's ears like teenagers—and slipped off through the crowd toward where I knew Karpovsky was still holding forth. The little holiday resort was just as we had left it—oh, maybe a tad more drunken, as it was later the same night—

still full of celebrants being militantly ethnic for the benefit of the hordes of loudmouthed, gold-card-toting tourists.

I was pretty sure that, in *this* world, no time had elapsed since the moment someone tried to abduct Our Lady of the Sluggish Tears. Which meant that Karpovsky was probably still in the same spot, buttonholing tourists and trying to get them to sign petitions for his grassroots candidacy. Yes, I could see him now. He was standing by a booth, against a backdrop of papier-mâché skeletons. A TV camera was rolling. It had a CNN logo on it, and the newswoman was saying, "But, Congressman, why are you in Mexico at all? There's a popular rumor going around that you feel that, with the trade agreement, Mexico should just be annexed and made into the fifty-first state."

Karpovsky laughed. "Very funny, Claudette," he said. "Personally I feel that Puerto Rico should come first. But no, I'm here—okay, I might as well be crass about it—for the photo-op. And the fact that so many of our citizens are spending their holiday dollars here instead of back home— why? Because a dollar will barely buy a Coke and a candy bar today."

He paused for effect, and then he pointed to the row of skeletons. "Do you see these?" he said. "We're all going to be looking like this soon, because none of us have health insurance—we're all going to be hanging in a row—unless my national health plan is implemented right away, and I intend to make it my top priority, understand?"

That's when he saw me.

"Excuse me for a moment, Claudette," he said, and walked in my direction. His place was filled by a dozen kids, jumping up and down and making faces into the television cameras.

"Serena," he said. "Where've you been?"

"Can we talk?" I said. "It's important."

He looked askance for a moment. But he saw that I was serious, didn't want to blow anything with the newspeople all around us, I guess, so he nodded. "Take five, guys," he said to his all-female, all-pneumatic staffers, and then we retired to a booth in an open-air coffee shop alongside the beach.

Karpovsky ordered a strawberry daiquiri; I ordered one too.

"I don't know about that," he quipped. "Are you of age?"

"I'm old enough to fuck, Congressman," I said.

That got to him. I'd never spoken to him directly about it before.

"Pretty strong language, Serena," he said.

"Something's happened to me sometime in the last five minutes," I said. "Well, it was only five minutes to you . . . but to me it was an adventure that like, spanned star systems and lasted lifetimes."

He was looking at me with utter seriousness now. I thought he'd act like I was crazy, but he didn't; there was a poetic side to this man, and I believed in him, in many ways, even when I was most mad at him.

I knew that there was a Serena who had never fallen prey to the congressman's lusts; she was a Serena who hid herself inside walls of lard, dreamed about Joshua Etchison, and finally sacrificed her virginity to bring him back from the dead. And there was a Serena whom the congressman had all but raped on the desk in his office between a bronze eagle and a crystal whale, a Serena who had never dared speak or point a finger or even resist because she was afraid. And there was a third Serena, who had reveled in the control she exercised over someone so much older, so much more powerful . . . a Serena who'd used her sexuality to shore up her sense of self-worth, who knew that, though she was at the bottom of the totem pole and he was at the top, in the bedroom their places could be reversed, and he could be reduced to a sniveling wreck with the threat of blackmail or exposure . . . all three Serenas had existed, and I was the sum total of all three . . . for just as each moment in time contains the potentiality for millions of possible futures, so also each moment is the junction of a million pasts . . . the River flows backward as well as

forward . . . and everything you can conceive of is, somewhere, the truth.

The drinks came. The congressman was looking kind of
nervous. I wondered which of the Serenas he remembered.
Probably a little of all three.

I said, "You probably don't remember the confrontation
we had back there in the cartoon city . . . you know, when
I was in the form of a dragon . . ."

I thought Karpovsky would probably think I was insane,
but in fact he began to stare at me strangely. "Are you
psychic or something?" he said. "I've been having these
dreams . . ."

"Did you dream about fucking me on top of your rain-
forest-busting mahogany desk right there in the Capitol
building?"

"I . . ."

I didn't know whether this was the Karpovsky who had
done these things to me, or whether he had only thought
about it or . . . dreamed it . . . but he said, "My therapist
tells me I'm just acting out my inner desires . . . and that
it's better that than actually going around . . . you know . . .
harassing . . . well . . . you know what I mean. Things are a
lot better now. I'm a flawed man, Serena, but you know, I
believe in things . . . I want to make things better."

"Well, maybe you'll understand if I just go ahead and
act out one of *my* fantasies."

"What, right here in the coffee shop?" he said, and I wondered whether he thought it would be the dragon-skinned
Serena who would rapaciously devour him on the spot.

"Nothing kinky," I said.

I got up, and I picked up my daiquiri, and I emptied it
over his head.

Something snapped in both of us, then. I mean, I don't
know if *this* Karpovsky raped me in his mind or in his office.
But I knew there was something between us, something that
needed to be washed away.

And you know what? The congressman like got up, and
he sloshed the rest of his drink on my dress. And we began

laughing, I mean, laughing so hard we were crying at the same time, and the daiquiri glasses might just as well have been the Holy Grail with the healing blood of Christ, because when the red liquid soaked into my pores, I began to feel cleansed of all my bitterness.

"Jesus, Congressman," I said, "what's happening to us?"

"Our wounds are going to get healed," he said. "Because we're able to forgive each other. Because we can look past the terrible things we do to each other, day in, day out, the searing hells we put each other through, often as not in the name of love. And maybe, just maybe, I'll even win this fucking election."

chapter twenty-five

Making Love

Phil Etchison

In the hotel room, we made love. The curtains billowed in the open window and the fireworks in the night sky flashed against the peeling paint, and their thunder drowned out the squeaking of the bedsprings. How does it feel to make love to someone you have known for twenty years, who has been so much a part of your life that there seems to be no pore or crevice that does not contain her? God, it was like making love for the first time. It was as though she had returned to me from a long and terrifying journey, from sickness or from madness. How else can I describe that night? At first we were like children playing doctor, discovering the intimate secrets of our bodies for the first time. Then we were like adolescents, our hormones raging, thrusting awkwardly . . . I knocked the lamp off the nightstand, Mary fell off the bed howling with laughter . . . oh God I love you I love you I said over and over and over . . . and over. And then we made love slowly, like the late baby-booming yuppies that we really were, for the music outside our window had changed from percussive salsa to a slow waltz . . . and then, strangely, during the afterglow, it transformed into a lugubrious funeral march. The Chopin thing, even more dirgelike because it was pouring forth ponderously from off-key tubas and trombones and punctuated by the flat thud of an untightened bass drum.

"Oh, turn off the music!" Mary said, laughing.

She got out of bed and went to the window. I followed her. We stood there, heedless of our nakedness, watching the parade of death-masked Mexicans go by.

"I wonder where our son is now?" she said softly.

"In your womb," I said. I bent down and put my ear to her flat belly, knowing full well I would not hear any kicking for many months to come, and that Mary would make fun of me for doing it, and that I would accept her chiding with good humor. All that happened.

But then, looking away, far away, across the crowd, across the brass bands, across the dancing celebrants, seeming almost to be looking to some distant universe, she said, "No, I mean our other son."

"Are you mad?" I said. This festival . . . breaking down the barrier between the dead and the living . . . it was making us both a little crazy . . . That was why it seemed that we were seeing each other anew across a tremendous gulf of space and time. "You know you lost our child . . ."

I thought of Theo, how we'd placed him in the cold earth, up north, in Arlington, a stone's throw from the Pentagon.

I didn't want to think about the past. "We're going to start again," I said. "We've been living through a nightmare, but now we're going to have a family, and we're going to be happy. A miracle has happened to us."

The funeral march went on up the street, and a new band was beneath our window. They were playing a jaunty tango-like song and it made me want to dance. I caught my wife in my arms, wrapped her hair about my face, kissed her several times, lifted her in my arms and gave her a whirl, carried her back toward the bed.

"Still," she said, "I wonder where he is."

book five

the forest of ice

TALES OF THE WANDERING HERO
by PHILIP ETCHISON

5: AT THE END OF THE FOREST

And so, at last, I left the darkling wood.
I came to the cave where I had left my mother,
The hearth I loved, the bed in which I'd dreamed
Of these adventures.

              I came upon my kinfolk
As they supped, telling old tales to warm their nights.
I said, "Mother, I have returned, with gifts
And stories, conquests, jewels, and a bride;
I have slain man and dragon; I have ravished
Maiden and crone; I have lived dangerously,
Stooped, beast-like, to drink water from the stream,
And quaffed celestial manna from gold goblets."
My mother said, "My son, take out the trash."

"But, but," I said, "what of my lurid tales,
My battles and my witty conversations
With saucy knights, my exploits in the bedroom?"
"Yes, yes, my dear, but first, go wash your hands,
Or you may not sit down to sup with company."

Only that night, when I lay down to sleep,
Did she consent to hear my tales of woe,
Of joy, of passion, courage, and survival;
And then she wept full sore, because the son
She loved had been through so much suffering.

Then she did kiss me gently on the cheek
And say, "The places you have been, the conflicts,
The fierce encounters, and the nights of passion,
These places all are marked upon a map;
The map is called *The Human Journey*.

                                        "So,
Although, my son, you have traversed the world,
And conquered love and death, and grown from child
To man, there is another thing to learn:
Your journey is the journey all men make,
An exploration of the human soul;
And I am still your mother.

                        "Let me kiss you,
And tomorrow I will bake you a fresh loaf
Give you a new condom and clean clothes,
And you shall venture forth again.

                                "The journey
Is forever."

epilogue

Theo

Theo Etchison

. . . "King Strang! King Strang!"

I'm calling out to him across the howling void. I don't know the name of this world and I don't know the name of the one we've left behind. Where we are now it's a world of ice and snow and our raft has been moving doggedly upstream for it seems like a year now. Corvus is piloting. I don't know where Ash is, but I think he is watching, waiting for the moment of reconciliation.

The king has stepped ashore to ask directions of a bear-like creature who sits, cross-legged, like a snowstrewn Buddha. He's been in that position for a million years and speaks to no one, but I think he will speak to us; he has, you see, been waiting for us.

Our journey is fulfilling a lot of prophecies. The gateways between the universes are shutting down or getting clogged. We do what we can to keep them open. My powers still work a little; on a good day I can clear a little pathway, enough for the River to run raging through. It makes me feel good.

The king and I don't speak much. I am his fool, and I tell him bad jokes from time to time, and he tries to laugh. Mostly we just sit in silence. He has his lucid moments. That's when he tells me stories about the old days. Spectacle and bloodshed beyond imagining. All I can tell him are stories about being picked on in school, or smoking in the boys' room, or Mrs. Dresser's social studies class, stuff like that. For him, though, my stories are of equal moment to his own; in a sense, I suppose, they are.

I wonder whether Josh is born yet.

I know that he'll be a far more powerful Truthsayer than I could ever have been. His father is a Truthsayer and his mother is the world. I can't wait to hold him in my arms. I'm no longer young, even though only a year or so has passed between now and the time that I thought I would live forever, the time I held those shiny epiphanies in my hands like so many bright new glistening marbles; I'm no longer a child even though I'm only slowly moving out of my childish appearance and getting ganglier and having wet dreams and all that shit; I'm no longer young because I've left my innocence behind me forever, floating downstream in the River like an unborn hero.

I don't know if I'm happy yet, but I know that now I can dream.

Fucking Jesus it's cold. The wind is like whipping us and screaming like a banshee and it gets inside our blood and you feel like you're going to split open, like a beer can in the freezer . . . but the cold means many things. It means we are getting closer to the source. That's why there is no sun. It's a twilight world here. A dark world, a dungeon among worlds. But we keep going.

One day we're going to reach the River's source. One day my brother the Truthsayer will come bursting through the spaces between the universes, and there'll be a final healing. But fucking Jesus, I did the best I could.

I tried to wash the memory of me from my Dad's mind. He'll think I was only a dream. He'll be happy now.

Maybe he'll even believe himself to be a poet, in the end.

Bangkok, Los Angeles, 1991–92

About the Author

Somtow Papinian Sucharitkul (S.P. Somtow) was born in Bangkok, Thailand, and grew up in Europe. He was educated at Eton College and at Cambridge, where he obtained his B.A. and M.A., receiving honors in English and Music.

His first career was as a composer, and he has emerged as one of Southeast Asia's most outspoken and controversial musicians. He has had his compositions performed, televised and broadcast on four continents. His most recent compositions include the dazzling *Gongula 3* for Thai and Western instruments, commissioned for the opening of the Asian Composers Expo, and *Star Maker—An Anthology of Universes*, for large orchestra, four sopranos and other soloists, recently premiered in Washington.

In 1977 he began writing fiction. He was first nominated for the John W. Campbell Award for best new writer in 1980, winning in 1981. Two of his short stories, "Aquila" and "Absent Thee from Felicity Awhile," have been nominated for the coveted Hugo Award, science fiction's equivalent of the Oscar. He has now published twenty-five books, including the complex, galaxy-spanning *Inquestor* series and the satirical *Mallworld* as well as the philosophical *Starship & Haiku* and two short story collections, *Fire from the Wine-Dark Sea* and *My Cold Mad Father*.

S.P. Somtow's career as a novelist has expanded beyond the boundaries of science fiction. His horror novel *Vampire Junction* was praised by Edward Bryant as "the most important horror novel of 1984," and the New York *Daily News* called it "the grimmest vampire fantasy ever set to paper . . . sure to become a cult classic." His second mainstream novel, *The Shattered Horse*, has been compared to Umberto Eco and was called, by noted author Gene Wolfe, "in the true sense, a work of genius." A young people's book, *Forgetting Places*, was honored by the "Books for Young Adults" program as an "outstanding book of the year."

His second horror novel, *Moon Dance*, is already being hailed as a landmark in the field and has been nominated for the American Horror Award; it also won the Rocky Award and the HOMER Award. Critic A.J. Budrys has compared the work to Henry James and Nathaniel Hawthorne. It is a vast novel in which a pack of Eastern European werewolves settle in the Dakota Territory in the 1880s. Somtow spent six years researching the novel, himself traversing every inch of his characters' odyssey from Vienna, Austria, to California, and studying Native American languages. *Moon Dance* sold out before publication date and has gone back to press three times. His most recent horror novel is *Valentine*, a long-awaited sequel to *Vampire Junction*.

The horror film that S.P. Somtow wrote and directed, *The Laughing Dead*, has been called "a horror film for the 90s" by *Cinéfantastique* and "one of the best independent productions in a long while" by Michael Weldon of the *Psychotronic Review*. It has been released in Europe and will appear in the United States later this year.

Riverrun is a trilogy of which *Forest of the Night* is the second volume. The final volume, *Music of Madness*, will appear next year.

RETURN TO AMBER...

THE ONE *REAL* WORLD, OF WHICH ALL OTHERS, INCLUDING EARTH, ARE BUT SHADOWS

ROGER ZELAZNY

The Triumphant conclusion of the Amber novels

PRINCE OF CHAOS   75502-5/$4.99 US/$5.99 Can

The Classic Amber Series

NINE PRINCES IN AMBER	01430-0/$3.99 US/$4.99 Can
THE GUNS OF AVALON	00083-0/$3.95 US/$4.95 Can
SIGN OF THE UNICORN	00031-9/$3.95 US/$4.95 Can
THE HAND OF OBERON	01664-8/$3.95 US/$4.95 Can
THE COURTS OF CHAOS	47175-2/$3.50 US/$4.25 Can
BLOOD OF AMBER	89636-2/$3.95 US/$4.95 Can
TRUMPS OF DOOM	89635-4/$3.95 US/$4.95 Can
SIGN OF CHAOS	89637-0/$3.95 US/$4.95 Can
KNIGHT OF SHADOWS	75501-7/$3.95 US/$4.95 Can

NEW BESTSELLERS
IN THE *MAGIC OF XANTH* SERIES!

PIERS ANTHONY

QUESTION QUEST

75948-9/$4.99 US/$5.99 Can

ISLE OF VIEW

75947-0/$4.99 US/$5.99 Can

VALE OF THE VOLE

75287-5/$4.95 US/$5.95 Can

HEAVEN CENT

75288-3/$4.95 US/$5.95 Can

MAN FROM MUNDANIA

75289-1/$4.95 US/$5.95 Can